HOME

MY LIFE IN THE UNIVERSE

Enjoy the adventure
with best wishes

Mark ·⋆·

'The character development throughout the novel was fascinating,
I definitely felt like I was almost growing up with Leah
and even some of the other characters…
I hope that this book is a huge success;
it is one of the best I have read…
I would recommend it for novel loving
and philosophical book lovers young and old.'
— *Goodreads* Review

'Leah's adventure is like no other and is a story
which young people of all ages can unite over'
— Reader review

'A good book to read when you are growing up. It makes you
think about where you belong and what you want from life…
Everybody who reads this book will interpret it slightly differently.
The true nature of a book that pulls at your heartstrings and
makes you think about your own journey through life.'
— *Goodreads* Review

'I really enjoyed the wider questions Home provides its readers…
I think this is a great book to read to inspire young minds
and to teach important lessons about acceptance, teamwork
and standing up for what you believe in.
A great book for inquisitive readers!'
— *NetGalley* Review

'Home is a joy to read and a crucial reminder that
life is a profoundly mysterious adventure'
— Reader Review

By the Same Author:

Courting the Future
Why is the Human on Earth?
A Second Chance at Life
A Short Journey of Poem Spirals

HOME

MY LIFE IN THE UNIVERSE

by

MARK BALLABON

with illustrations by
Grant MacDonald

Eminent
PRODUCTIONS Ltd

HOME
my life in the universe
Mark Ballabon

Illustrator: Grant MacDonald
Layout: The Flying Fish Studios
Production: Nick Ross

First Edition. Published in the UK in 2022 by:
Eminent Productions Ltd. The Centre, Bath Place, Barnet EN5 5XE England

Printed in the UK on FSC certified paper by:
TJ Books, Trecerus Industrial Estate, Padstow PL28 8RW England

A CIP catalogue record for this book is available from the British Library.
ISBN: 9780955948770

FSC Certified

#LeahsUniverse   www.leahsuniverse.com

Inspired by true events
and real teenagers

THE GALLERY OF WINDOWS

This story is dedicated to the young in spirit.

Wherever on this beautiful planet you live,
and whatever conflicts surround you,
may your courage and passion for life
ease away the shadows of impossibility.

All the technologies you will ever need
are those you were born with;
your mind the most powerful technology of all.

Our purpose and destiny in life are ours to choose,
if we get the chance.

You are
here!

I am here too.

We're spinning through space and time, on the edge of our Milky Way galaxy. I've seen a glittering arc of it on a pitch-black winter's night.

And it made me wonder...

...where is home?

My name is Leah.

I could never have imagined that I'd be stuck in this depressing place, still in pain. I turned 14 last Tuesday but only found out two days later. I'll explain more when they finally let me out of here. But I can't wait.

So I'm writing this out in my old journal. I think you can tell so much about a person from their handwriting — like the way they curl or slant their letters. Mine's a dead giveaway, isn't it? Overdramatic and oversensitive.

At least I've got this glossy postcard from Sean by my side. It shows the crystal blue ocean at Fintra Beach, along the coast of Donegal where he's from. My memory of him keeps me going, but summer camp seems a long time ago.

৭ ৭ ৭

I'm looking out of the open window in this sterile, white room. A scent of autumn rises up from a heap of leaves below, and over on the left, someone's neatly planted a circle of purple and yellow pansies.

I gaze out into the distance far across brown fields and suddenly, I'm running scared through the forest to get away from... oh. Sorry. I must get to the point of this. The doctor's due back to see me again in ten minutes.

I really need to share my story, because for the last few days I've been feeling desperate... like I've got to write this down before I forget why I need to.

I'm writing this for anyone who's ever had an experience that no one could explain, or asked a big question that no one could answer. It's also for those adults who really need to listen more (I've got a few in mind).

At first, I thought my story might sound too weird, but my best friend Taka snuck in here yesterday with dark chocolate smuggled in her back pocket and told me not to change a word... well, not until I get her final edits.

With her 'no messing' stare and hands on hips, she snapped at me, "The stargazers, the survival group and climate activists from camp will fall in love with your story. The school bullies will totally hate it. So get writing! But just because you're a spelling bee champ, don't get cocky using long words I can't understand."

Taka is an Aries, and whatever anyone thinks about astrology, she is the ultimate ram - nothing gets in her way once she's made up her mind. She's already decided to be my editor, and now she's told me I only have three months to finish this - no pressure then.

The thing is, I've always loved reading true stories, especially about teenagers going on crazy adventures inside never-ending caves, out on survival trips or solving impossible mysteries. But this is the first time in my life where I have my own story, and I must tell it.

Some stories take you to a different world, but it's as real as this one. Like when Taka hung this giant, full-colour poster of the Andromeda Galaxy above her bed

– that's the nearest big spiral galaxy to our own. It's a close neighbour... only trillions of miles around the corner! If you gaze at it for a minute, you get sucked into its sparkling whirlpool of billions of stars, taking you to another world.

I sometimes imagine myself at the centre of the Andromeda Galaxy, in a life different to the one I'm in now. Maybe someone else out there imagines waking up one day living in another part of the universe.

So I wonder if what's happened to me has ever happened to anyone else.

*

*

*

I was going through a very stressful time a month ago, and that's when I began drafting this in my journal... which took like ten times longer than typing! Yet writing it out by hand slowed me down a lot and let me relax. It helped me to meditate more deeply on the special people I've met and the experiences I never believed could have happened to me.

The streams of my story are turning into a flood now and I mustn't stop the flow – it's too strong. I mean, only fish like salmon can swim against the currents. So I have to write this out live, right now, even from this miserable room.

Lastly, before I forget.

Although Taka and I are both fast readers, she reckons this story needs to be read s-l-o-w-l-y. My Uncle Jake agreed with her. He said that reading it too quickly would turn it into a greasy, fast-food takeaway book - and that wouldn't taste great.

Also, I find the word 'chapter' kind of annoying. It reminds me of an English lesson where Mr Eaton gave me an earful in front of the whole class for not remembering the title of chapter 1 in a very BORING, classic Victorian novel. Blaaah!

So instead, I've used the word 'window', as that's what I'm looking through right now. Through this window, I can clearly picture each event in my story.

And an image from the mystical island near where I grew up is already in sight...

WINDOW ONE

MY LIFE-CHANGING ESSAY

My Life-Changing Essay

At last. I'm back home and totally relieved to be up in my cosy bedroom, typing away on my tablet. The first four days in hospital were the strangest time of my life. I later found out from my Uncle Jake that I might have been through... well, something I'd never heard of before called a 'near-death experience'. Hazy memories are coming back to me about it... but my story doesn't begin there.

It began in January this year with that stern English teacher, Mr Eaton, and what was a nanosecond away from a shouting match with big Ed in class.

"Yeah, right, so I never did that grammar exercise you set. So what?" Ed shrugged, glancing behind with a big fat smirk to his back-row gang of mates.

"Grammar's rubbish. It don't teach you nuffin' you need to know in real life. You wouldn't understand that. Anyway... never 'ad time... been takin' care of my mum for months now, ever since the doctor told her she 'ad c..."

"Stop!" shouted Mr Eaton, losing his cool.

"No, I won't. You don't get people like me, do you? We're not good enough for you lot, are we?"

Mr Eaton flushed red across his whole face. Beads of sweat were soon snaking down his forehead. He wiped them off with his shirt sleeve, his hand shaking.

"I understand about your mum, Ed. Believe me, I understand. I'm very sorry she's not well. You can tell me about her diagnosis after school, and then I'll tell you about mine."

The class was instantly hushed by the shockwaves. What diagnosis? Mr Eaton leaned sharply forward in his chair, gripping his head with both hands and bracing himself as if he was about to crash on board a plane.

Ed sat down sheepishly as Mr Eaton stumbled to his feet. We'd never seen him lose his temper this way before. He must have shocked himself to openly admit that he was ill.

"I'm sorry, I'm really sorry. You don't deserve my anger. But I've not been well for almost a year, and the frustration and fear have become almost unbearable. I must apologise."

Mr Eaton gathered himself, sighed and walked to the back of the class, leaning stiffly against the radiator. The school bell wrecked the silence, but no one budged.

"It's ironic," he said softly. "This week's homework essay is going to be very different. I want you to write freely. Let your emotions and reasonings flow, without worrying about grammar or spelling. Yes, that *is* what I just said.

"This essay has to be authentic. Because the topic I've chosen for you is… 'Understanding people'."

He paused to compose himself. "And to be very frank, perhaps that's an essay I need to write too."

Muffled laughter broke out, melting the icy atmosphere as the class began to shuffle out of the room. I'd never heard a teacher speak about their personal life before with their students. It was very brave.

As I was passing him on the way out, I had to stop and look up. I'd always thought that he had issues with me and the way I challenged some of the world's greatest novelists as being too predictable or prejudiced. But my words leapt out.

"It's alright, Mr Eaton. We never knew. It's understood. I'm going to write that essay with everything I've got."

He half-smiled, with an emptiness in his gaze. But I meant it. He'd triggered something from deep inside. I wanted to understand people, whatever that took.

☆ ☆ ☆ ☆ ☆

My homework began the next morning before breakfast as I was approaching the bathroom. The door was ajar, and I saw Mum frowning as she examined herself closely in the mirror. She caught me peeking.

"I must get my hair done. I can't keep these greys at bay any longer. But the cost of highlights… and my credit card's already creaking."

"At least you have hair to worry about," grumbled Dad, half-joking. He joined the bathroom queue behind my eight-year-old brother Aiden, in his new sea-green rugby shirt. "Come on, Mum. I need to go now," he piped up.

Sisu, our beloved cat, darted between Mum's legs and mine, plotting her exit – she knew to scram whenever a whiff of worry filled the air.

Then I had a wild idea. For my essay on 'Understanding people', I could actually write about my family… without telling them, of course!

Who would everyone else in class write about? Celebrities, sports heroes, maybe their neighbours? Mmm. No competition. My family would be much more interesting.

After school that day, I couldn't wait to begin. I poured some fresh grapefruit juice, rushed upstairs and switched on my tablet.

Understanding people. Where to start? With myself or my family? Maybe one would lead to the other.

I decided not to overthink it, gulped down half the glass of juice and began tapping away non-stop, trying to capture the speed of my train of thoughts.

Understanding People through their Stories

Leah Greene. 11th January

Part 1. My Funny Family and I

Mum and Dad fell in love on a boat when they were both 22. I know that sounds very romantic, but I do have a lot of evidence that it's true!

My mum grew up near the great lakes in Killarney, Ireland. And when she began studying to become a midwife, she had to work to pay for it because her family were in debt. So she took a part-time job as crew on one of those little boats that ferry tourists from Ross Castle to the mysterious island of Innisfallen on Lough Leane, which means 'Lake of Learning'.

My mum loves telling me their story, which becomes more exaggerated every year.

"Your dad was on that little ferry boat one summer and he got clever when it was nearing the island. He clambered up onto his feet to prove how good his balance was on a moving boat, but jumped off too soon before docking and belly-flopped straight into the deep lake. My best friend Chloe and I had to dive in and rescue him as he hadn't tied up his life jacket properly – it was half strangling him!"

That's my mum's version. Dad swears he didn't need rescuing. That says a lot about their different characters.

Nearly drowning in a lake is a pretty dramatic way to get to meet someone for the first time. Anyway, Dad's a slow burner. When he returned the next summer to Killarney, it was love at second sight. Those warm summer breezes by the lake intoxicate people. He proposed to my mum in the Abbey ruins on that island, and a year later I came into the world.

Their stories help me understand why my mum worries a lot about money and why my dad is afraid of water. And I get why they both love being out in nature and discovering secret places… the lakes and haunted sites around Killarney are full of unsolved mysteries.

I had to wait five and a half years to get a brother. I'd always wanted a brother who I could spoil and tell scary stories to.

Aiden was a quiet baby and would spend hours staring into space… until he learnt to walk. Then he became an expert in knocking things off coffee tables and taking apart every piece of equipment he could find – especially alarm clocks for some reason. Now I understand why he already sees himself as the greatest scientist on earth.

I also understand where my looks come from. It seems that my sandy blonde hair comes from my dad's Norwegian father (thank you, Grandad), and my naughty pixie nose and love of the wild comes from my great aunt who was a famous explorer. As for my big ears, I've no idea where they came from or what they're doing there. All this spells mischief, which is where I got the nickname 'Miss Chief' from when I was a child. My nickname didn't last long, but the mischief did.

I spent my first six years near the lakes, and many magical hours playing among the ruins on the island – just me and my wild imagination. I was there to protect the island from pirates with sharp swords and tourists leaving rubbish. I remember when I was only six, I spotted a man dumping a bottle, plastic cutlery and a used paper plate and then walking right off. I ran up to him and shouted, "Who are you leaving that for, mister?" This was my little world, and no one was going to spoil it.

It makes me understand my love of adventure books and why I'm always trying to find ways to protect the planet and people who can't defend themselves.

Since we moved near Trent Park in North London seven years ago, the Japanese Water Garden near the centre of the park has become my new island. That's where I met my best friend, Taka. We both used to love running across the wooden bridges and hanging upside down from the rails. We even tried to swim in the ponds there during a summer heatwave and catch little fish with our hands – we didn't, but we loved cooling off and getting muddy. Even then, though, I realised we were very different.

She was the bold, brave and popular one at school. The red streaks on her long, curly hair were a little warning sign that she was not to be messed with. Whereas I was often to be found eating lunch on my own or reading at the back of the library. It's changed a bit though. I'm still the quieter one, but much more outspoken in class now.

Everyone says we're like sisters. It's in the stars too – Aries and Librans are sister signs. My mum thinks our differences make us much more interesting. She told me that, "Quiet folk and chatty folk mix well. They each have something the other needs."

That makes me think that different people don't need to fight each other about being different. They can enjoy their differences and learn from them.

Most adults, who believe that they really get me, usually describe me as 'precocious'. They use that label to criticise me in different ways: either, 'she's gotten too big for her boots since she became the under-15's school spelling bee champ'; or, 'she uses way too many long words for her age'; or, 'she's unusually cute and clever for someone who's so weird'.

So basically, they don't get me at all. How can you understand a person if you squeeze them into a tiny box containing one word, like 'weird'? Boxing is easy and understanding is not.

And that's the whole point, I think. We don't understand people because we're always assuming that we do.

The essay felt alive. And until now, I hadn't realised that this was how I thought about people, including myself. I'd forgotten to mention Uncle Jake though, but he'd never find out.

I twirled one of my braids between my fingers, wondering how to continue. I had zero ideas for Part 2. So I read Part 1 out loud.

'Mmm…' I wondered, 'this is beginning to sound more like an essay about myself'. And as much as I didn't believe that adults understood me at all, it left me doubting how much I understood myself. That thought turned my whole brain inside out. Understanding myself was something I'd never consciously tried to do before.

A little volcano then erupted in my head. A volcano called 'Maia'! Why hadn't it even crossed my mind until now? That's it! If anyone on this planet understands human beings, it's Maia. She's the coolest, wisest adult I've ever met and a close family friend.

Part 2 was now downloading super-fast into my head, and I had to start writing and stop thinking.

Understanding People through their Stories

Leah Greene. 11th January

Part 2. Maia at the beach

"Understanding other people depends on how much you understand yourself. Every single relationship you build with other people depends on your relationship with yourself."

That was Maia's wise advice to me once.

She used to teach a philosophy course at university, but eventually gave it up because she said that the course was so stuck in the past that she feared her students would get stuck there too. She tried to change things, but change wasn't in the uni's philosophy.

Philosophy means 'love of wisdom' and Maia explained to me that, "You don't have to study famous men in Ancient Greece, Rome or anywhere else to find wisdom. Just speak to a taxi driver, tour guide, parent, farmer, child… or listen to yourself speak sometimes. Everyone is a born philosopher. Maybe they don't know it yet."

I think that Maia should be a world leader – but that's just my view. And I want to share a snapshot of her story because she understands people like no one else.

My parents met Maia when I was about seven. We were on holiday on the island of Crete, and she was staying in the same hotel writing a book about the meaning of dreams.

I remember we were all on the beach one day, and I was crying because I was terrified of going into the sea. Other children around were pointing at me and laughing. Mum told me that Maia was standing nearby, saw me crying and ran straight into the sea, shouting out madly, "It's sooooo cold. But I love the wobbly waves!" Apparently, I switched from crying to shrieking laughter in seconds.

Maia looked so silly diving into the water with an oversized orange baseball cap on, which of course flew straight off with the first foaming wave! A few minutes later she ran out of the water smiling mischievously, with seaweed dripping from her hair.

My parents and Maia then got chatting, while I started walking down to the shore on my own, and then, step by step, into the cold sea – right up to my elbows. I'll never forget those mixed feelings of danger, joy and daring. I felt proud of myself and very happy that my parents didn't stop me – although they were watching through the back of their heads, of course!

Now I understand what Maia was trying to do; in being silly and then charging into the sea, she was trying to get me to relax and make it easier for me to overcome my fears. She gave me the courage to dare to do something that was so challenging at the time. She really understood me.

Since then, she's been such a bright light in my life, especially during some very lonely times. Like when Taka was off sick for a month and there was only one other girl at school I could talk to.

Maia would remind me that you may feel very lonely, but you're never alone. "You can always be friends with yourself, Leah, and with the natural worlds."

Now I enjoy being on my own sometimes. And when I am, I try to clear my mind of regrets and other clutter... like tidying the mess on my bedroom desk. Sorting through stuff helps me unwind.

So, I think Maia has been helping me to understand myself better – not by telling me how I should think, but by showing me other ways to think.

This all flowed out in one go, as effortless and fun as skimming stones across a lake – once you get the hang of it. I was nervous, though, that Mr Eaton would find my essay too personal or emotional. "Essays need to be eminently logical," as he loved to put it.

Concentrating so much on this essay had left me exhausted. Understanding is hard work, I realised. Yet I'd enjoyed digging deeper and uncovering things about people that could never be found on the surface.

As I was switching off my tablet, the word 'understand' suddenly shape-shifted in my head, broke in two and came out as, 'under stand' and 'stand under'. That was another clue, but my brain was overheating now.

Not to gloat on it, but when we all got our essays back, I found out that Mr Eaton had given mine the highest mark. "You are beginning to understand what motivates people to do what they do, Leah," he announced to the class. "And you're right, it's in their stories. Your essay demonstrates a lot of insight for a teenager."

Although the 'for a teenager' bit made me cringe, it didn't last long. I was so happy to be recognised, and right after that, I became Miss Popular in class. Even everyone's best friend, Lina Hart, who'd never once spoken to me, tried to get chatty. Well, all that didn't last for more than a few days, of course, but from then on, Mr Eaton stopped treating me like some stroppy girl with an attitude problem.

There was still something though about 'understanding people' which got right under my skin. It felt like I'd already begun writing another essay in my head.

I spent both afternoons that weekend closeted in my bedroom, writing, doodling and not wanting to speak with anyone, except for Taka, who called on Saturday.

"Still obsessed with that essay, Leah?"

"Well, maybe. I don't know."

"But it's not school homework anymore. It's over. Done. Let it go!"

"It was never homework for me in the first place. Mr Eaton opened this small window and now it's like… I've got to understand what motivates people. I mean… does that make any sense?"

"I'm not sure. All this seems to be making you super-serious."

"Oh. Sorry. I hope it's not making me boring to be around. It's just that this essay writing is making me happy…"

"Well, that's alright then. And don't worry. You're anything but boring… although you definitely need to understand yourself better!" she cackled.

I went back to scribbling away and watching people hurrying past on the street below, each with their peculiar walks. I was consciously searching for more clues, but to what?

Then a funny memory of Mr Eaton appeared. Since speaking openly about his illness, he'd become much more mellow and free. I remembered him standing on a chair in class almost singing the whole of Hamlet's brilliant speech, "There are more things in heaven and earth, Horatio, than are dreamt of in your philosophy..."

He then jumped down gracefully and gestured us to gather around him, and with the air of a wizard casting spells, he said, "So find out the mysteries of heaven and earth. Find out where you've come from... where your real home is."

Mysteries? Home? My home was in Stafford Close. He was obviously talking about some other home. What was he trying to say?

I began drifting away into a daydream about 'home' as haunting sounds of Mum's favourite cello suite – a famous one by Bach – floated up from one of our neighbours. I saw myself as a child playing with emerald green dragonflies by the shores of the lakes in Killarney. Other images came into view, in vivid colours, full screen, with surround sound of birdsong, people's voices and folk music.

I was transported to my last birthday on the island. There was 'Old Man Matty', who was one of the boat crew, my mum and Chloe, plus her daughter who was a year older than me. Dad was at home, looking after baby Aiden.

Mum loves Irish folk songs and with Matty on mandolin, we all sang our hearts out and ate way too much soda bread pudding.

There was a strange magic in the air that day, like we were being joined by dancing spirits or the ghosts of monks and choirs from hundreds of years ago. Before we left on the boat, Mum suddenly stopped. She stretched out her hands like she was trying to touch the air and whispered, "Feel the presence."

I wasn't sure what she meant, but my hands and cheeks went ice-cold and tingled with some kind of electricity.

Chloe felt it too. "The fairies and elves are sleeping, like stars hidden by the daylight – unseen, yet present. I wonder what illumined people once lived on this island, surrounded by these enchanting waters. A powerful event has happened here."

She turned pale, and I began to see a faint glow of purple around her head and a shimmer of silver pass over her face.

The cello music became louder and I woke up in the present. Wherever my daydream had taken me, I knew that I'd experienced one of those mysteries in heaven and on earth which Mr Eaton had told us to search for.

And I felt part of the mystery. Because I realised there was so much that I still needed to understand about people, especially myself.

WINDOW TWO
☆
THE CODE OF FIVE

The Code Of Five

Mr Eaton retired a few weeks after his illness was sadly diagnosed as terminal. He wrote this amazing letter to our class, saying how much he'd learnt from us and apologising again for being too strict. "Now I'm going to visit the birthplaces of every one of my favourite English poets," he wrote. "That will be heaven for me."

It was a farewell letter, and when the Deputy Head read it out, a rush of emotion swept the classroom and touched everyone, even Ed. I watched him carefully out of the corner of my eye as he tried to make out he was scratching an itch on his eyebrow – but he was cleverly using his thumb to wipe away his tears. We were all going to miss Mr Eaton.

Taka wasn't in my class, so I told her the story at lunchtime.

"He might die soon, maybe months. It's so sad. But he's going travelling around England now to visit…"

I put the brakes on, seeing Taka grimace.

"I hate talking about death. Have you forgotten what I went

through last year? Allana should never have died in that car accident."

"Sorry, Taka. I know. Your cousin was so young… I'm sorry."

She looked away and the moment passed. But there was a thirst in me to discover what dying was really about. Some adults were still telling me that I was too young to understand. So why did they always have a look of fear when I asked? That didn't seem natural to me, but dying somehow did.

That evening, my mum helped me write a letter to Mr Eaton.

Dear Mr Eaton,

Writing that essay you gave us on 'Understanding people' has been life-changing for me. I know that sounds dramatic, but it's true. I'm grateful you taught us to think for ourselves and to always be open to what we don't yet know.

You've inspired me to want to discover what else exists 'in heaven and earth' and where I've come from. I feel like I've just begun and am now reading Hamlet – although I haven't got past the first few paragraphs yet. Shakespeare's language is another mystery!

Enjoy your travels. You will always be a great teacher.

With my best wishes,
Leah Greene

After I'd given the letter to the Deputy Head, I was overcome with an unexpected sense of having outgrown school… or maybe needing to think about it in a fresh way. It left me with a very new thought – if I was to understand people better, maybe I should try to look a bit differently at the teachers and students who I mix with at school.

That thought was a bit depressing, though, because Taka is my only real friend there. And for me, our school is only exciting when there's an arts and crafts project, a sports day or a special field trip to somewhere far away. Otherwise, it's as annoying as our history teacher, Mrs Maynard — talking down to students with her fake posh accent is bad enough, but banging on about her grandmother who married a royal no one's ever heard of… why does she keep doing that?

Our art teacher, Mr Kowalski, is easier to understand. He does everything in slow motion and tells us amazing stories about painting on his own near the edge of cliffs. If things are less than perfect, however, his bottom lip starts twitching and he looks like he might burst out crying.

Mind you, I'm a bit of a perfectionist too, especially about my braiding techniques. I do French braids, fishtails, braided ponytails, buns, the lot. I enjoy doing plaited twin tails for school, as that seems to annoy people who think they look childish. They mock me by calling them 'girly pigtails', but that just makes me laugh.

I do get on with a few of the teachers and students, but I can't understand why I get picked on a lot. It's like Anunda and her best friend, Rhianna, who've never forgiven me for fouling them both in a school football match. I told them I was only going for the ball, but Rhianna growled, "Yeah, right. They all say that, don't they?"

They threatened to get me after school, but so far, they've never dared gang up on me because they know Taka would come after them. Other girls aren't so lucky.

Looking at people differently was going to be a steep uphill climb.

☆ ☆ ☆ ☆ ☆

One afternoon during that spring school term, Taka and I were taking a longer route home through Trent Park. There was a path halfway that led to a stream, where we sometimes bumped into Aiden and his mates. On this afternoon, however, as we got closer to that path, we heard a commotion and scuffled noises coming from behind a clump of trees on the other side.

I heard a boy cry out. We both ran, full speed. My God, it was Aiden.

"Leave me alone! Please. Let go."

"You're a waste of space. Little turd. What a loser," someone was shouting menacingly.

As we reached the trees, there was a bunch of teenagers just hanging out and doing nothing except watching Aiden getting beaten up. "Stop!" I shouted out furiously. But the two Bentoni brothers, who we instantly recognised from behind, had already shoved Aiden to the ground. His short, skinny body rolled over and thudded hard against a tree trunk. They were about to kick him, but by this time Taka, me and another girl called Ava had already rushed over to stand in their way.

The Bentonis laughed viciously. "Oops. Girls to the rescue. What a wimp." They slinked off, turning around at one point to show their big smirking faces to the crowd.

I snarled and swore loudly at everyone standing around as we lifted Aiden carefully to his feet. He was struggling not to cry.

"I'm okay. Don't make a fuss."

"Aiden, you're bleeding. You've got a cut across your forehead and cheek. And you must be bruised all over."

He let me wipe the blood from his face with a tissue as he pressed around his ribs.

"Just bruised. Not much pain. It's okay."

His hands were trembling though, as he wheezed and coughed. He sat down, looking utterly dejected. I guessed this wasn't the first time.

"We need to go to the police," insisted Taka.

"No way. They'll make me pay for it at school."

I took his hand, but he snatched it back.

"How long has this been going on for?" I asked.

"I'm off."

"Aiden!"

"Forget it. And don't say a word to Mum or Dad."

He limped forward a few steps, wincing, and then managed to sprint away.

The Bentonis had a bad reputation in this area. Even older students in my school tried to avoid them.

Ava was in Aiden's class and told us some of what had been going on. "I reported them once for kicking and punching another boy in the playground. They enjoy picking on people who they think are weak or uncool… almost got expelled for it once. They always look angry and ready to take it out on anyone they don't like. I've seen Aiden run away from them before. I didn't know he was your brother."

"Yes. Thanks, Ava. I've got to go."

"Call me if you need me," cried Taka, as I raced off.

When I got home, I rushed up to Aiden's room doing my best to remain calm. I was already calculating how to take revenge on the Bentonis when I remembered Maia calling revenge 'a fool's game'. I deleted all my thoughts. My brother simply needed me now.

"Aiden!" I called out. "We need to talk about this. Come on."

Nothing. Seconds flew past. I called again. Eventually, he opened the door a fraction and peered through the gap, looking despondent.

"Shhh. Dad's going to hear."

"What's been going on?"

Aiden stepped back and as I came in, he slumped down on the

floor in the corner, pressing his head into his knees. I waited, but he said nothing. So I sat down opposite him.

"Aiden. Let me check your wounds."

"Shhh. Keep your voice down. I washed the blood off. Put two bandages on. The bruises don't really show yet."

"Okay, but… look, you need to tell me… what's been happening?"

Aiden hesitated. I waited again. He finally opened up and spoke shakily about the name-calling, shoving and kicking which the Bentonis had been doing to him and two of his classmates since term began. I was burning inside. It was painful to hear. At least he felt he could confide in me, but what could I say or do to help him?

Maia had shown me how she would sit down with a blank sheet of paper whenever she was facing a big challenge. She would make notes and sketch out the bigger picture of what was going on and then place herself in it. "Always start impersonal first. Then personal. Otherwise, all you have is your view, not the overview," she'd explained.

I understood that, but the problem in this case was that I didn't know what the bigger picture was. Anyway, this was my brother. Of course it was personal.

After Aiden finished talking, I caught the thread of an idea. Could my essay help solve this?

Still struggling to keep cool, I said, "I think most bullies are insecure people who try to act strong by picking on someone smaller than them."

"But I *am* smaller than them," Aiden mumbled.

"They're also weak. Bullies are always trying to prove themselves, which only weak people do."

"Yes. But they beat people up badly," said Aiden, now getting teary. I began to lose the plot here and my only thought was to storm into his Head Teacher's office the next day and demand that she lock them both up in a dark cell.

I tried another tack.

"Look, Aiden. I heard the Bentonis live with their stepfather who's a control freak. I know that's no excuse, but behind their anger and boasting, maybe they're just looking for respect or attention?"

"So now you want me to make friends with them?" he fumed.

"I'm sorry," I said, realising that I was making things worse. "I know it hurts."

I so didn't want my brother to feel this fear. I closed my eyes and took in a deep, long breath.

"Some animals, like dogs, smell fear. Bullies do too, so they attack... I mean, you remember Dad explaining that to us once?"

Aiden nodded reluctantly, but then snapped, "I told you not to tell Dad or Mum."

"It's okay. I haven't. But you must."

"Yeah, but you didn't tell them when it happened to you once."

"Well, I was wrong... and anyway, as soon as I found out the name of that girl who'd been leaving those hate notes for me in the classroom, I reported her to the Deputy. Plus, Taka always has my back. If anyone is picking on me, she somehow miraculously appears around a corner or at the end of a long corridor. She has this way of standing tall and looking mean, which backs off the bullies big time."

I stopped. Aiden's face had scrunched up. He wasn't going to take in another word. I realised my big mistake – Aiden didn't have a friend like Taka and my little speech had just made it worse, again.

I needed to put my essay into practice differently and understand my brother, not just bullies.

"Aiden. I'm with you. I understand your fear of bullies. It's okay, you've got me. You're not alone. I've got your back. This is going to stop."

I meant it.

Aiden swallowed hard.

"Look, I know Mum's out for an hour, but why don't we go and talk to Dad right now? Yes?"

I sensed Aiden shudder inside. Clutching his ribs, he followed grudgingly behind me as I tracked Dad's voice to the kitchen, where I overheard him finishing a work call.

Dad was puzzled at the hasty entrance of the two of us, standing side by side like we were a delegation from the local youth club. Aiden's bandaged forehead and the dirt marks all over his shirt sounded the alarm as Dad's eyebrows arched high. I waited to give Aiden the space to tell his story, which he did in graphic detail.

When he described the first bullying incident, Dad looked distraught. As Aiden went on, Dad's face sank in horror as he grasped the extent of what had been happening. He clasped his hands tightly.

By the end, Aiden was choking up and Dad went over and hugged him like he'd never let him go. "I'm truly sorry you've had to go through this. It's devastating to hear. But I'm very relieved that you've told me. And I know what I need to do before we go any further."

Dad grabbed his phone and ran straight out of the kitchen and into the back garden. Baaammm! The door slammed shut.

"Let's eavesdrop," I whispered, pointing to the kitchen window. Aiden discreetly opened it.

"No. I can't wait. Please tell her it's urgent," we overheard Dad arguing. "She needs to be aware of how bad the bullying is getting at her school. She needs to know about my son."

Dad rarely raises his voice, but when he was speaking, we were worried that both neighbours and half the road would hear every word. Right afterwards, he came back into the kitchen looking satisfied but shaken.

"It's going to be okay, Aiden. Please, don't worry. I spoke to the Deputy Head. She's on the case right now, not only for you. There are others. Anyway, do you want to have a chat about it?"

I'll never forget that talk between my brother and Dad. It was as if each word was meant for me too. He didn't offer Aiden a theory or tips on bullying. He offered his experience.

"Remember when I was working as a construction manager on big building sites in central London? Well, on one major contract, I was running a team of over twenty tough men and women, under the pressure of deadlines. I had to break up several fights and even got threatened physically myself.

"After six months of this, I'd absolutely had enough. So, I developed what I called a 'Code of Five' and trained all my teams in it. I can still recall it word for word:

1. **Avoid dangerous situations, if you can.**
2. **Don't let anyone wind you up.**
3. **Breathe deeply, stay calm, get help.**
4. **Know what you won't do.**
5. **Learn from every challenge.**

"This 'Code of Five' was a bit of a lifesaver for me and my teams. It might help you a lot. You can find your own, too."

Dad wasn't telling Aiden or me exactly what to do, but he was certainly showing us what not to do. Aiden sighed, relaxed his shoulders, and sat upright in his chair. At the same time, I could feel my spine straighten and this surge of strength pulse through me.

Over the following week, I noticed that something had toughened up in Aiden.

On the Friday after school, Taka and I were wandering through the park when we saw Ava striding towards us.

"Leah, I wanted to tell you about your brother at school today."

"What?" I asked as a wave of anxiety rippled through me.

"Well, I watched him walking down the main school corridor this morning. I was at the other end, only a couple of metres away from the Bentonis who were lurking there. There were no teachers around, and I knew they were going to go for him.

"I was about to step in, but Aiden was strolling towards them with this amazing air of confidence. He didn't stoop or look down at his shoes. When he got closer to them, he looked both brothers straight in the eye for a few seconds and walked off.

"You should've seen the surprise on their faces. One of them swore at him, but they never laid a hand on him."

I was so relieved and thanked Ava for her care. Taka hugged me close. "Whatever happens in the future, your brother's become a lot braver and smarter at outfoxing the foxes." I glowed with pride.

Just before half-term, the Bentonis received a final warning. When we told Dad about it, he smiled. "Well, just remember that the Bentonis are not your enemies. Creating enemies is a complete waste of energy and time. You could spend that time with your friends, yes?

"People who feel inferior often create enemies. That's what bullies do. It makes them feel superior."

I wrote Dad's words below his 'Code of Five' and made it into a little card – I carried it in my backpack for whenever I needed to remind myself. This entire experience had helped me become a little calmer and more in control of my own reactions.

What felt urgent now, though, was to become more confident in myself... something which came so naturally to Taka. I knew that I was still a kind of nervy girl and too self-conscious, but I could feel that was changing.

Then, as if something in heaven or on earth had been listening in, an awkward situation spun my thinking 180 degrees.

I was waiting for Taka by the gates after school had finished, and saw her in the distance chatting with a little group in front of the library entrance. I began walking over, and as I got nearer, I heard her cracking jokes and winding up the boys, obviously unaware that I'd already been waiting quite a while for her.

I stopped a few metres away and sensed this nasty storm of jealousy and irritation brewing up inside me. I was about to make a dash for the gates, but in the next instant, Taka spotted me.

"Hey, Leah. Come and join us. We're just joking about the new Head Teacher and her ridiculously outdated navy-blue outfit. Power dressing it is not!" They all sniggered, but I would have sprinted away if I could have. I didn't fit in and didn't want to.

"Got to get home now, Taka," were the only words I could manage, as I broke out in a raw blush of embarrassment. My face was almost burning as I turned to leave.

"Oh, okay. I'll say goodbye then to this sad little bunch of teacher's pets!" They all let out another roar of laughter.

As we walked out of the school, Taka faced me with a look of sheer confusion.

"I don't get it, Leah. What's up with you?"

"Nothing. Really… I mean, well, it's just that you always seem so confident around everyone, even the boys. And I…"

"Don't compare us, Leah. You know we're very different," she tutted. "You don't need to be like me. Don't forget that I'm a fiery Aries and you're a cool Libran! Remember what your Uncle Jake told us about that? I barge straight in on things, and you tiptoe carefully around the edges.

"Anyway, I'm not as confident as you think."

"Really?"

44

"Well… yes. I mean, I'd like to trust myself more."

"What's that got to do with being confident?"

"A lot. You know my mum studied English Lit at uni, and she told me once that the word 'confidence' comes from Latin. It means, 'with trust'. So she often reminds me that if I want to be more confident, I need to trust myself more."

"Wow. Trust. That's so strange. I've been thinking for weeks that I need to trust myself more."

"Well, start now!" she teased, laughing to herself.

My face had cooled down, and the stress began to drain out of my body. I skipped around her, feeling a ton lighter.

"Good to see you a bit less serious, Leah!"

When I got home afterwards, I went straight down the narrow side entrance and out onto the small, square lawn in our back garden. I took off my shoes, lay down, and let my fingers comb through the crisp, fresh grass. A parade of brilliant white clouds drifted slowly overhead.

Maybe I was beginning to understand more about why people do what they do. I was certainly starting to understand more about the world I was growing up in. And as those clouds disappeared from view and blue space opened overhead, this warm sensation of calm washed over me.

I had a picture of me standing on a wide pathway that led into a vast forest… like I was about to go on a journey into the unknown. All I had was myself. But now I understood myself a little better.

Everything had gone quiet.

I stood up, tall. With arms reaching upwards and feet wide apart, I made a star shape with my body.

Feeling a rush of strength, I heard myself say, "My name is Leah."

I don't know why, but it made me feel like I was really worth something.

WORDS, SWORDS AND DANCING LETTERS

Words, Swords And Dancing Letters

There were two firm knocks on my bedroom door. I knew those 'one loud, one louder' knocks as well as Sisu's miaow.

"Hi, Taka. I was just thinking of you," I said, welcoming her into a jumble of papers, hair bands and cushions scattered across the floor.

"Hey, Leah. I got stressed hearing my parents arguing again about whatever – I had to get out of the house. So… your dad said you've been banging around up here all day."

"Well, I read my mum's book on clearing out clutter and thought half-term would be the perfect time. Sorting through stuff calms me down. So, here I am, in a total mess!"

Taka surveyed the various heaps of stuff and picked up a salmon-pink pair of trainers.

"Yeah, pink was my colour then," I muttered, slightly embarrassed. "But check this out!"

I held up a chunky handmade journal that my parents had bought me on an outing to a craft fair.

"What's in it?"

"Some secrets which Maia showed me."

"Are you still on about the mysteries of understanding people and Mr Eaton quoting Shakespeare while standing on a chair?"

"Yes… and no! It was what he said when he got *down* from the chair! Anyway, don't you think that finding the mysteries of heaven and earth sounds exciting?"

Taka hesitated. "Well… I guess so. But how do you find them?"

I flopped onto one of the big velvet cushions, still holding onto my journal.

"What did Maia tell you?" asked Taka suddenly, as if I was hiding something from her. "You know, I boasted about your essay to everyone, but you've only ever told me snippets about Maia. What's she really like?"

"Well, I guess she's almost 60 but looks sooooo young. You should have seen her cool jazz dance vibe at last New Year's Eve party!

"She's quite tall, with warm, amber-brown eyes and black, bushy hair with silvery wisps."

"Okay," interrupted Taka, "but I meant, what do you actually talk about?"

"Ah, do you want to hear this?" I pointed to pages 26 and 27 in my journal, which I'd been reading before she arrived. Taka put two thumbs up.

"Okay. Mmm… it starts here, last summer…"

Sunday, June 24th

Maia showed me the most amazing thing today. She explained how important it is to look inside things, to discover their magic or their 'essence'.

When I asked her what she meant, she whipped out an apple from her big old leather bag, opened up her penknife, and sliced the apple right across the middle. And there it was, shazam! I couldn't believe it... a star, a perfect star! Aiden's going to be amazed when I show him.

Maia called the star a 'pentagram' – a five pointed shape that she said 'appeared on earth' many millions of years ago.

I didn't believe her at first and she knew it.

So she reached back into her bag and carefully pulled out something intriguing. She told me it was from one of her many trips to coastlines around the world, where she loved rummaging around in rock pools.

It was a sea star. She'd found it dead while rock pooling on the coast of North Wales and had preserved it – so this one was still pinkish.

People also call it a starfish, but it's not a fish at all. It's a beautiful little sea animal in the shape of a five-pointed star. And Maia was right. I checked it out. There were sea stars 500 million years ago! Astonishing... a pentagram shape appeared in the form of sea stars and sea urchins, millions of years before humans ever walked on earth.

I wonder where else I can find natural things like a sea star, with five arms or five points...

"She's amazing! I can't wait to see the star inside an apple! Do you still have that sea star?"

"It's on the corner shelf over there. Careful. It's fragile."

Taka stroked her fingers across its prickly surface and giggled as it tickled her.

"Listen to this then!" I enthused, flicking speedily over the pages.

Saturday, July 7th
I was climbing an oak tree today in Trent Park. I could easily hang from this big, low branch and even swing about on it. As I did, I found myself looking strangely at my hands... my hands! Five! Why five fingers? Why five different lengths? What does five mean? What are numbers? Why do I ask so many questions that no one ever seems able to answer?

Except Maia, that is. She doesn't always know the answer, but then she always has a way better question.

I closed my journal and looked up keenly at Taka.

"Those mysteries... that's awesome. And I love your questions. Did you tell Maia about your essay, then?"

"I only read her Part 1 over the phone. She said I was a young philosopher... so I think she liked it."

"Is that her?" Taka asked, instinctively picking up a photo half-buried in one of the piles. "Where's she from? How come I haven't met her yet?"

"She goes away travelling a lot, and often visits her family in a little village in Nepal called Solambu. She can see Mount Everest from there."

"Wow! I've always wanted to climb to the top of that mountain one day and see the whole world... and then hang glide back home to London..."

"Taka, you're crazy!"

She looked more closely at the photo, squinting at it like a detective examining evidence. New questions tumbled out.

"Is she one of those clairvoyants, then? Does she see into the future? What's her secret?"

"I can't answer all that. But I know that one of her sort-of 'secret powers' is language."

"What?!" said Taka, wide-eyed.

"Yes… she listens to the tone in people's voices and what's really speaking through them. She's a magician with words and brilliant at reading body language… you know, posture and stuff."

Talk about body language! Taka crossed her arms, frowned and made a long, drawn-out sigh.

I was hoping that I hadn't given the wrong impression of Maia, or made her out to be some kind of prophet or guru. But Taka didn't like a mystery she couldn't quickly solve, and Maia was a big one.

Taka's arms uncrossed, and the lines on her forehead arched up.

"I want to meet her. Can I come next time you go to see her?"

"Yes. Let's do it! She lives in Clapham, south of the river."

"Great. Maybe when we go to see her, we could also visit the Observatory in Greenwich? I've been there once and actually stood on that meridian line they say separates the East and West of the planet. Imagine having one foot on each side of the world! I'll take you there, but you've got to watch out for the hordes of tourists battling away with their selfie sticks!" Taka said excitedly.

"Sounds interesting, but who decided to split the planet in two? It's one world. Anyway, you'll have to lend me your selfie stick to defend myself!

"I'm sure Maia's going to love meeting you. She's a Leo, by the way – fearless and funny. And she told me that she chose the name 'Maia' for herself on her 18th birthday. Isn't that cool?"

"So what's her real name?"

"Aahana Lamar. What name would you choose for yourself if you could?"

"Mmm. Don't know. Molly Brolly?! But why choose your own name?"

"Not sure. Maybe because it means something special to you. I think I'd call myself… Hope. Anyway, let's ask her when we meet up. I just got a postcard from her saying that she'll be back in London in a few days. She's doing volunteer work out in Colombia."

"She sounds kind."

"Yeah. I'll text her and let you know what she says."

"I'd love to hear more of Maia's secrets… but you so need to get your mess sorted. I'll see you tomorrow in the Water Garden. And make sure I get to meet Maia when she's back!" she ordered, scooting out the door.

I couldn't wait to see how Taka and Maia would get on together. I'd already checked that out in my astrology book, and read that Aries and Leo are both fire signs, and can easily get into heated arguments. They're both very independent-minded and stubborn. But as a Libra, I could be the peacemaker!

Having finished texting Maia, I reflected for a moment about being independent-minded. The thought that my teenage life was, as my mum once put it, 'engaged in an existential struggle to become an independent woman' made me smile.

I knew that I was willing to be the odd one out – I usually am. In my whole class, I'm the only student who doesn't have a smart-phone. I did get one last Christmas, but it gave me a real headache, even with earphones. Plus, the daily social media shaming triggered my anxieties. I'm not going to compete with photoshopped and filtered teenagers who claim to be 'living my best life'. Whatever that is, I don't want to live their version of life.

Also, some images gave me nightmares for weeks – one image a boy sent me still does, really. How come tech companies aren't able to stop cyber-flashing and online bullying when they know the harm it causes?

So, I have this dumb phone which only does calls and texts. It's much smarter.

Last time I got out my phone after class, Ed took one look at it and announced, "That's the most uncool phone I've ever seen. I guess you can always message a dinosaur with it!"

The thing is, I prefer having conversations face to face and writing letters, shopping in shops and finding my own way to places. I enjoy working things out for myself. Why do I need the stress of following everyone else, or straining to get a gazillion followers? Anyway, my mum and Taka let me use their phones if I really need to go online when I'm out.

The door swung slowly open and in walked Dad.

"Here you go, love," he said, cheerfully passing me a steaming mug of fresh mint tea and a bar of organic dark chocolate. I'm sure that no one in school ever touches this stuff, but it's my favourite treat.

Ping! Maia responded saying that she would be in Barnet, North London, on Sunday morning and could drop in on us afterwards. Within minutes I'd spoken to my parents and Taka and set it all up for 1pm. Taka fizzed and sparked at me down the phone when I told her. At last, she was going to meet the woman I'd described as having almost supernatural powers.

☆ ☆ ☆ ☆ ☆

When Sunday arrived, my dad was buzzing around tidying up the kitchen, while Mum was out in the garden picking herbs and winter lettuces. Aiden was watching football replays in the living room, and I asked him to mute it so that Taka and I could share the latest gossip going around school about the new sports coach.

The doorbell rang, and it was like watching iron filings gather around a magnet. In an instant, we'd become the front-door welcoming committee.

Maia entered, looking relaxed and beaming away as she slipped off her lemon-yellow canvas shoes and began the hugging. Taka was looking unusually shy. Maia took a step towards her.

"I've been so looking forward to meeting you, Taka. From what Leah says, I know that you're a true friend, which is rare."

"Ah, mmm… thanks, Maia," replied Taka, blushing. "She is my best friend, and she's told me some incredible stories about you."

Sensing a bit of awkwardness, Mum hugged Maia again and almost dragged her into the kitchen.

"I've just baked one of my famous carrot cakes, Maia. Come on in."

I watched Maia sit down neatly with the poise of a ballerina. Her mind seemed to be somewhere far away, but she was clearly enjoying being spoiled.

We were happily drinking and wolfing down the carrot cake, when Dad said, "You must tell us about your trip to Colombia, and the mediation training you gave in villages."

"Don't ask her about work. The girls were so eager to see Maia and just have a chat," Mum interjected, quickly changing the subject. That gave me the green light.

"I was telling Taka all about you last weekend, Maia. I told her you had a sort of superpower."

"A superpower. Wow!" repeated Aiden.

"I don't think so," smiled Maia, amused.

"Well, you once told me about the power of language…"

"Yes. It has its own power. But it's only when you mean what you say, and say what you mean, that it becomes a superpower."

"What? I mean… what do you mean?" I asked, tripping over my words.

Maia grinned mischievously, like she was plotting something.

Taka went all timid again, but that vanished when Maia literally leapt up from her chair, cleared her throat and looked ready to make a speech or something. We shuffled our chairs backwards to get out of the way. Maia was always surprising, and I was loving this already.

She sang out the word 'universe' at the top of her voice.

"Universe, uni–verse, one verse, one song, one life, one great, amazing happening!"

Sisu bolted straight out into the garden and we all froze. Maia looked in a trance.

"Isn't it absolutely extraordinary? 'Universe', get it?" She said the word three times slowly, with emphasis – but we all just stared back blankly.

"Look, I'll write it down for you!" she persisted.

I knew that Maia loved using large sheets of paper, so I pointed her towards my art drawing pad leaning up against the wall. She grasped it firmly with one hand and held it up in the air like a lightsaber. With a whack, she threw it dramatically onto the floor, getting down on her knees as she began to write.

We hastily lined up our chairs around one side of the pad and watched Maia write down the word like this:

UNI – VERSE
UNI – SERVE
ONE – SERVE
SERVE ONE – serve one what?

We were slightly less blank now, but Aiden was having none of this.

"It doesn't make sense," he said bluntly.

Aiden prided himself on the fact that he knew far more than anyone his age, and that even teenagers were mostly 'way too illogical'.

Maia laughed heartily.

"Mmm," she said, being careful not to contradict Aiden. "Consider for a moment the words 'university' and 'universe'.

You should be studying the universe when you get to university, shouldn't you?"

Aiden was speechless for a change. But I began to see that Maia was sort of diving deep into the word to fish out its true meaning… its essence? Taka looked totally mesmerised.

Maia sprung up from the floor, hovering above the sheet of paper like a hawk. Ignoring the sudden buzz-buzz of Dad's phone, she swooped back down and excitedly wrote the words:

EXPRESS. IMPRESS. DEPRESS.

"Now, that's all about pressures, isn't it?" she declared, pointing to each word. "When you ex-press something with your emotions or words or movements, you let pressures out, don't you? But when pressures get into you, they im-press – they make an impression. Providing you don't get too de-pressed, of course! That's when all the pressure gets you down, isn't it?!"

Taka shot up like she'd had an electric shock. "What about the word 'compress'? You missed that one!" She sounded thrilled to slot in another piece of the puzzle.

"Indeed! Com-press. With pressure. Like when you've had a nasty cut and someone gets an ice pack, wraps a towel around it and presses it against your wound to stop the bleeding – a cold compress. Nice one, Taka."

Our heads were spinning now and before we could work it all out, Maia had triumphantly written down two words in big blue letters:

SILENT. LISTEN.

"The letters in both words are exactly the same. When you are silent inside, that's when you really listen. Don't you think that's true?" asked Maia, with a glint in her eyes.

She chuckled to herself. "Don't you see? Letters love line dancing, waltzing and swapping partners… which is when they become words. Dance forward and you get the word 'live'; dance backwards and you get the word 'evil'; stop dancing and a 'veil' might come between you and your partner! 'Words' are a 'sword'… they are both capable of protecting or cutting people.

"It's astonishing, isn't it?! And didn't you notice before, when I wrote those letters down, that they began to twirl and swirl around in an enigmatic dance? Language is alive. It only dies when people lose their love of it, or use words to harm."

I looked again at the drawing pad… and wow! I swear those letters began to shift, separate and join up again like colourful little puzzles. Maia looked like she was 'away with the fairies', as my mum used to say. Hey… maybe I was away with the fairies too, wherever that was.

Mum had been observing this quietly. "I've always believed that words have the power to heal or hurt, to encourage people or make them feel worthless. But isn't it the intention behind words that matters?"

"Yes, I think so too," agreed Dad. "People can say the wrong thing, but they often don't mean any harm by it. Other people mouth all the right words, but their intentions are deceptive."

Taka, Aiden and I yawned in a domino effect. This had been a words marathon, and although we wanted to go on another sprint, we were already over the finish line.

By the front door, I watched Maia and Taka hug each other as only good friends do – the kind of hug where you feel the other person's care seeping through your whole body.

After Maia had left, I thought that maybe Mr Eaton would have been proud of me. I'd taken another step towards understanding people better. Last month, it was through their stories. Today, it was through their words. What would it be tomorrow?

☆ ☆ ☆ ☆ ☆

Back up in my bedroom that evening, I was trying to finish some homework for my first day back after half-term. But I couldn't focus. The experience with Maia had left me not only wondering where words came from… it left me wondering where I came from.

I had an overwhelming instinct that my world was about to get turned upside down – not by anyone I knew, but by something that I couldn't predict or prepare for.

WINDOW FOUR

*

VOYAGE TO THE STARS

Voyage To The Stars

It was a wild, blustery day in early March. Winter was melting away and snowdrops were peeking through everywhere.

By around 5:30pm, the winds were dying down as Uncle Jake arrived for a coffee and chat with my dad about gardening. They could natter on forever about growing vegetables and what were the most humane ways to stop slugs eating their lettuces – apparently, luring them into a dish of cheap beer works a treat!

I was in the middle of reading a book about how to survive in nature, including what plants and insects are edible. I guess cooking ants and steaming snails might make a tasty meal if you'd remembered to pack lots of soy sauce! I'd only camped out once – in a field for two nights on a school trip – and I was imagining what you'd have to do to survive in a tropical jungle where leopards hunt after dark.

There was this fascinating chapter about survival in a forest: how to build a shelter, make fire, forage and find water. I loved the section on locating stars to find your direction and lost myself in the amazing pictures of space – it was like being carried on the wind across the treetops in Trent Park. I'd ziplined there several times before – along canopy high tree-to-tree crossings – but this felt like doing it without the zipline.

In one movement, I put my book down and stood bolt upright. It was as if the trees were calling out my name.

"I have to go to the park now," I announced, in a voice that sounded more like a robot's than my own.

Dad looked oddly at me. He must have been wondering why I was acting strange – although I was wondering about that too.

"But you've never been to the park on your own before in the evening. It'll get dark soon…" he said with concern.

I could feel my face tightening up. I was determined to go, but Dad still looked worried. So I said, in a sort of 'it's no big deal' kind of way, "Look, the park's only a few minutes away. It's still light and I'll be safe." My confidence surprised me, but since that conversation with Taka, I was starting to trust myself more.

I leaned forward and whispered, "Don't worry, Dad. Mr Hardwick, the park keeper, is usually scouting around and stopping people trampling over his lavender bushes and pansies."

Dad's strained face melted into a faint smile. He knew that once I'd set my heart on doing something, any speech from him would disappear like a helium balloon blown skywards.

He glanced across the table to double-check with Uncle Jake, who just smiled as if to say, 'Well, you did teach her to be independent'. It was true. Dad was always encouraging me to be daring and to follow my instincts.

I pulled on my thick, green woollen hat, wrestled on my duffle coat and slipped a pair of gloves into my pocket in case it got really cold. I grabbed the front door keys and rushed out. But why the hurry? I began walking and, soon, running towards the park.

As usual, I darted inside through a gap in a side hedge – no need to take another five minutes to get to the main entrance when there's a neat little shortcut. I paced briskly along the avenue of towering silver birch trees, almost running to get away from something... to get rid of something... to be free.

At one point, I stopped and tilted my head upward to see the crowns of the trees which surrounded me now. I looked closer.

Then I became aware of something so obvious. Every single tree, every single branch, every single leaf is different. There aren't two leaves in the entire world that are exactly the same. I found that stunning – but what did it mean? And every tree has its own family – the Birch family, the Oak family, the Willow family. So, what does that mean?

I could feel my mind opening, opening wide, wondering, opening wider still. The park was so quiet and empty. In the next moment, I was transported to another world, whisked away, travelling at speed. Then images burst into my mind from a book on the natural worlds I'd read... a sequence of colour photos of different praying mantis insects from over 2,000 of their species. Such awesome, bizarre shapes, sizes and colours.

In the next instant, my mind flashed up some of the photos of the hundreds of different types of beautiful hummingbirds that exist. How is it possible that some of them can beat their wings 80 times in only one second?

I turned around as if I was being watched, only to see a huge, gnarled oak tree looking back at me. The book said that there were nearly 500 different types of oak trees around the planet. But why such incredible variety?

Something was pressing the 'urgent' button in my mind.

I remembered a biology lesson in which the teacher had said that millions and millions of sperm are released, but only one fertilises the egg. Why only one in millions – what does that mean? Incredible wonders, way beyond the grasp of my mind. In an instant, everything was new.

These thoughts were coming thick and fast now, one quickly overlaying the other, overlaying the other, and again, and again. No answers, more questions, no stopping. It was rapidly taking me to a place far beyond my imagination.

It seemed as if I was losing my mind, but maybe I was about to find it. It all felt so weird. I thought I might be dreaming, but I could feel my heart beating faster and harder against my ribs. I began to feel scared, vulnerable, alone. I walked on, speeding up. Mustn't turn back, not now.

Before I knew it, the evening skies had faded into black. I stopped, pulled my hat over my ears and quickly slipped on my gloves.

All at once, my feet were rooted to the spot in the middle of the wooded part of the park, trees closing in all around.

Then, strange sounds. A busy rustling not far behind me... was that a deer, a badger? What if it was a group of foxes and they wanted to attack me? I'd heard stories...

As I grew more anxious, a huge bird swooped right across me, its wings almost brushing my face. It happened so fast. Was it an owl?

I panicked and started running and weaving through gaps in trees, but couldn't find a clearing... and no pathway, no exit. I'll shout out Mr Hardwick's name. No. He's gone home. What time is it? Where's the path? It's so dark now. I can't find it. Keep running.

Ouch. That really hurt.

I'd tripped over a fallen tree trunk and slashed my cheek and ear on one of its spiky branches. I jumped to my feet and wiped some of the blood away. It still hurt but... must keep going now.

I brushed off most of the leaves, mud and twigs which covered the front of my coat, took out my last tissue and wiped the blood again.

My heart was still pressed tightly against my chest, pounding. Thoughts blurred. Run. Run. It seemed like ages. I had to find the exit.

But then I stumbled across a big clearing, which must have been right in the middle of the wood. I knelt down and cried. I'd never felt so on my own or so scared.

My brain was racing with worries. What if I can't find the exit? What if no one finds me here? How will I survive? Books are one thing, but what if...

The whole side of my face was hurting now. I got up, looked around and could partly see through some of the trees, straight ahead, into the distance. There seemed to be the faint glow of a streetlamp and I thought I recognised the back of a bench there that I used to play on. Then the glow disappeared. My legs felt unsteady and I had to kneel down again.

Catching my breath, I pulled myself up, feeling strangely calm, like I was meant to be here. I sighed and closed my eyes. "Stop. Don't run away," something whispered.

Then, ever so slowly, I raised my head up into the sky. It was almost pitch black now. And there, arcing high above... the stars, the glistening stars. Light and dark everywhere, surrounding me. The stars had appeared as if out of nowhere. My gaze reached higher, higher, scanning the heavens, drinking in the dark, the brightness, the wonder.

Millions of stars. Dazzling, diamond white. Brilliant, enchanting. I was soaring high up towards the constellations, flying beyond. I wasn't in my body at all.

Somehow, by some mysterious change, my mind had become

like a tiny space rocket, travelling far into the atmosphere, effortlessly launching into deep space and jumping across from star to star. And, ohhh... I was spinning and skipping on air.

Was I that body I'd left behind? Or was this really me, gliding across the skies, weightless, free?

And then it happened. The strangest sensation ever. The stars were alive in me... deep inside me. Their light was pouring through me and out of my eyes, like the lit-up windows of cottages on a dark winter's night. Light, so much light. Then silence.

The stars were trying to speak to me, or hum, like a choir inside my head... no words or melodies, only this warm feeling of friendship. And in that moment, an insight dawned... and it thrilled me.

I knew that whatever tiny sparkling gems the stars were made of, they were the same shining gems I was made of. I felt it, really felt it. And it lifted me higher.

I was alight, floating, fearless. Down in the park, my body wanted to dance... but I wasn't there to move it. I was so happy dancing up here. It was everything I wanted. I'd come home.

Now I was like a golden eagle, rising up on the warm air currents, soaring higher still. A word then glittered inside my head. 'Stardust'.

There I was... a force, shining from space, a tiny globe of shimmering lights, radiating white and rainbow colours, like the sparkling fires of an opal gemstone. Stardust. Was it now in me? Had it always been there?

Then my mind did a backflip. A voice whispered, "You are made of stardust, Leah." Woosh. I suddenly grew taller than Big Ben.

That spun my mind upside down, where it landed on a question. A question that stunned me. A big question. And I wanted to shout it out at the top of my voice... like if I shouted it out loud enough, someone somewhere would answer. I had to ask it right now. I had to know.

Then time split in two. Footsteps stomping, rustling nearby. No.

Woosh, again. With a high-pitched whistling sound, I was dropping thousands of miles down from the sky.

Hovering for a second above the earth's atmosphere, I caught a glimpse of wonder. The fragile, blue and white marble, precious planet, floating in darkness. She was breathing light and sadness. I wanted to protect her with my life.

Thud. Back into my body. Numbed. Stranger in my body than travelling the skies. But the awe, the awe of a universe that was no longer a stranger.

Crunch, crunch, snap. The heavy footsteps were getting closer, louder. This wasn't a deer or fox. This was a person. Torchlight shot past me.

In shock, I tried to run, but my body was sluggish. I looked towards that bench I'd seen in the distance. The footsteps were racing closer, the light searching me out. My legs and arms loosened. I ran for my life.

Whack. I tripped again. Couldn't believe it. This was it. My arm was bruised and throbbing, my left glove ripped, blood seeping through. I pulled it off and wiped my hand on some nearby damp moss – a tip from my survival book.

I scrambled to my feet. My left ankle was hurting. Keep going. I broke out of the forest, panting and sprinting along a rough path towards the bench. I was getting closer, but had to stop. The footsteps behind me had stopped too. I was trembling and couldn't go on.

Looking over my shoulder, I glimpsed the outline of... well, what seemed to be a tall man approaching. I was terrified, stiff, my T-shirt and jumper were soaking. Must keep running... but my energy was completely drained. Then a voice broke through the darkness.

"Is that you?"

The torchlight caught me and cast a shadow. I froze and something in me woke up as if from a nightmare. I didn't flinch. Did he recognise me?

At first, I thought it was Mr Hardwick, out searching for me with the police, maybe. But the voice sounded younger and more familiar. I had to work it out. Think. Yes, that must be it.

Dad must have sent Uncle Jake to get me because he wouldn't want me to think that he was being overprotective. I glanced over my shoulder. Yes. It was him.

I wanted to run into his arms and cry. But as soon as I realised that I was safe, my big question came flooding back.

My uncle knelt down beside me. "Are you okay, Leah? You're bleeding."

He handed me a tissue. I smiled awkwardly. I was sweaty and still shaking, but couldn't resist looking back up into the starry night. Back to where I'd come from.

All of a sudden, I realised I'd been alone in the middle of the park for over an hour. An icy shiver of fear flushed through my whole body, yet nothing would let me walk out of the park now. The stars hadn't finished our conversation.

Uncle Jake didn't move. The twinkling night sky had gripped him too. He switched off his torch, and we both gazed upwards in wonder. A wonder deep as the ocean floor – curious, inviting, nearly out of reach.

Then silence.

"Look, Uncle. See the fields of lights. I've been there, through constellations, among great crowds of bright stars. They're still talking to me."

Silence again. I could sense my uncle holding back his questions.

"They're saying that they are my friends. We're alike and travelling together through time and space. They will teach me secrets. I want to go back and meet them again."

I wasn't sure if I understood what I was saying. Uncle Jake didn't respond. Maybe he thought I was talking gibberish. I was still looking up in awe.

"I see my face in the stars… like I am up there with them now, yet still here. There's no distance. I feel at home with them, even though they're trillions of miles away."

I was beginning to struggle now. My mind was running fast… desperately seeking words I didn't have or didn't even know yet.

"We are made of the same… I mean… am I made of stardust?"

Questions pooled together, like ice cubes melting into each other in a glass. A bigger question was about to cascade. I wanted to shout it, but it came out as if I was trying to sing it.

"If I am made of stardust, then why? Why am I made of stardust? Why?" My voice faded into a murmur.

I turned around again. Uncle Jake looked astonished by my question. He gazed out into space like a child for the first time.

"Leah. I love your question. It carries an echo… a memory from my childhood, bursting back into life with a mixture of grief and joy."

My vision reached up into the universe again. "That's it! Don't you see, Uncle? We are connected. Everything out there in the skies is in here, in me, in you. We are made of stars and space… aren't we, Uncle? But if that's true, then why?"

I needed to know and turned to face him again.

I rarely saw Uncle Jake get emotional. I'd seen him keep his cool in an emergency, an argument and even when watching a weepy romantic movie – unlike me. But I noticed a few tears begin to trickle down his face, reminding me of raindrops streaking down my bedroom windowpane.

"Why are you crying?"

"I don't know, Leah. I really don't. It's wonderful to think that… that we can shine like those stars out there. Are we made of light too? Perhaps some form of life out there wants to meet us… and when we shine, it can find us."

It can find us? When we shine… like stardust? I knew that wasn't science fiction. It was beautiful and I could feel myself holding back my own tears now. But something stopped me. I had just asked the most important question of my life.

I gasped for air. My mind was speeding again.

I felt my sweat-drenched clothes, now cold and clingy. Touching the fresh blood on my palm and cheek brought me back to the moment, the quietness, the presence of my uncle.

A few tears welled up in me. I wasn't sad. These were tears of joy. Not just the joy of being happy. It was… like being in love with a great mystery.

I'd always been attracted by curious questions. Why do fireflies glow? Why were the pyramids built? Why is each snowflake different, yet all are patterns of six? I felt sure that these were some of the wonders in heaven and on earth that Mr Eaton had opened my mind to.

Switching his torch back on, Uncle Jake came over and hugged me. I needed his warmth. "Your face looks so pale, Leah. You've got this glassy, far-off stare," he said with concern. "And we must clean those wounds. Come on, let's go."

I fixed my gaze on him and spoke as if I was addressing a big audience. My words sounded… well, like someone else was speaking. Or maybe something else was speaking?

I found myself emphasising every word, each one a precious jewel I was polishing. It was that question again. A golden key to a secret treasure. I said it out loud.

"Why – am – I – made – of – stardust?"

The words held there in the cold night air. Did anyone have an answer?

My uncle wrapped his arm around my shoulders, and we headed for the exit. I couldn't look up anymore. I was leaving my friends behind.

My big question thrilled and frightened me. And my fear in that moment was that no one on earth knew the answer… or maybe everyone had forgotten it.

DOES MAIA KNOW?

Does Maia Know?

What happened in the park and the skies that night was like nothing else I'd ever experienced, heard of, or read about. Literally out of this world. It made me wonder who else had been on a voyage into the universe before, making friends along the way. Had anyone? If some had, then they probably didn't dare talk about it in case others thought they were just dreaming it up, or lying.

After leaving the park, Uncle Jake and I hadn't said a word to each other. And now, as we were approaching my house, I signalled to my uncle to stop. I asked him for a fresh tissue and dabbed as much dried blood away as I could, hoping that my parents wouldn't notice.

"Before we go back in, please, can you keep this a secret? I'm not ready to talk to anyone about what happened. Not yet," I insisted.

"I can't get my head around what went on there, Leah. But I do understand it's precious to you. Believe me, I won't tell anyone."

My parents opened the door before I could even put the key in the lock.

"We've been so worried!" Dad exclaimed.

"It's okay. I just got a bit lost. That's all. Good night, Mum, Dad… night, Uncle Jake… thanks for finding me. I must prepare for school tomorrow. Night, night."

Before my parents could ask anything, I'd dumped my coat in the hallway and was already halfway up the stairs. I turned around briefly to see them standing at the foot of the stairs, mouths wide open.

"What happened?" asked Mum, while Uncle Jake was trying to joke with my dad and calm him down.

"Can we speak in the morning? I'm so tired now." And with that, I disappeared into the bathroom and showered off the blood and traces of soil. Fortunately, in the mirror, the cuts along my cheek and ear looked more like grazes. And I only needed a plaster on one hand and some arnica cream on my ankle and bruised arm.

Back in my bedroom, I lay down and soaked up the warmth and comfort. But something deep inside felt different, changed. I instinctively reached for my stargazing book, fumbling a little as it dropped to the floor. As if by chance, it opened out onto the centre spread pages, showing the constellation of Orion.

I gasped, as I instantly remembered travelling across the three stars in Orion's belt and having the crazy idea to design a waist belt made of stars. Then I smiled as I noticed that one of those stars is called Mintaka. Was this where Taka came from?!

I recalled Mr Eaton saying, "Find out where you've come from…
where your real home is." Well, I'd felt at home with the stars,
wrapped in the spiralling arms of the Milky Way, held like a baby.

Such odd ideas and clues were spinning and whirring around
inside my head like a full tumble dryer. I had to meet Maia as
soon as possible. And, as if she'd been watching my thoughts on
a screen, the day after she unexpectedly texted an invite to me
and Aiden. 'Come over. Afternoon tea. Saturday, 2pm? Favourite
lavender scones!'

What a chance to ask Maia about what had happened to me in
the park. If I can travel to the stars and look down at my body,
does that mean that I am not my body? And if I am not my body,
then what is me?

I love questions, but these scared me. I'd never asked such big
ones and never heard anyone else ask them either. Maia once told
me that she was captivated by the biggest questions about life, and
thinking of her calmed me down a little. She would understand,
wouldn't she?

☆ ☆ ☆ ☆ ☆

Mum dropped us both off at Oakwood tube station on Saturday.
"Call me when you get there, and don't expect Maia to have
answers for everything," she advised, knowing what I was like.

Travelling to Maia's place near Clapham Common across the
river was a great adventure, and we only had to change trains once.
I was fascinated watching families as they stepped onto the train,
debating who would sit where. Sometimes they laughed or argued
or were deep in conversation, but they always tried to protect their
own space, piling their bags on empty seats or outstaring anyone
who came near.

When Maia picked us up at the station, she gave us both one of her warm-blanket hugs. It was like nothing could ever harm you when you were with Maia.

Her house was one of those stylish Victorian terraced houses with a big bay window. The tiny front garden was blooming with yellow, white and purple crocuses.

She invited us in, guiding us along the hallway, through her cosy kitchen and straight out onto the patio facing the sunny back garden. She'd set out three high-backed wicker chairs with orange cushions, around an old iron table.

Maia had that faraway look again. It reminded me of a school trip I'd gone on to the British Museum where I became almost hypnotised by the eyes of a pharaoh. Watch out. Those eyes don't look back at you. They pierce right through you and far out into space.

Maia pointed to a pot of fresh mint tea and a glass of apple juice – she knew exactly what we each loved to drink. She sat down, each of her movements precise and unhurried, as usual.

My big question was about a breath away from bursting out of me, when all of a sudden Maia presented one of her own.

"Do you know about the brightest star in…"

"Sirius! It's Sirius!" Aiden shouted, grinning proudly. He sounded like he was making an announcement on a megaphone.

Maia sighed, smiling. I imagined thousands of large and small cogwheels in her brain spinning away happily. You never knew what might pop out next.

"I didn't ask about the brightest star in the sky," said Maia, now laughing. "Look at my eyes and tell me what you see?"

Aiden went very quiet. He wasn't used to not getting the right answer to a question. "Well, your eyes are sort of light brown, I mean bright brown. Very bright, like…"

Aiden looked hypnotised himself and I could see why. I'd never looked deeply into her eyes before and now they seemed to shine back at me like two…

"Stars!" I called out, thinking this might be where the expression 'starry-eyed' comes from.

Maia looked as if she'd entered another world again.

"From South Africa to Hawaii, mainly on mountaintops around the globe, you'll see these massive high-tech telescopes pointing skywards. Some astronomers are searching for black holes out there in the universe. But why don't they begin by looking into their own black holes? Their pupils," she said, firmly pointing into the middle of her eyes. "These two tiny black holes work the same as those gigantic ones out there. So why not be a scientist and study the universe in yourself first? Then you can begin to grasp what's really going on out there…"

"I know this!" I cried out quicker than I could think. "When I was in the park at night stargazing, I felt the universe out there. I did. And… well, I also felt it in me too, like I was breathing it, in and out and in and… it was so…"

Maia said nothing. I saw blue light pouring out of her eyes. She leaned in towards me and I could sense her mind tuning in to mine. "Yes, you do know it, Leah."

Aiden, however, seemed confused. "I still think the answer is Sirius," he protested half-heartedly.

"Yes, Aiden," said Maia, softly. "But why not discover what elements stars are made of… then picture those elements inside you now, because they're all zipping around in there, inside you, right now.

"You are breathing in oxygen and nitrogen, which is all out there… the calcium in your bones, the iron flowing in your blood, the sulphur in your cells and tissues – it's all out there too. We are each made of stardust.

"Molecules, atoms, electricity, magnetism, light, consciousness, feelings… they're all alive in you right now, as they are up there in the skies. You come from the universe. It's your greater home.

"Down here is only a smaller, different version of what's up there. You're a living, breathing universe."

My mind and eyes and mouth opened wide. Each of her sentences transformed into swirling shapes, colours and pictures inside my head. I'd been searching for a long time for what she'd just revealed.

"Look at your fingerprints. That's the universe's unique signature, isn't it?" Maia said, closing her eyes and seeming to drift away. We both looked at them intensely.

I'd never noticed the detail of those amazing looping, whirling lines. Aiden couldn't stop examining them and comparing each fingertip.

And I was absolutely stunned. How had Maia known about my big question? Had it somehow travelled from me to her when I was in the park?

She'd read my mind and my feelings many times before. Some people think this is very spooky, but I'd experienced this kind of thing myself a few times… like knowing exactly what someone's going to say before they say it.

As I was wondering how this worked, I remembered an extraordinary music lesson last term when my teacher, Mrs Adler, was showing me a special tuning for my guitar, called an 'open D'. She pulled out of her music bag a pair of two-pronged metal forks, fixed on top of a hollow wooden base. They're called tuning forks, and these were tuned to the note of 'D'.

She placed the first tuning fork right in front of me on top of the table, and then walked across to the other side of the room. Placing the second tuning fork on a shelf, she then hit it with a little stick and it rang with the note of 'D'.

Well! Even though no one had touched that first tuning fork in front of me, it began to vibrate and ring clearly with the same note. The sound waves had travelled, unseen, across the room… like magic.

Mrs Adler had seen my amazement. "That's why tribes used to listen to the wind. Sounds, messages and ideas travel through air. How did an ancient design like a pyramid get to Mexico from many thousands of miles away in Egypt?"

So, as surprised as I was that Maia had known my question, I pictured that music lesson. It made me realise that thoughts can travel across a room, between people, around the globe.

And so, what if… what if the stardust in me had lit up and sent some light across to the stardust in Maia? Did that light carry with it my big question? I know that a text message can whizz across from one side of the planet to the other in seconds, even though no one can see it.

It all sounded so bizarre, but real. And it explained how Maia had answered the most important question I'd ever had, without me even needing to ask it.

Then I wondered why people keep saying, 'She's a star', or 'You're a star'. There must be something in it. Everyone looks up to stars, don't they? I mean stars in the sky, but yes, often people too. Funny, isn't it?

So if we're made of stardust, that must mean we're directly connected to the great universe out there.

Then I suddenly remembered what Maia had said to us weeks ago: "You should be studying the universe when you get to university."

☆ ☆ ☆ ☆ ☆

There had been a long pause in the conversation, filled up nicely by the munching of delicious lavender scones with cream and jam. We ended up talking about my latest braids, football tactics and how to grow lettuce from seed. I love growing vegetables, and Aiden and I have got our own little raised bed in the back garden.

During the train journey back to Oakwood station, for once, Aiden had way more questions than me: "What's the difference between the pupils in my eyes and black holes?", "Where does electricity come from?", "Why are so many galaxies and seashells in the shape of a spiral?" As the older sibling, I thought I should have all the answers at my fingertips. Mostly, however, I simply replied, "Well, I don't know, Aiden. But what a brilliant question."

☆ ☆ ☆ ☆ ☆

I slept deeply that night and when I awoke, my mind felt as open as a desert. It seemed as if I'd become a different person... like a visitor from outer space.

Vivid images of that evening in the park and up in the skies were lighting up in my mind. I'd been taken to a world which maybe few had ever seen. And to me, that sparkling, mystical world felt more real and more important than my tiny world of school, TV, tablet, texting and school again.

I had to call Taka now about my voyage to the stars – she didn't know anything yet. I wasn't sure how to explain it, though... I could hardly explain it to myself.

"… so I ran through the park and into that big forest…"

"Why were you running?"

"I don't really know. I was sort of running to get away from something, and before I knew it, I was in that clearing…"

"You mean, where we had that picnic… you know, where you brought stale bread and mouldy cheese?"

"Yes, but… well, anyway, when I looked up at the stars, they were calling to me and…"

"So, you were dreaming?"

"No. No. Listen. I was rising into the skies and I was able to look down and see my body, and…"

"Oh, come on, Leah! You *were* dreaming."

"No. I was awake up there and then the starlight started pouring through me, and… Taka, stop giggling."

The call ended soon after and I decided not to mention it to her again. She obviously didn't believe my story could be true unless I'd been dreaming. I did start to doubt myself… but only for a few seconds. I absolutely knew that I hadn't dreamed it all up.

Later that day, I was about to call Zara, the football captain, to check on my position for our next game, when a cold and uneasy sensation came over me. It was a hollow feeling, and it made me think that I really knew nothing… like I was lost in space somewhere.

Did I actually understand what Maia had said? She'd explained so beautifully about the stardust in each person, but I never asked her 'why?'. I should have asked her, '*Why* am I made of stardust?' That was my actual question. That's what I really wanted to know.

A week after the experience in the park, I'd put my question directly to my science class teacher, but she just gave me a lesson on hydrogen and helium without even referring to my question. I guess she wasn't really listening.

So I knew I had to find out on my own. I had to go out myself and search for clues. But why was I getting so frustrated and excited about one question? Then a quiet voice inside my head said, '… because this means the world to you'.

I went to look at myself in my bedroom mirror. Wow! My hazel eyes were full of different colours, shining so brightly that it seemed as if they would laser two neat holes straight through the glass.

And as I saw my face looking back at me – a bit lonely, hopeful, desperate – I knew exactly what I had to do.

No time to waste. I'd made up my mind and had to leave as soon as I could. I had to get away, urgently.

WINDOW SIX

≋

FEAR

Fear

I was desperately hoping that it wouldn't be too late.

Earlier in the year, my parents had told Aiden and me that they'd saved up enough to send us to an international summer camp in Sussex. Although I knew that Taka was going, I was feeling so anxious then about my grades at school and the super-competitive culture. So I'd told them that I didn't want to go.

I remember there was also this fear in me of being in a strange place and sharing a cabin with loads of other girls I'd never met. They'd probably laugh at my dumb phone, my ears or my plaits. And Aiden wouldn't go unless I went, so I felt terrible about that.

But now, I knew I had to go – even if I didn't want to. I needed to get away from everything and everyone and find some answers. The experience in the park had inspired me to feel a part of worlds so much bigger than mine. At the same time, it had made me feel very different from everyone else… like I didn't belong anywhere. 'The school weirdo' was what they called me behind my back.

I had to break free.

At breakfast on Monday morning, with Aiden reading his graphic novel and my parents on their second coffees, it seemed a good time to speak up.

"I've been thinking again about your offer... you know, for Aiden and me to go to summer camp? Well, I know it's very late now... but..."

I came to a complete stop. A rush of anxiety swept through my body like I'd been shoved under a cold shower. I couldn't believe what I was about to say. I gathered my courage.

"Well, what I mean is... I really do want to go to that international camp that you found. The one that Taka's going to. Please, can I go?"

Mum spluttered on her coffee, Dad dropped a spoonful of marmalade, while Aiden swung around abruptly on his chair with eyebrows raised. Not the reactions I was hoping for.

"Why have you changed your mind?" asked Mum, frowning.

"Well... I just need to go," I babbled. A twinge of worry resurfaced... of staying in an unknown place for three weeks with teens I might not get on with. I began to sweat. Why was I so afraid of the unknown?

Dad looked up. My answer surprised them... probably because it wasn't an answer at all. This was getting very awkward. I had to offer a better explanation.

"Well, the activities look interesting... I mean, very interesting. Especially the water sports and survival stuff. And Aiden is going to love it there!" I didn't have a clue what else to say. Thankfully, it was enough.

Mum smiled cautiously. "Okay, love. I'll phone the camp after breakfast and see if the registrations are closed or if there are still places. Do you want to go as well, Aiden?"

Aiden looked down, kicking his legs nervously back and forth. "I think so," he muttered. I should have spoken with him first.

As it turned out, that very morning the camp had received two cancellations. Maia had spoken to me once about destiny, and even though it was a bit vague in my head, I thought to myself that this was destiny. I was going. It was on.

I was so excited to tell Taka that I phoned her straight after Mum had told me the news. She screamed with joy and then listed all the things that I needed to bring – including extra hairbands, a swimming costume, tinted lip gloss and insect-bite spray.

"Why the lip gloss?" I asked, a bit shocked.

"Well, I know you're not into makeup, but you'd look great with it. I'll help get you ready for camp. I'm going to get my hair done with carrot-orange highlights, although I'm worried they'll scare my mum. She'll think I'm getting ready for a Halloween party, not camp!

"Anyway, if you want, I can lend you my lip gloss. Try it out. I've got three different tints."

"But… why…?"

"Well, you know, it makes you feel good… and think of all those guys from around the world!"

"But I'm not looking for a boyfriend."

"Yes, you are."

I didn't answer. Taka laughed. She knew me well.

"Must go now. Too much happening here. Got a drum lesson in ten minutes. And my parents had another mad argument this morning. Mum says she needs some space. Whatever. Oh, I almost forgot… you might need to bring a compass and a torch for survival training."

I grinned. This could be my big chance to practise what I'd been reading about in my survival books.

☆ ☆ ☆ ☆ ☆

The next few weeks and months came and went with the usual mix of boredom, stresses and tensions at school. But my stardust experience, my big question, and Taka kept me from getting too depressed.

Taka's birthday adventure during the Easter holidays was definitely the main highlight. Her mum took us both to Kew Gardens, where we walked 18 metres off the ground along the Treetop Walkway, which has amazing views. From that height, it's like you can see what a tree sees.

Inside an enormous glasshouse, we saw a giant, disgustingly stinky corpse flower and other huge sci-fi-like plants. We're both into insects and spent ages in The Hive installation, where you enter the magical world of bees. We even tried copying their waggle dance. If only people could communicate as efficiently as that!

The end of term and beginning of summer holidays finally arrived when I most needed them to. My fears about camp were gradually turning into excitement and expectation.

With some very rushed preparations and panicky moments, we were gearing up to go on August 5th, tomorrow! Oh no. That meant I was going to miss Maia's birthday on the 15th. Although we'd spoken about camp, we hadn't been in touch for a couple of weeks.

I reached for my phone, hoping she'd be in.

"Hello?"

"Maia. Hi. It's me."

"Great to hear you, Leah."

"How are you?"

"That's a big question! But in a nutshell, I'm in good spirits and enjoying my current work – training teachers and teenagers how to mediate and resolve conflicts at school."

"That sounds amazing. I'd love to hear more about it. But I'm calling as we're off to camp tomorrow! And I'm so sorry that I won't be around for your birthday. I haven't even got you a present yet."

"Oh, please don't worry about that. But tell me, are you looking forward to going now?"

"Er... I was... until last night."

"Why's that?"

"Well, some stupid fears kept me awake, like... well, I've never been away from home on my own for so long. And although Taka and Aiden are coming, there'll be teenagers from around the world and... will they think I'm too frumpy, weird, uncool? I know I need to get away from everything, but I'm not even sure why I'm going to camp. It's just too..."

"Unknown?"

"Yes, that's it."

"Right. Mmm. I get it.

"You know, when I was eleven, my parents took me to Heathrow to board a long flight to Kathmandu on my own. I was going to stay with my uncle, aunt and cousins. My first plane journey ever was far less terrifying to me than the prospect of meeting family – I hadn't seen them since we'd moved to London when I was five. It was all so unknown.

"But over the years, I've developed a love affair with the unknown. Because... well, imagine all there is to know about a galaxy or a sun, the human brain, an ecosystem, deep-sea creatures, lightning, viruses, conflict, healing, death... there is so much unknown, isn't there?

"So I've discovered that the only way to get to know myself and this world better is to explore the unexplored, the unfamiliar, the unseen. To search and research. To discover and uncover. To dare to be curious. To find the questions which no one's asked yet."

"Are you saying that most of life is unknown?"

"Yes, I think so. A human, for example, is a complete mystery – almost. People can say they know themselves well, but do they appreciate the vast powers of their own mind, the function of their own instinct, the cause of their deepest fears or longings…"

"Right. Wow. Yes. Well, I wonder if I'll get to know myself better at camp… what if I don't like what I find?"

"You know yourself well enough to realise that you mean no harm. That's a vital place to begin. And you can always learn so much about yourself from watching how you react in challenging situations with other people. I certainly do!

"So, enjoy the experience and expect the unexpected!"

I soaked up her words and came off the phone feeling much bolder about facing this great unknown – super-excited even! I texted Maia to thank her and promised that I'd find her a very special birthday gift when I got back from camp.

I continued packing and slipped in a postcard which Maia had sent me years ago of a vast cave in Spain – 'Cuevas del Drach' in Mallorca. It shows hundreds of these stalagmites towering up from the ground, and huge stalactites pointing down from the ceiling. Maia described discovering the meaning of beauty in that cave – it was like poetry.

I gazed out of my bedroom window, hugging Sisu as she purred so loudly that her whole body vibrated through mine. I closed my eyes. My question flashed up in my mind like a neon sign written across the sky.

It really was time to go.

☆ ☆ ☆ ☆ ☆

We set off the next day under gloomy, dark-grey skies and driving rain. As we all crammed into the overloaded car, I began feeling more depressed than anxious. I'd only discovered the night before that Taka wasn't able to come for the first two days of camp – she'd only said that it was 'family stuff'.

It was probably to do with her parents' possible separation. She rarely talked about that to anyone, but over the last month at school, she'd been slouching around and frowning a lot – not her usual bouncy self. Hopefully, she was soon going to enjoy being away from the stress.

In the back seat, I glanced across at Aiden, who seemed quite relaxed. But I suddenly woke up to the fact that I was going to need to look after him as well as myself. My stomach knotted and a cold quiver slid down my spine.

Then I remembered what Uncle Jake had said when I refused to go out on a rowing boat with him once on a gusty day – I thought we might drown. "Come on, Leah. I was the rowing team captain at uni. Relax. It's all about balance." He taught me different rowing techniques, but what I really learnt was how to be more centred in myself and let my instincts guide me.

I relaxed. If Aiden got bullied again, I knew exactly what I was going to do before calling my parents; go through the Code of Five with him first. I'd tucked the card in my backpack.

There were still another two hours of driving, so I leaned back and took out my latest book. It was the true story of a seriously ill boy my age, who'd been miraculously healed through a special diet, exercise... and angels, so his family said. Angels? I was getting to the part where the boy begins to describe in detail the angels he saw, when Dad banged the dashboard and exclaimed, "I'm no longer lost! We'll be there in ten."

The rain was only drizzling when we finally arrived at the end of a narrow dirt road, with rolling open fields on either side. There was no gate, just a big old sign with fading green letters saying,

'Welcome to Bridgewell Camp'. It didn't look welcoming at all, and I noticed that I was clenching my teeth as we drove into the camp. Aiden was looking down sheepishly at the floor.

We got out at the car park right opposite the main entrance. This was it. The first time away from home for three whole weeks for the two of us. I tried to look grown-up and tough, but I was blinking back the tears. Mum was all smiles at first, but Dad got so emotional he could barely speak. Aiden still had his head bowed.

"Remember, you're here to enjoy a unique experience," Mum said, not managing to hide the worry lines creasing up all over her forehead.

Dad stepped in. "Be careful and… well, I hope that you make one or two good friends. Remember, everything that's on the outside of a person is not necessarily what's going on inside."

I was not up for a philosophical conversation, but I did want to understand this.

"What does that mean?"

"It means that people can have an identity and appearance on the outside, which may be deceptive. They can hide their intention behind words – remember, we spoke about it. You're very trusting, Leah. That's good. Just don't get fooled by people's expressions and fine talk."

I knew what Dad meant, and I wasn't sure if I was going to be able to trust anyone.

We quickly hugged each other. I was probably going to miss them much more than I'd admit.

Suddenly, this big old wooden door swung open and two adults, who looked as if they were in charge, strode over to meet us with their broad smiles and crushing handshakes. Wearing bright-orange, crisply ironed shirts, with 'Bridgewell Camp' neatly embroidered across the top pocket, they could have passed for high street store managers.

"Welcome! You're Leah, aren't you? I recognise your pigtails from the photo!" I didn't like that. They were not pigtails. They were my own style of snake braids.

"And you must be Leah's brother, Aiden. My name's Emilia, and with Kamlesh here, we are the Bridgewell Camp team leaders. We'll take you straight to your cabins so you can settle in."

I couldn't believe that they didn't invite my parents to at least see the cabins, but Emilia just shook their hands and said, "Nothing to worry about. They're not going to want to come home! See you at Presentation Day in three weeks. Bye."

We all hugged again, and Mum and Dad left swiftly like they'd been dismissed. Despite Emilia's bluntness, I felt a warmth from her and Kamlesh, which made me relax more.

Emilia began leading me over to my cabin, which I was going to share with seven other girls, while Kamlesh walked off with Aiden in the other direction towards his cabin. Turning around to wave at me, he now looked transformed and beaming with excitement – he'd already told me in the car his plans for every one of the camp activities.

Emilia was quick to pick up on my anxiety, and reassured me that our cabins were only about 400 metres from each other – that wasn't much, but it seemed too far away.

"When will I see Aiden again?" I asked sharply.

"Soon, Leah. Don't worry," said Emilia, softly. "Everyone's meeting in the main hall in an hour to set up and prepare for dinner. You can each sign up when you get there and choose what job you'd like to do."

I started coughing as soon as I entered the cabin. It smelled damp and dusty, and there were cobwebs around the window frames. My bunk bed was on top, and I'd never slept up high. I don't mind roughing it a bit… but this cabin was gross!

"Yeah, it's not five-star," said a short, freckled, ginger-haired girl who was unpacking. She must've noticed me turning my nose up as I sniffed around the cabin.

"My name's Skye. I'm from Aberdeen. This is my sister, Isla."

Their rounded faces, pixie-bob haircuts and funky clothes seemed to be… well, almost exactly the same!

"Yup, we're identical twins," Skye grinned.

"My name's Leah. I'm from North London. It's great to meet you both."

"You look a bit worried," said Isla, with genuine concern.

"Oh, it's just that I'm not keen on sleeping on the top bunk and…"

"Don't worry. We both love top bunks, don't we, Skye? It means we can look down on everyone!" They both laughed and Isla lobbed her backpack up on my assigned bed. "You take my bed, Leah. You'll be under Skye. She's fine, except when she snores!"

I could have hugged the twins, and I left the cabin with a warm glow of relief.

When I arrived at the main hall, I was pleased to see on the notice board outside that Aiden had already signed up to help set up the chairs and tables.

I signed up for peeling potatoes, took a deep breath and walked through the big doors into the main hall, where loud music was thumping away and lights were glaring. Young people of all ages, shapes and sizes were buzzing and darting around excitedly, with different languages whizzing past my ears. I did recognise some Spanish! It was like a youth circus had arrived in town and I started to get excited too.

One of the youth leaders, Sarah, led me to a big kitchen at the side, where about a dozen others were busily washing, chopping and frying up. She pointed to a huge pile of potatoes where a girl who looked a bit older than me was already happily peeling away at the sink. We were about the same height, and I instantly liked her sleek and straight black hair, with a single braid to the side.

"Hi, my name's Leah. What's yours?"

"My name is Natsuki. I am from Kyoto, in Japan."

I knew that Japan was in the East, somewhere on the other side of the planet, but I wasn't exactly sure where. I had learnt a lot about the famous Mount Fuji, though, from a project I did on mountains of national pride.

"You must have had a long flight, Natsuki."

"Yes. Fifteen hours. No stopping."

"Did you travel on your own?"

"Yes, alone."

"Wow. That's brave."

"My parents want me to speak good English and meet young people from many countries."

"Your English is amazing. I wish I could say something in Japanese."

"You could learn 'hai'! It means 'yes'."

"Hai! Sounds nice. You must show me how to write it in Japanese."

"Sure. Later I will show you."

"Are you into astrology?"

"I am a Scorpio."

"Wow. So is my uncle – he's really smart and honest. I'm a Libra."

We had a speedy chat about our signs, our favourite movies, the teachers we love, the bullies we can't stand and braiding, ponytails and double buns – she knew the names of almost every style! It was such a fun way to spend 45 minutes peeling potatoes. Natsuki was kind, and so fearless to have travelled thousands of miles away from home on her own – the first time she'd ever been outside Japan.

With dinner ready, food queues moving quickly and people swarming out to tables, Natsuki and I sat down with the twins, a girl called Raya from Mumbai and a tall boy from South Africa with great jokes and a long name. "Just call me Jabu," he grinned.

We each shared how nervous and excited we were and what activities we wanted to do – Jabu had a hilarious story about each sport that was mentioned. Taka would have loved his jokes.

That first night swept past like a noisy blur, and it was fun. Natsuki and I staggered back late towards the cabins, exhausted. Fortunately, we were sharing the same one, but I still wasn't looking forward to sleeping there. My anxiety returned as I breathed in the damp and mould.

All the other girls were sound asleep. As Natsuki climbed into bed on the other side of the cabin, she gave me a little wave. "Sleep with peace, Leah." I felt her warmth pass across the room.

Then I realised that even though I'd seen Aiden, I hadn't checked on how he was, or even if he'd found his way back to his cabin after dinner. Maybe he'd got lost or something, and Mum and Dad would hold me responsible.

As I quietly wriggled into my bed, trying not to wake up Skye, I realised that I was way too tired to worry about anything or anyone anymore. I gripped my pillow and prayed that I'd be able to fall asleep quickly. Tomorrow was going to be a big day.

WINDOW SEVEN

GROWING CONFIDENCE

Growing Confidence

My alarm was beeping, and the sun was streaming through the open window. "Meeting in the main hall before breakfast!" someone yelled. I leapt out of bed, astonished to discover that I'd fallen asleep the previous night with my clothes on – first time ever.

Most of our cabin had already left, including the twins, but Natsuki was kindly waiting for me. So, after a quick shower, I dressed up in my new strappy black top, denim shorts and white trainers, and we jogged over to the main hall.

Despite her confident look yesterday, Natsuki seemed a bit on edge now. But then so was I. It felt like we were hanging onto each other, unwilling to admit we were feeling shy and awkward. I was frustrated that my confidence was so up and down.

The hall was packed and we were obviously late, because apart from a few empty chairs, everyone was already sitting and waiting for Emilia and Kamlesh to start. Embarrassed, we snuck into the back row and, as I sat down, I noticed Aiden two rows in front. He was on the edge of his seat and already chatting loudly with a boy next to him. He gave me a thumbs up and I winked, breathing out a long sigh of relief.

"Well, good morning everyone, and a very warm welcome to Bridgewell Camp. We hope you slept well, and we're so happy to see you here together," said Emilia, with an angelic smile.

I scanned faces around the room. It made me relax a bit to see a few other stressed-out teenagers like me, with the kind of fearful looks you get in a doctor's waiting room. I guess I was trying to spot those who looked like I was feeling… but actually, most people seemed totally thrilled to be there.

Emilia continued enthusiastically. "We are very pleased to see so many people from around the world. There are 53 of you here from all parts of the UK, and 37 who've travelled from Kenya, South Africa, Germany, India, Spain, Ireland, Japan, New Zealand, the USA, China, Egypt and Denmark."

Emilia then asked if people from each country wanted to stand up in turn. As each person or group rose to their feet, an unusual surge of joy fountained up inside of me. How exciting to see such a range of nationalities all together in one hall. A recognition of unity, one world. Did we have the same hopes and dreams, or the same big questions?

Meeting people around my age, from so many different cultures I knew little about, made my heart glow. Was I beginning to fall in love with the unknown, like Maia? Now that thought made me chuckle.

"Thank you for coming all this way to join us," Emilia continued. "And now I'd like to introduce our international team of experienced youth leaders." One by one, they shared with us their enthusiasm about being at camp and described their background, favourite hobbies and the activities they'd be leading. It was gripping.

"You can always find at least one youth leader here in the main hall if you need to ask anything. And now Kamlesh wants to go through some practical things with you."

He rattled through a long list of very boring things to be mindful of. The only thing that scared me was his warning about not using matches in the wood cabins. That made sense, but how was I going to sleep tonight worrying about whether someone would sneak over and set fire to our cabin? Then I realised how ridiculous and stupid that sounded – but possible!

Thankfully, Kamlesh's list came to an end and Emilia stood up again, still beaming.

"Now, I'm sure that you've read through all the amazing activities which you can do over the next three weeks, and you may have already chosen the ones you'd like to do.

"However, why not consider doing something you've never done before? Because we're hoping that during camp, you'll not only experience great teamwork and adventures and make some good friends, but that you'll also be able to build confidence in your ability to do things you've never even tried."

'Wow,' I thought. 'Is that why I've come here? To grow confidence and try out things I've never done before? But how, what? And will it help me answer my burning question?'

Emilia's tone of voice was friendly and hopeful... much like Maia's. I relaxed back in my chair and was starting to feel a bit more at home now, in myself that is... which was a really strange thought to have. At home in myself? Well, yes, I think so.

Emilia pointed to a list on the whiteboard.

"Here's the complete range of fantastic activities you can choose from in the first two weeks of camp, A to Z: from archery through to visiting a small zoo not far away. You can choose to do two different activities each day."

I whispered excitedly to Natsuki, "Let's go white-water rafting and rock climbing together," and she nodded keenly.

Emilia then mentioned something I'd completely forgotten about. "During Week Three, you'll get an opportunity to work in small teams on a special creative project: writing and acting in a play, composing music with a band, choreographing a dance, making original pottery or ceramics, designing an app, producing a short film, building a website or creating a science project. Each team will then stage a performance or demonstration for families, friends, youth leaders and everyone at camp for the last day... the big Presentation Day."

As Emilia had been speaking, a growing volume of excited chatter had been breaking out. Everyone was eagerly asking everyone else which project they were going to choose for Week Three, and probably making on-the-spot decisions about who they wanted to be in a team with.

One project caught me by surprise. Producing a short film. That wasn't something I'd ever thought of doing... no experience, either. It made me wonder.

Emilia then told us that after breakfast we were going to have a tour of the whole campsite together, followed by an afternoon for all kinds of sports activities.

☆ ☆ ☆ ☆ ☆

The tour around the buildings and grounds, with a swarm of 90 of us struggling to keep up with ten youth leaders, was like herding squirrels all scampering off in different directions... great fun and so noisy you had to shout to be heard.

But the nearby forest was peaceful. It was like a larger version of the wood in Trent Park where I'd had my extraordinary journey soaring to the stars... an experience which had strangely brought me here. I wandered off for a few minutes on my own and nearly got lost. But it gave me some very interesting ideas for Project Week.

Back at the main hall, it was time to choose our sport for the afternoon. I love football, especially playing in goal, even though I'm not that good or tall enough. What excites me is leaping into the air, punching balls, diving dangerously and getting muddy. I've even saved two penalties – more by luck than skill!

Although he's a brainbox, Aiden also loves football and he immediately chose that. His favourite position is in defence and because most boys only want to be strikers and score lots of goals, he often gets picked to play in teams. He becomes a different person on the pitch and goes flying in fearlessly with sliding tackles, even from behind.

I was going to join him, but my hand shot up when Camille, one of the youth leaders, mentioned hockey. I'd never held a hockey stick before or played the game, and I reckoned it would be exciting to give it a go... a little sports adventure into the unknown.

So that afternoon, I joined a team of mainly older teenagers, as we rushed out onto the hockey field and began swirling our sticks around as if we were having a sword fight. Some players were a lot bigger than me, but I had the same size stick and I was going to use it.

The hockey game was a total mess, with most of us madly charging around after this one hard ball – I only touched it twice in an hour of playing. But I loved the feel and the cracking, echoing sound of whacking it right up the pitch somewhere... anywhere!

After the game, as I was walking back to the cabin on my own, I had this exhilarating feeling pouring through me, like standing by Torc Waterfall near where we used to live.

Then a phrase appeared that my mum used sometimes when she got an intuition: "Some good news is on its way. I can feel it in my waters." Well, I know that our bodies are made up of about 60% water, and in my waters, this fresh feeling came bubbling up that a big change was about to happen soon. Good or bad, I had no idea.

☆ ☆ ☆ ☆ ☆

The next morning warmed up quickly and I couldn't wait. I'd put my name down for a day's foraging and survival course with Kamlesh, who marched a dozen of us straight out into the forest. I didn't know that there were so many things you could actually eat to survive. We picked and ate delicious blackberries, wild strawberries, mint, and even dandelions!

We boiled water from a stream for nearly ten minutes to purify it, poured it into a tin teapot with some wild chamomile, and had afternoon tea together in the middle of the forest – unfortunately without scones. The tea tasted awful, but Kamlesh assured us that it had some 'excellent antioxidants' in it – whatever they were, they certainly didn't make the tea taste any better.

Afterwards, we gathered around as he demonstrated the basics of building a lean-to shelter. He got some of us preparing the ground between two trees and checking the wind direction, while the rest of us went off to scout around for materials: a long, sturdy branch for the ridgepole, bare branches and heaps of bracken and moss. Then, using these materials, plus rope, a tarpaulin and Kamlesh's big hands, we put together a frame that eventually became a strong shelter. We all huddled together underneath it like a bunch of mischievous elves. It was so cool.

After dinner, with torches in hand, Kamlesh led us back into the night-time forest to check out our lean-to shelter... which now looked like a Hobbit hole! In the middle of a big clearing nearby, we sat around a large camping lantern and became like wide-eyed children clustered around the storyteller, as Kamlesh charmed us with his incredible survival stories.

He then showed us how to navigate with a compass, tie knots and do basic first aid. I was gripped and soaked up every detail. At last, the pictures and diagrams from my survival books were coming to life.

"Now let's try to make a fire without matches, using a piece of steel, a flintstone, and tinder. Watch this!" he cried out, as he gripped the steel tightly and scratched it along the flintstone. Sparks flew everywhere, but not onto the little bed of tinder below.

"Sorry, I do this all the time, but it's different when you're teaching it," he said, beginning to sweat a little. There was a lot of sniggering going on.

"Okay, you try it then," he huffed, handing the tools to a boy who was laughing the loudest. The boy scraped away furiously, but with few sparks and no fire. Eventually, Kamlesh let a few of us have a go in turn. After a screechy few minutes of rapid swiping, Isla was the first to set fire to the tinder, but it blew straight out. So, with a trick from my survival book in mind, I had a go. The tinder exploded first time into a little ball of light and everyone cheered.

We soon had a glowing bonfire and began to tell stories and sing a few songs. It was a bit cheesy at first, but when Sean, one of the Irish boys at camp, sang a couple of folk songs... well, I think I entered dreamland.

His silver, rope-chain necklace hung neatly over his yellow T-shirt, which stretched tightly across his chest. He had longish dark-brown hair, with a wavy fringe that swept over his olive-green eyes whenever he swayed his head to the tune. His distant look brought memories of the stars and I... well, he was... okay, I really liked him.

We found an old Irish song we both adored singing – 'Whiskey in the Jar' – except he knew every verse compared to my two. Most everyone joined in with the chorus, though. And as I listened to him take over the singing from verse three, I realised that I'd been singing this song with my mum since I was five and I didn't have a clue what it was about. Most astonishing for me was to hear Killarney mentioned in the last verse!

"And if anyone can aid me 'tis my brother in the army,
If I can find his station in Cork or Killarney..."

Sean's raw energy and husky voice brought this tale of robbery and betrayal to life, especially when he sang directly to me. I was breathless in those moments and my heart was somersaulting out of control. On the last chorus, he looked at me with a cheeky grin spread across his lips, which set the skin on my face and arms tingling with an electricity I'd never felt before.

Was he feeling anything? What did that cheeky grin mean? Was he really singing to me? Wow! I totally hadn't expected this to happen on day two. Taka was going to want to hear every detail about this, and more.

Before I knew it, I was strolling back to the cabins, side by side with Sean!

"So, where are you from?" he asked, turning his head ever so slightly towards me.

"I grew up near the lakes of Killarney. And you?"

"Donegal. So, we're both Irish!"

"Yes. Although we moved to London when I was only six. I've never been to Donegal."

"My whole family live there and most of us sing in pubs on weekends – like the Clannad family used to do. You know, you've got a beautiful voice for Irish folk songs."

"Well, I used to sing a lot with my mum," I said, trying not to blush.

"I once went hiking with a mate around Killarney. I love the hills and waterfalls there, and the history."

"I love that too," I gushed, realising I was coming across as too keen. My attempt at not blushing had now failed, but at least it was dark.

"I also love camping out in the hills near Donegal. The skies there are so clear and when I stargaze with my little telescope, I can sometimes see the clouds of stars in the Milky Way. It's awesome."

"I love that too," I replied, too quickly, realising that I'd also repeated myself.

Although it was a chilly night, I could feel myself beginning to sweat. Sean's dazzling eyes had drawn me in, like the deep waters of Lough Leane... full of hidden stories. My words dried in my mouth before any more could come out.

As he said goodbye, he brushed my arm and hand lightly with his fingertips before walking away. It sent shivers of delight through me. I wasn't sure what it all meant, but I assumed Sean was being deliberate. Taka would know for sure.

When I got back to my cabin, I peeked around the door and saw that everyone, including Natsuki, was fast asleep. My head was still buzzing away, though, so I sat down outside on the steps. I couldn't stop thinking about Sean and that touch. I started sifting through every word that he'd said. I couldn't remember my responses, except that they were mostly silly, repetitive and obvious.

However, as soon as I crept back into the darkened cabin, my mood changed completely. I became filled with dreams and pictures of myself teaching children foraging skills. There I was, surviving bravely against all odds, showing everybody how to build a shelter and find edible plants, as they followed me with eyes full of admiration. But was I really just dreaming about how I could impress Sean... or everyone at camp?

Being popular felt good, even in my imagination. But did I really want to be popular? On my last birthday, I made up my mind that I wasn't going to play the social media game of 'likes' and 'followers' and happy-clappy photos posing at concerts. I decided that this wasn't me.

Then an image of Sean singing appeared, and I drifted off into a deep sleep.

☆ ☆ ☆ ☆ ☆

I woke up half an hour before my alarm went off. I knew Taka was due to arrive very early at camp and couldn't wait to tell her everything and ask for her advice... although I knew she'd give it to me anyway.

When I breezed into the main hall for breakfast, I was amazed to see her already queuing for food. I ran up behind and tapped her on the shoulder. "Leah!" she shouted at the top of her voice, even before she'd turned around. A lot of curious faces swivelled in our direction, as they watched us both in a flurry of hugs and outbursts of squawky laughter.

"Let's go to that table in the corner – it's the least messy!" I said, grabbing Taka's arm. We gulped down our food in the few spaces between endless catch-up chatter and jokes.

At one point mid-sentence, I instinctively looked up and glimpsed Natsuki eating away in the opposite corner. Curiously, she looked up at exactly the same time and almost knocked over her table as she crossed the room towards us.

Natsuki knew that this was Taka from my previous description of the carrot-orange streaks in her curly, chestnut-brown hair. And when Taka stood up, they both hugged like they'd been friends forever. We then shared with her many of the fun experiences from the last couple of days: from foraging, hockey and disgusting cups of tea, to an archery session where Natsuki had stunned the teacher by getting five bullseyes. I didn't mention Sean – that was for later.

Taka didn't explain why she'd missed the first two days, but she was her usual bubbly self, so maybe things weren't as bad with her parents' separation as she'd feared. I decided not to ask about it. I knew she'd share those things if she wanted to.

"My cabin doesn't sound as bad as yours," Taka told us. "But there's this girl, Anja, who's already ignored me. Her makeup routine this morning took forever... although she failed the catwalk supermodel test when she fell over squeezing into her tight shorts."

"Ha! Sounds hilarious. Although... well, I'm starting to feel a bit intimidated by a few girls I've seen around who are acting like they're at a fashion show, not a summer camp," I said, thinking out loud.

"Who cares?" said Taka, shrugging her shoulders. Natsuki shrugged along and gave a dramatic swish of her long black hair while pouting her lips, as we all burst out laughing.

"Oh, and I know all about Project Week," winked Taka, changing the subject. "I'm going to join the band. They'd better be ready for me. I don't want pop, hip-hop, jazz, classical or any of that stuff. It's rock or nothing!" I thought that maybe I should warn the other musicians.

Although I was disappointed that we wouldn't be in the same group, I absolutely knew that she was going to choose the band as her project. She's a talented drummer and has her own kit at the back of her parents' garage. She practises for hours on weekends and has such a natural sense of rhythm. And although I play a bit of flute and guitar, I didn't think I'd be nearly good enough to join a band. Anyway, I had other plans.

Natsuki told us she'd make a last-minute decision about her choice of project, and Aiden had already told me that he was going to join the science group.

I gave Natsuki and Taka strict instructions to look out for Aiden, although he'd quickly made friends with some boys from Wales who were as clever at science and maths as him. They stuck together for most of the activities, choosing to do a lot of indoor tech and science experiments – a good excuse for getting hours of video game time, I guessed.

☆ ☆ ☆ ☆ ☆

With Taka now at camp and my friendship with Natsuki, I was so looking forward to each new day. For the three of us, it was outdoor adventures all the way. We became inseparable, and my anxieties steadily faded into the background.

I could feel my confidence growing; a confidence to just be myself and worry less about what everyone else was thinking or doing. And this gave me a curious idea.

I love growing things from seeds, especially herbs, tomatoes, lettuce and sunflowers. Learning how to prepare the soil, watering, checking the weather and watching the first green shoots sprout up make me so happy.

So, was it possible to seed confidence in someone? Was I watching a seed of confidence grow and flower in myself?

WINDOW EIGHT

BEAUTY

Beauty

The white-water rafting day later in the week was definitely the wildest and wettest. Taka had been rafting twice in Lea Valley, London, so at dinner the night before, she gave us a lecture about all the safety issues.

"Okay. I know you're a strong swimmer, Leah. How about you, Natsuki?"

"I am champion for backstroke in school and I can rescue if you fall into deep water."

"Ah. Right. That's good then," said Taka, surprised to discover that Natsuki was obviously a better swimmer than her.

"Okay, but do you both know how to put on a wetsuit and a lifejacket properly?"

Natsuki and I stared at each other blankly. This wasn't such a big deal to understand, but we both admitted that we weren't totally sure, which gave Taka an opportunity to explain in great detail. For something so simple, she made it sound slightly confusing, but at least Taka enjoyed teaching us.

Of course, on the day, the instructors spent half an hour taking us carefully through all the safety concerns and demonstrating using the equipment itself. I winked at Taka as if to say, 'Yes, we know all of this already because of what you taught us.' She winked back, grinning.

Our guide, Jessica, demonstrated how to use the paddles, and then walked us to the raft and showed us how to 'read' the river. I loved watching her hands glide and twist as she described the different currents in the river – strange new words like 'downstream or upstream V', 'strainers' and 'eddies', and innocent-sounding words like 'holes' and 'pillows' which were far scarier than we thought. But I was super-excited to get going.

The first group of six of us climbed into the raft as Jessica looked far down the river and then at each of us in turn. She dipped her hand into the water and said a curious thing before we launched.

"You know the expression 'go with the flow'. Well, if you can feel the rhythm and pulse of this river – its speeds, currents and bends – then you will go with the flow too… and you'll have the best smooth and rough ride of your life!

"This river is like life – it's much bigger and more powerful than you. So, listen to it and let it move you."

Jessica spoke as if it was the river speaking. We listened in awe. Time froze.

I began reflecting on her description of the river when the sunlight, glistening with the ripples across the water, caught my attention. And there it was. Still and quiet. The presence had appeared. The same presence I'd felt on Innisfallen.

It settled like a fine mist on the water right opposite where I was sitting on the raft, and seemed to wrap itself protectively around everyone. I wondered if it lived on water, on earth or in the air? Maybe there were presences all over the planet.

But what did they do? I only knew what my mum had told me… that they bring healing and guidance. To me, they also brought a deep feeling of safety. The presence was like a shield against harm. Could it also guide me towards an answer to my question? If only…

With a sudden jolt, we were hurtling down the rapids with white water lashing up and over the sides of the raft, as this bunch of teenagers squealed with delight. It felt totally out of control and safe at the same time… although with all the bobbing up and down, it was like our insides had become our outsides!

After the trip, Jessica looked around at all of us dripping with water, cheeks fresh and rosy, everyone elated. She told us how well we'd done in navigating the rapids and staying focused. Yet, as she helped us out of the raft, without explanation, she almost pleaded with us, "Please remember. People often stick their stupid words on nature, like 'violent'. Nature is wild, but never violent or cruel. She's always herself – always moving in harmony and balance, unless humans interfere."

☆ ☆ ☆ ☆ ☆

Almost every day of those first two weeks was packed end to end with activities – probably too many because, just as the three of us were really getting into one of them, it was time for another. We had no complaints, though. We loved all the outdoor activities and the youth leaders were caring and fun. Above all, we loved getting to know each other better. I no longer felt on my own. I now had two close friends and wasn't looking for any more. Well… maybe one more… with a wavy fringe!

Apart from the survival evening, I'd hung out with Sean another two and a half times. I mean, one amazing chat in the dinner queue, one little walk and talk near the cabins and one sort of quick 'hello, hi, which activity are you off to next?'

It was that dinner queue chat, however, where something unexpectedly sparked off.

"Do you like reading?" I asked, hopeful.

"I love books on folklore, legends and angels."

"Really? That's incredible, because I was reading a book on healing angels during the car journey to camp! It's the true story of a family who have a farm on a remote hilltop in Kilkenny, and their son has a serious illness which…"

"I've read that one!" Sean interjected with delight. "I love it. I think that angel was real."

Out of all the millions of books, this was more than a coincidence, and we both stopped and just gaped at each other. My body became light and airy. Some sort of powerful energy passed between us.

We soon went back to being awkward and stumbling over our words and feelings. But we'd connected in some way.

Before going off to our different tables, he asked about my cabin. When I mentioned the damp and mould, he said, "I can come over and help clean it sometime if you want." That was sweet. Or was there a message in that? There was definitely something going on.

Over dinner, I updated Natsuki and Taka on the latest with Sean. Natsuki was quiet and attentive, but Taka blurted out that, in her opinion, we were already in love.

"I know these things, Leah."

"So, what else do you know?"

She scrunched her face mischievously and stared into her glass of water like it was a crystal ball.

"I can see it now, Leah. You'll marry him in your twenties, go back to Ireland and live together on a sheep farm." She pressed her hand over her mouth to stifle a huge laugh that was about to erupt.

"So how many children will we have then?" I teased, as the three of us broke out into a fit of giggles.

Natsuki then turned serious. Her first response was much more practical.

"Do not forget to exchange phone numbers as soon as possible."

"Mmm. Good idea. Although my dumb phone might put him off."

"Nothing gets in the way of true love," chuckled Taka.

After dinner, I began walking over to the forest on my own. I had to get my head together.

All sorts of electric new feelings sparkled through me when I was with Sean, but at the same time, I also sensed a strange power calling to me. It was to do with my experience in the park and knowing that I was on a special quest to find answers to my question. So, I decided to just let things happen, rather than make things happen. That felt right, and sounded like a wise thing that Maia might say.

Maia! 'Oh, no, it's her birthday today – must call now. It's late. That's okay, she's a night owl.' I turned around to walk back to the main hall as there was a bench not far from the rear entrance, which was usually a private space. As I passed along the side wall, I overheard two girls around the corner speaking loudly in posh accents. I stopped.

"Love your style, Anja. You've gone really high end and sparkly on all your outfits. It's so cool that we're into the same designer brands."

"Why go cheap and common, like some of those girls in town? They look so plain."

"Nothing worse. I've seen a few girls here like that. Ordinary. Plain clothes and matching faces."

I waited half a minute, adrenaline pumping fast. I then turned the corner, carefully keeping my distance and looking ahead like I hadn't even noticed they were there. But then, as I walked away towards the bench, almost out of sight of the girls, I heard Anja's high-pitched voice again. I wish I hadn't.

"Hey, look. There's one of them over there. Check out her supermarket bargain trainers. Top plain Jane that one."

She must have assumed that I couldn't hear her or wouldn't know who she was talking about – or she simply didn't care.

I headed out to the car park, wanting to hide and feeling sick to my stomach. This must have been the Anja from Taka's cabin. I hadn't met her, but her words stabbed hard into a sensitive spot – talk about words being swords. I've heard a few girls call me 'plain' before, yet somehow, hearing it now hurt a lot more.

I've always been worried about how I look. It's not so much to do with what I wear. I don't have any supercool designer clothes, but it doesn't bother me much. I brought a new purple hoodie and matching trainers to camp, which I think look cool with my cropped blue jeans… although probably no one else does except Taka.

I do worry about my face, though. My family, neighbours and even some teachers have always told me how pretty I am. But I've noticed that they never talk about my face. They only talk about my hair, its colour, my ponytail or braids, how cute… they don't mention my face.

Maybe it's because my nose is a bit too narrow or small, although I've seen even smaller. My ears are on the large side and do stick out, and my eyebrows definitely aren't as thick as those of some of the girls at camp. I know it's negative to compare myself to other girls… but I guess they also compare themselves to me. So it's hard when everyone does it.

I do look in the mirror quite a lot, and that word 'plain' sometimes writes itself across the surface… as if someone's scrawling 'plain' in lipstick, like they do in those horror movies. It feels awful.

I wonder sometimes if it's my plain looks that make people ignore me at school. I know who all the pretty girls are, or at least who everyone says are the prettiest girls at school – the 'Insta plastic gang' or IPG as me and Taka call them. They're into curls, curves, bling and photo filters. I don't look anything like them, I know that. Sometimes I don't care at all and sometimes it makes me feel sad… like I'm not worth much.

I heard some music thumping away in the distance, and it broke my depressed state for a moment. It was now nearly 9:30pm, and I still hadn't called Maia on her birthday. I felt emotionally all over the place and didn't want her to hear me sounding so low. But without thinking, I was already phoning her and trying my best to sing her a happy 'Happy Birthday'.

Of course, she wanted to hear about the camp activities and new people I'd met. I tried to sound bright in telling her about Natsuki, the white-water rafting, foraging for plants and my ideas for Project Week. But my voice sounded flat and, like my mum, Maia could always tell when something wasn't right.

"You don't sound very inspired, Leah. What's wrong?"

"Nothing major… I'm actually really enjoying it here, except that there's something…"

I struggled to speak about this, even with Maia. I'd never brought it up with my parents, only with Taka a couple of times. And now I was worried that Maia would think I was being immature. But I had to tell her.

"Please don't say anything to my parents about this."

"Why would I?"

"Because… it's about my looks. I'm embarrassed to even mention it."

"Leah. Speak freely."

So I did. I started with the girls I'd just overheard and then recalled every time someone had described me as 'plain'. Even once when our neighbour's teenage daughter told her mum that I was "… not so much ugly, but definitely very plain." I remember that the word 'plain' hurt me more than the word 'ugly'.

"What do you think, Maia?"

She didn't respond. That wasn't unusual. She listened so carefully that it took her more time than most to answer. Except that she answered with a question.

"What is beauty?"

I'd never asked myself that before, and now it seemed like an essential question.

"Beauty? I don't know. I've seen some beautiful actors in movies. Mmm… our cat Sisu is definitely beautiful! I love sunsets, lakes and… you said those caves in Mallorca were beautiful. But I'm not sure if that's what you mean."

"Is beauty a pretty face?"

"Well… yes. I mean, there are models and singers who I think look very beautiful."

"Do they look beautiful because they have pretty faces?"

"Well… maybe not all of them. Some look a bit…." There it was again. That word. 'Plain'. It kept swirling around my head. I looked down feeling a bit ashamed. Maia read my mood.

"Do you mean they weren't so much 'pretty faces', but they were very attractive in some way?"

"I suppose so."

"So what makes someone attractive?"

"I don't know. I don't… well, maybe it's to do with how you feel."

"Mmm, yes. I think you're right. It's how you feel about yourself, not worrying about what everyone else thinks of you or how you compare to the latest celebrity model.

"Because when I reflect on beauty, I don't start by thinking about faces or bodies. I mean... I believe that beauty is in moments like this; rare moments between people where they feel free to speak their minds with no fear of being judged. I find that so beautiful."

I imagined Maia's face shining as she spoke.

"It's just my experience, Leah, but I see beauty in a person who listens deeply, or in someone who does an act of kindness, expecting no recognition.

"And to my eyes, the tiny world of a seed or a cell in our body, and every design, shape and colour in nature, is beautiful beyond words. Even for people with no sight, speech or hearing, there's always the beauty of the mind, the heartbeat, our ability to touch and feel.

"There's beauty in breathing and in moving.

"And what about being able to sleep and rest, while some special healing force repairs and refreshes your whole body inside out – and you don't even have to think about it. To me, that is beautiful.

"So I think that beauty is life, in motion, flowing through us now and right across this universe. It's ever changing and graceful. And it always starts unseen, deep inside, with feeling good about who you are."

Maia paused.

"Does this make any sense?"

"It does. It really does," I said, feeling like she understood me. I'd never thought of beauty like this.

"Did you obsess about your looks when you were growing up?"

"Yes. A lot. But when I was in my late teens, I remember looking at my face in the mirror one morning and thinking that I didn't want to measure my value by every detail of the face looking back at me.

"I realised that measuring your own or other people's worth according to their looks – their face, whether they have makeup on, what brand they wear – often hides your own insecurities or jealousies… that's what you're really measuring.

"So I believe that one of the hardest, most important things for human beings to grasp is actually the simplest. That true beauty always comes from the inside out."

There was a wonderful silence. It was as if we were the only two people alive on the planet. It was, well… a beautiful moment.

I thanked Maia from my heart. I didn't think that I would ever look at my face in the mirror in the same way again. She'd helped me change how I see myself.

From that day at camp, the word 'plain' hardly ever came into my head again. 'Plain' wasn't me. It was just a word that someone who didn't know me once used.

☆ ☆ ☆ ☆ ☆

As I made my way back to the cabin, it suddenly hit me that we were at the end of week two and about to begin Project Week on Sunday. There was already a loud volume of chatter building up about it at camp.

I still had no idea what project Natsuki would join… or Sean. However, I'd now made up my mind. No question. I had to join the filmmaking project.

I hardly slept that night because I was imagining all the amazing things I could film… my ten favourite braiding styles, growing herbs from seeds, how dragonflies are born, where to find stardust, or maybe… where to find home.

I wanted my parents, Aiden and Taka to be proud of me on Presentation Day. Well, I might not to be the star of the show, but… a star?

A LIGHTHOUSE
IN THE STORM

A Lighthouse In The Storm

That Sunday morning, I was the first up in my cabin and the first showered and dressed. I'd left before Natsuki and the twins had even woken up. The introduction to Project Week was going to start in an hour, and I was beyond keen.

When I arrived at the main hall, it was locked; there was no one there yet except a girl who looked about sixteen, maybe more. Her oversized black sweatshirt, ripped jeans and edgy combat boots made her seem older.

"Hi, my name's Leah."

"Hey, I'm Kayleigh."

"Where are you from?"

"Lewisham, South East London. I've been looking forward to Project Week, like forever..."

I was just about to ask her what project she'd chosen, when the doors flung open and Kamlesh and Emilia strode out, looking very focused. A few youth leaders were already inside, and we helped set up the hall as we eagerly awaited the arrival of the whole camp.

When everyone was seated, Kamlesh talked us through each of the eight different project areas in detail. Of course, I was only interested in the filmmaking project, and Emilia announced that the youth leader and facilitator for that was going to be Tanguy.

All I knew about him was that he was from Chad – a big country in central Africa – and that he now lived with his uncle in England somewhere. I guessed he was around 19 or 20 and he had this intriguing, serious expression on his face.

I sometimes get an intuition about people, and in Tanguy's eyes I saw a great leader. There was a sense of strength and safety about him, like one of those tall, sturdy lighthouses by the coast. I also saw pictures of deserts and danger. What was his story?

"Please decide which project you want to do in this last week, and then check out the board next to me, here, to see where your meetings will be. Then get going after breakfast!" said Kamlesh, in a loud and commanding way – not his usual laid-back self.

The filmmaking group were given the spacious gym, which was only a minute's walk from the main hall. It was a new building with a high ceiling, a wooden floor and large windows all around. As soon as I entered, I got a mouthful of the stinky mix of sweat, floor polish and rubber that filled the air. A couple of the team were already flinging the back door and windows open.

When everyone had arrived, it hit me again that Sean wouldn't be coming. After breakfast, I'd seen him running off with the dance team – they were already doing spins, jumps and stag leaps as they dramatically flew out of the main hall. I imagined Sean would be a street dancer, a natural. He was probably already in a dance crew back in Donegal.

I was thrilled, though, to see that Natsuki had joined this project. We did a big high five in the air to each other from across the gym.

Kayleigh was also there, and when I saw her, I gave her a big smile… but she blanked me. I reckoned she was one of about 40 teenagers at camp who were older than me, and I got the feeling that they didn't want to mix too much with anyone my age. I wondered if I'd be the same in a couple of years.

"I'm delighted to be your facilitator and meet every one of you today," beamed Tanguy, running his fingers through his short, tight dreadlocks and low fade haircut. "I'm sure that you're into a great range of films… and over this week, you'll have a fantastic opportunity to make a short five-minute movie of your own, on a topic that you're really passionate about.

"The idea is to listen to each other, experiment together and build real teamwork in creating an original film. You'll be showing it to the entire camp, to your families and to friends on Presentation Day this coming Saturday – that's a lot of people.

"Now, let's start by getting to know each other a little. Please introduce yourself to the group, with your name and the town and country where you come from."

Out of the eight of us, I counted seven different nationalities – so amazing! But from the whole group, apart from Natsuki, I'd only met Rhys – one of the younger Welsh boys staying in the same cabin as Aiden – and spoken briefly with Kayleigh. There was also a Danish girl, Helena, and a Spanish boy, Antonio – both maybe sixteen – plus two younger guys who I'd seen hanging out together: Darweshi from Kenya and Joe from the USA. We were like 'around the world in eight people'!

Tanguy walked towards a corner full of filmmaking equipment.

"Okay. We have this first-rate equipment here, which one of the parents has very generously loaned us. It includes a professional video camera, so you're very lucky. You'll get much better quality images and sound from this than on your phones.

And you're going to enjoy the experience of learning how to use it!"

Tanguy was methodical as he showed us the key features of the camera and how to set up the tripod, the sound equipment and lighting. We looked on with delight. Soon we'd be shooting with a proper film kit.

"Okay. I hope you get the picture!" he said, laughing at the double meaning. "Please don't lose, drop or scratch this camera in any way, or touch the lens. This is expensive professional equipment. I recommend that you read this instructions booklet later."

Tanguy sat down casually on the edge of a table, with an air of satisfaction. "You know, we're doing a lot more here than making a film. This is about building trust and excellent teamwork. Are you with me?"

"Yessss!" we gushed.

"Okay, good. So, your first task is to discuss what your topic will be and come to an agreement you're all happy with. Then I'll leave you to it."

No sooner had Tanguy finished than Kayleigh's hand shot up.

"I want to make a film about why the climate crisis is a final red alert for the whole human race. And I've got some great ideas about what to include and what the message must be."

"I've heard some of her ideas already," Helena chimed in, "and I'm totally on board. In Denmark, this is what we talk and campaign about all the time." Darweshi and Joe nodded excitedly.

Tanguy looked pleased. "Well, it looks like you don't need an extensive discussion. I'm also very concerned about the climate crisis and environmental issues. So... is that what you all want to do?"

Everyone, including Natsuki, put up their hands and said 'yes'. Everyone, that is, except me.

Suddenly, I felt all eyes zooming in on me... especially Kayleigh, who was scowling from across the room. My face flared with heat and I looked down at my trainers to avoid being stared at.

"Isn't that something you'd want to be a part of too, Leah?" said Tanguy, carefully.

I couldn't believe that this was happening and kept my head down. I had that awful churning feeling in the pit of my stomach, like I'd had many times before when I'd been the odd one out.

"Are you okay, Leah?" asked Tanguy, calmly. I had to find a way to explain.

"I... I do think that the climate crisis is... well, probably the most vital issue we're facing. I've read so much about it, and it makes me sad and anxious. I've also been on demonstrations in London... but... I've been dreaming about a project that is... well, a bit different." That came out clumsily.

Looking up, I caught Joe and Darweshi smirking and Helena glaring straight back at me. There was now this uneasy tension in the room, which made me swallow the words which were queuing up to find a voice in me. But my voice was buried under a heap of insecurities.

I closed my eyes, breathed in deeply to slow myself down, and sensed some of my strength and confidence returning. Confidence means 'with trust', I remembered. I had to trust myself now.

All at once, an idea inspired by my experience in the park came together so clearly, like when you turn the focus wheel on binoculars to change a blurred view into high definition. I had to be bold.

"I want to make a film about 'home'. A film about, 'What is home?' I mean, is the universe our home? Is the planet our home?"

I came to a sudden stop. My idea had only just hatched. What more could I say? I looked out of a tall window across the fields, then scanned a few of the faces staring right back at me.

Kayleigh and Helena tried to stifle their little sniggers. They probably thought that I was being childish, or even freaky. Tanguy took a step towards me.

"Well, that sounds very original. 'What is home?' Mmm... okay, would anyone want to join Leah in that?"

There was complete silence, apart from Rhys, who was sitting opposite me, fidgeting and scraping his feet on the floor. Suddenly, it seemed as if all my hopes and dreams for Project Week were now over.

"Yes, me!" cried Natsuki, coming to my rescue... even though she'd put her hand up before for Kayleigh's idea. Natsuki was smiling away and seemed completely oblivious to all the undercurrents in the room. I looked back at her with a nervous, grateful smile as she held up a sheet of paper with the word 'Hai!' scribbled in Japanese. It was like a friend's secret code. I wanted to run over and hug her to pieces.

"That's great. Now we have two strong groups – although you still need to practise your teamwork," Tanguy pointed out. "And as we only have one video camera and kit, you'll need to agree on how to share it between the two groups each day. Anyway, you won't need it all the time – you have lots of work to do researching your themes and planning each scene.

"So, this means that we're now going to have two short films for this Saturday, which is brilliant. And I really hope you enjoy working together. You know where to find me over the next five days if you need me. Are you all okay with that?"

Almost everyone said 'yes' and so Tanguy left, looking relieved and wishing us good luck for our first group meeting without him tomorrow, Monday.

The 'yes' seemed a bit half-hearted in some, and I was still blushing and feeling rattled. A few spiky looks came my way, and I thought I picked up Joe muttering, "Stupid girl," as he frowned in my direction. That upset me a lot.

Fortunately, the afternoon was free time and gave me space to reflect on what had happened. Although some of the team had sort of ganged up on me, I decided to let it go. I was just pleased to have been more in control of my emotions, with the strength to speak my own mind. Anyway, I got it... they were just passionate about their subject and irritated because they thought I wasn't.

Then the title of my school essay appeared in my head, like it was written across a big placard. I grinned. Understanding people was going to be a lot more challenging than I'd thought. Mr Eaton would be smiling if he'd heard me say that.

I decided to chill out later on with Natsuki, Taka, the twins and Aiden. We went to see a very funny animated movie showing in the main hall. Afterwards, frazzled from the day, I crashed out before anyone had a chance to start snoring.

☆ ☆ ☆ ☆ ☆

Natsuki and I hurried to the gym straight after breakfast the next morning. When we entered, there was this heavy, menacing atmosphere, like you get when a fierce storm is brewing. A clammy, sinking feeling came over me.

As soon as everyone had gathered, Kayleigh closed the door loudly and addressed everyone like she was now the leader and in full control.

"Well, as my group is the main group, we'll take the camera and equipment for now. I've set up four tables in the middle here for my team." There *were* only four tables in the whole gym. So, were we meant to work on the floor?

Then, without asking, Kayleigh casually picked up the camera, called together 'her team' and promptly ignored us. When she saw me still standing there, gaping at her in disbelief, she snapped, "Just use your phone to do the video."

"I don't have a smartphone," I blurted out, gritting my teeth. I knew what was coming next.

"You don't have a proper phone? What planet are you living on?!" she cackled, with Helena and Joe joining in. I'd had this before, and I just couldn't handle it right now.

I looked at Natsuki and, without a word, we turned around and walked out, slowly... I didn't want them to feel that we were scared. But I was angry and confused.

We wandered back towards the main hall in complete silence. 'How ironic,' I thought... 'I'd been worried that Aiden would get bullied, but it ended up being me.'

I stopped and turned to face Natsuki. "Thank you so much for standing by me. I really appreciate that, you've no idea. What happened in the gym was totally unfair. It hurt. Kayleigh wouldn't even discuss the camera. She just took over. Why does being the biggest team make them more important than us? What happened to agreements and teamwork?"

"Don't know, Leah. It is unfair. But listen. No one makes me feel inside what I don't want to feel. No one. So you decide. You make decision about how you want to feel," urged Natsuki.

I was amazed. How wise.

"You're right. It is my choice how I feel. Although I need to have a bit of a rant and let off steam sometimes."

Natsuki fixed me with a serious look. "You do not know Kayleigh. Maybe she will make a very good film, yes?" I nodded and looked down, a bit ashamed. Although I thought Kayleigh was well out of order, I knew that she was genuine about this project. But so was I.

"So, Leah… what is your big idea?" beamed Natsuki, suddenly getting excited. It was clear that she was not going to gossip or get involved about Kayleigh, and that actually helped me to just focus on our film.

"Well… I've been thinking a lot about what 'home' actually means. What is home for a bee, a tree, the moon? What is home for a human being? And for the first part of our film, I imagined recording some people live, answering the question, 'What does 'home' mean for you?'"

"Sounds a great idea. Let's go and do it now!" said Natsuki, lighting up.

We rushed off to the main hall to find some people to ask the question. But everyone was out working in their project groups.

Eventually, we found Sarah – the youth team leader I'd met on the first night – working in the kitchen. So we entered with a friendly hello and asked her, "What is 'home' for you?"

"Mmm… that's such an interesting question," she replied, gathering her thoughts as she stacked some plates into a cupboard. She walked out through the kitchen into the main hall and we followed close behind.

"I suppose… well, right now, home for me is this summer camp and the cabin I'm staying in with some of the other youth leaders. I feel at home here.

"I think home is also the community in which I live, because over in Llangrannog, Wales, you get this village community vibe. Most evenings, I can just drop in unannounced and see my friends in their homes. When we get the log fires burning and stay up late talking and sharing our music, it feels so homely. Yeah, I always feel at home when I'm with my close friends or family – even when we argue!

"And then… mmm… well, I go surfing most summers down in Cornwall at the beautiful Watergate Bay beach. There's this energy there… you know, I've never thought about it in this way, but when I catch the crest of a wave in rhythm and glide across it at speed… well, I feel completely at home on those waves… like 'in the zone', if that makes sense?"

"Wow! I'd never thought about 'home' in that way either," I marvelled.

"Is this to do with your film project?" asked Sarah.

"Yes, it is. But we're only just making a start," I answered, apologetically.

"Tell me more about your ideas."

"Well, it's like… you know, my home is in Oakwood, North London, and Natsuki's is in Kyoto, Japan. But then there are other kinds of homes, aren't there? Like in nature… there's the fox's home, the seagull's home, the home of one star in a galaxy, and … I just believe I'm onto something big here. What do you think, Sarah?"

"Well, I can't wait to see your film on Presentation Day!" she replied with a broad smile, flicking back her blond-streaked hair. It wasn't an answer, but it gave me hope.

I thought Sarah looked beautiful. It wasn't so much her face or hair or her totally cool clothes. I think it was her kind eyes, her honesty and encouragement. Those qualities are beautiful. I had to tell Maia that I'd got it.

The main hall door creaked open and in walked Tanguy. He seemed to look right through us, fixing only on Sarah. As soon as he noticed us, he stopped and hesitated. "Oh, I was trying to find… er, just wanting to check with Sarah if…"

"Yes. Mmm… we need to check the rotas for dinner tonight," said Sarah, striding across the hall towards an embarrassed-looking Tanguy. Something very odd was going on for sure. It seemed to me that Tanguy hadn't only come in to check rotas with Sarah. I started to imagine that they were probably… oh no, the filming! I'd almost forgotten.

"We could have recorded Sarah," I cried out, frustrated. But Sarah and Tanguy had already shuffled out the back door.

"You're right. Let's make a plan," Natsuki insisted, sounding increasingly urgent.

"Yes… and I think I know how our film needs to start."

We were alone in the huge main hall. We grabbed a couple of chairs and sat down at a long table by the windows overlooking the sports field. Natsuki found a big pad, and we started sketching ideas about what 'home' really means. Our diagrams looked like cave paintings with subtitles… but they made sense to us, and we were on a roll now.

Before we knew it, there was only an hour and a half to go until dinner. We had to make a start filming something, so we raced back to the gym to get the equipment – they'd had it all day. We burst in, puffing away, but no one even looked up. Kayleigh's team were sitting around busily typing away on computers, while Kayleigh walked from person to person chatting and checking their work.

"Oh, great!" I shouted out. "You're not using the camera and we need to do some filming right now. Can I take it?"

Kayleigh stared down at me as if I'd insulted her.

"This is our workspace now. Find somewhere else. We need the camera and all the equipment so we can film spontaneously. We'll probably need it soon… don't touch it."

"But we need it too. We're ready to film before dinner." I could sense Natsuki standing strong beside me. She had my back.

"Didn't you hear me?" sneered Kayleigh, tightening her lips.

"But Tanguy said to share it and..."

"Shut up. We're doing an important project here on the climate crisis. And what are you doing?" She stepped forward sharply, right in front of me, clenching her fists.

"Making a film about 'home' is ridiculous. Everyone knows where home is already. If you don't know where you live then you're a nutter, aren't you?" she snorted, while most of her team laughed along with her like a little robot army.

"Let's go, Leah," Natsuki said, gently tugging at my arm.

Helena then pulled this threatening face and snarled at me, "You're only doing a film about 'home' because you're a little baby who feels homesick. Why don't you just go and join the pottery group, or go back home to Mummy."

I froze, trembling deep inside. I tried to remember Dad's Code of Five, but in the heat of the argument, I couldn't even recall the first point.

I began stomping towards the exit, seething inside. But before I got to the door, I realised that Natsuki wasn't with me. I turned around and she was still standing there, locking eyes full-on with Helena. Natsuki looked defiant and wouldn't back off. Helena eventually took two steps back.

"Come on, Natsuki," I said, my whole body quivering now. "Bullies are all the same. They think that making people small makes them big..."

I wanted to vent every drop of my anger, but I could feel Kayleigh hissing back like a python. So what was the point?

Natsuki slowly came over to join me, and we walked out of the gym together. I slammed the door as hard as I could, and we made our way towards the forest. I wish I'd been as brave as Natsuki, but was still shaking and trying not to cry. Was Kayleigh about to get violent?

Natsuki touched my hand tenderly.

"Are you okay, Leah?"

"Not sure."

"I don't understand why Kayleigh and Helena hate talking about 'home'. And why others only follow."

"People follow when they become lazy and stop thinking for themselves," I said, sounding more like Maia.

"That makes a lot of sense, Leah."

"Yeah. But it still hurts. Do you mind if I stay here on my own? Please go to dinner without me."

"Are you sure?"

"Yes. Don't worry."

As soon as I was alone, I wished she had stayed with me.

I ran off through the forest, wanting to scream. The light was fading, but I was more upset than afraid. Taka was probably drumming away happily. She was with the band now.

I sat down on a tree stump in a little clearing where we'd had tea two weeks ago. I was so happy then, and couldn't believe how things had become such a disaster all in one day. It felt like I was being bullied to stay quiet and go along with the crowd.

My mind was running around in circles about what to do. I could complain, but who would listen to me? Anyway, that would cause more trouble.

It was getting too late now to get back for dinner, and I was starting to get cold. But I didn't want to move. I needed that camera urgently.

I slouched back to my cabin, feeling emotionally drained. The damp, lifeless air inside weighed heavily in my lungs.

Avoiding speaking with anyone, I sat on the edge of my bed, resting my muddled head in my hands. I desperately needed to sleep, but had to clear my thoughts for a minute.

I promised myself that I was going to stand up much more bravely for what I believed in. And I believed in the message of 'home'.

WINDOW TEN

BRAVE

Brave

I had nightmare after nightmare that night. In one, I was white-water rafting and Kayleigh tied the video camera around my neck and pushed me out of the boat. Jessica dived in to save me, but when she brought me back into the boat, Kayleigh had disappeared. In another, Sean and I were dancing on Innisfallen at midnight, when a gust of wind swept us onto the moon and we couldn't breathe. I can't recall what happened next, and I wished Maia had been around to interpret my dreams.

I awoke early to the sound of my phone vibrating under my bed. I dashed outside so as not to disturb anyone. It was Mum. She'd been speaking with Aiden more than me, but we texted each other every day. I missed my parents but wasn't homesick.

Mum loved hearing about Natsuki and Taka and our wild adventures in nature.

"How's the film project going, love?"

"Well, I'm not sure… it's… mmm…" I rambled, deciding whether I should mention the conflicts.

"Are you working together well as a team?" Mum had already picked up that something was wrong.

"Mmm… yes, well, no. I mean, Natsuki and I are really into it, but the rest of the group want to focus on the climate crisis – they don't get the meaning of 'home', or why it's significant. I can't explain it to them yet, because I'm still working it out myself. Anyway, they won't listen to me."

I decided not to tell Mum about the bullying, fights over the camera and feeling pushed into a corner. She'd only worry.

"Sounds like a perfect opportunity to continue trying to understand people! You know, working in teams needs skills like listening, good reasoning and loads of patience! It's not easy… so give it more time, love. You believe in what you're doing. They do too. You'll find a way to bring it together."

Mum's encouragement and the warm tones of her voice soothed some of my stress away. By the time we said goodbye, I knew that whatever would happen next, I was going to follow my instincts about 'home' and not let anyone or anything get in the way.

I crept back into the cabin as everyone was still fast asleep. I glanced across at Natsuki and wanted her to rush over, hug me and tell me that everything would work out fine. Yet while her friendship was important to me, I was going to stand up for myself.

I slipped on my tracksuit quietly and wandered out to the forest with a notebook and coloured pencils. That little spot I'd found in a clearing was becoming my safe space at camp.

After setting up there, I must have fallen straight asleep or been daydreaming for ages, because I felt my eyes squinting open as someone in the distance began calling my name.

"There. Leah!"

Natsuki's voice pierced through the silence and my sleepiness. She ran over and swung her arms around me, setting off a huge wave of relief. Then, as I looked up, I saw a tall figure approaching. It must be... it was... Tanguy. I was amazed that they'd both come to find me.

"Your friend Natsuki told me that you'd probably be here," he said, relaxed. "She's explained everything to me, Leah. But I also need to speak with Kayleigh. I've learnt that there are several sides to every story; there's your side, her side, and then there are the sides neither of you can see yet.

"Anyway, I'm not interested in that now. I'm more interested in discovering how you're getting on with your project on 'home' and, well... why are you doing it? What is home for you?"

I was surprised that he didn't want to hear my side of the story now – just my project ideas.

But I felt an immense force shining out from him as that image of a lighthouse appeared again. I've always loved those solid, red-and-white-striped lighthouses that you sometimes see rooted to the edge of a cliff. Well, in that moment, Tanguy had become like that lighthouse, guiding me away from the rocks.

I studied his face and posture as he stood there, and a ton of self-pity slid off my shoulders. It left me feeling as high and light as those feathery, cirrus clouds.

Catching Tanguy's eyes, I remembered his question.

"I know that home is not just the place where you live. And earlier this year, I had the strangest experience in the middle of a wood, similar to this, where..."

I had to stop. My experience in the park was still a secret. And would they believe me anyway? Could I trust them not to tell anyone? They both had this wide-open look in their eyes and my instinct told me that it was safe.

"... every tree, leaf and sound seemed new. I questioned everything, and began running until I reached a clearing. I gazed skywards, and in the next moment, I felt myself gradually leaving my body and rising up into the night sky. I was weightless, high on the air, surfing among the stars. I felt like they were my friends… their lights were passing through me and making me shine from inside out.

"I sensed that the universe was my real home. I looked down and could hardly see the trees, let alone my body, until… look, I know this might sound crazy to you… but it's why I need to understand the reason I'm made of stardust and discover the truth about home."

I'd just squeezed months of my life into a minute. They were both looking intensely at me. Something unusual was happening. Time was slowing down.

"I'm with you," said Tanguy. "I don't understand what happened to you, but it sounds extraordinary."

We sat down on the forest floor. Tanguy peered through the treetops.

"You know, the night skies over Chad sing timeless melodies. They share wonders and carry you far away from all your worries. You feel loved, held close."

"That's poetry," I said. "I want to see those African skies. I want to be up there."

Tanguy's face suddenly aged, like a shadow had surrounded him.

"Are you okay?" I asked anxiously.

"No… not really. I miss that special feeling. I miss my roots, my people."

He paused, deep in his thoughts. I wished I could fathom what was going on in him.

"Can you tell us about your hometown, Tanguy?"

As soon as I asked this, I realised I was entering a world that maybe I had no right to enter. I waited.

"I don't know whether I can tell you any of my story. I don't know if I should." He paused again, looking searchingly at the two of us. We held his gaze for a few seconds as his lips widened into a glimmer of a smile.

"Yes, please... your story..." Natsuki chimed in, sensing there was an opening.

He bowed his head, took a deep breath, and waited for a while. The forest was still full of birdsong and yet I only heard silence.

"I don't know where to start. Because, well... it seems this world is never enough for some, when we take more than we need... and more than the planet can ever give. Is any nation different, I wonder? My story happens in many places.

"I was born in a small town which used to be right on the edge of Lake Chad before it started shrinking. My great-grandparents and grandparents fished in the lake and worked closely together. They needed to. It was a very tough life and there was often some kind of violent trouble going on.

"Despite this, they made a good life there and had fresh food and fresh air – my parents too, mostly. They managed to send me to school to get a good education. All the children loved to learn. Then we'd spend hours playing in and by the lake. It wasn't all wonderful, but we were satisfied with what we had.

"Within a few years, thousands more people had settled around the Lake Chad Basin... many of them refugees, with their hopes for a better life. Then came the overgrazing, overfishing, too much irrigation. More factories followed, as well as air pollution, some of it carried across on currents from beyond Africa.

"Then the impact of global warming. Temperatures soared. This was too much for an already dirty, shrinking lake, with some of the land cracking up badly from drought.

"My father was a fisherman there, but he became a farmer when the fish catches declined. My parents and uncle were wise… they could see where this was going, not only in Chad, but across the planet. They felt the pain of it too, because they were strongly connected to the land.

"When the rain began to fall less and conflicts and corruption grew more, they faced the toughest choice of their lives…

"I was only nine. My parents sold most of our cattle, and with some money they borrowed from family, they sent me away with my uncle. I was heartbroken, but I never questioned it. I trusted them completely.

"We travelled through the desert to Libya, aiming for Europe. Almost a year later we managed to cross the sea to Italy. You can't imagine the horrors of this whole journey, and I will never speak of it to anyone." Tanguy stopped and closed his eyes tightly. His voice had almost become a whisper.

"Eventually, we reached France and stayed with my uncle's cousin there, until we finally got into England after many dangerous attempts. We arrived with only a name. Refugee. It got us into this country and I am very, very grateful for this. But that name is not my name."

Tanguy had to stop again. I felt torn inside with a sadness I'd never known before. An icy chill raced through my whole body and stayed. I couldn't imagine having to leave my family and country like that.

Maybe Tanguy thought that we couldn't take any more. I was about to thank him for trusting us with his story when I heard him sigh.

"What my parents did was heartbreaking for them too. Imagine sending your son far away from home when he's just a boy… probably never to return. I think it was the ultimate sacrifice. They love me deeply, I know that. And they love our country. But they saw no future for me there at the time. So that must have been the worst moment of their lives. It was for me."

Tanguy's voice cracked as he covered his eyes.

Silence.

"I've never heard such a tragic story in my life, Tanguy. It must be so painful not having seen your parents and family for so many years. And the hell you suffered in escaping must have been…"

Tears welled up from so deep inside it hurt… but I couldn't cry. I thought of the millions of refugees and homeless people all over the world, and couldn't take it all in. Natsuki looked away, speechless. When she turned back to face Tanguy, she was wiping her eyes and straining to find the right words.

"Sorry. So sorry. You are very brave. I hope change will come in the world… maybe when there is no other choice."

"Yes," he said quietly. "Anyway, I've cried my tears on this and have no more left. But I carry many precious memories from Chad… and one day, if you're able to go to Zakouma, you will see beauty your eyes won't believe. You will see how people, the planet and wildlife can live in relative harmony." Tanguy's face lit up.

"And next year, if I can, I'm hoping to go back to see my family and friends in our town. And that, for me, will be the best moment of my life."

He smiled. Bitterness and history loosened their grip. He seemed free again.

☆ ☆ ☆ ☆ ☆

The three of us stood up and started heading back towards camp.

We reached an old bench by the main hall and sat down together. It was already early afternoon, and the camp was quiet. Everyone was busy with their projects, and we needed to refocus on ours very soon. But I was feeling down… Natsuki too. Tanguy's story had moved us to the core.

"Thank you so much for sharing your story," said Natsuki.

"Yes, thank you. I felt it in every space of my heart," I added. "What I don't understand is why everyone in this world can't work together day and night, so that no one will ever have to be a refugee. There must be a way for every person on the planet to have a safe place to live… a home."

I felt helpless and naïve.

"How do these crises come about? Are there too many people, or is there too little care?"

"Yes, Leah, there is much to put right in this world. But it's difficult for people to build a future if they cannot escape their past," reflected Tanguy.

That made sense. His life had forced him to grow up fast, and I wanted to understand more. One question was still lingering in my mind. I hesitated. I didn't want to be insensitive, yet I couldn't let the moment pass.

"Tanguy, can I ask… you don't have to answer, of course… but, well, you've come so far from home. You've travelled through many different towns and countries, through deserts, over oceans… and you reached England.

"So what is home for you now?"

He took a while to answer, glancing over his shoulder, back towards the forest.

"I don't know, Leah. I still miss my parents a lot, even though my uncle has been very kind to me. My family and friends, the town and the lake were all my home. And now England has given me a chance. But it's not my home yet.

"So, all I have is me. And I think 'me' is… well, perhaps 'me' is home now."

Everything went quiet. Thinking about what he'd just said made me sigh in awe.

Tanguy stood up and stood tall, despite a load of troubles that seemed to be weighing down on his shoulders. I gazed up into the sky, wondering and praying for a better world. My worries seemed so shallow now.

"My story is not that unique. It's the story of what so much of this world has become. But look at us here, now, in this international camp. We can demonstrate that we're able to listen to each other and work well together… all nations, all colours, all viewpoints.

"Our generation can bring change. And change must come."

In the quiet that followed, the presence gathered again. I recognised its field of energy, its stillness and the feelings of hope that it inspired. It was becoming like some kind of a spiritual travelling companion. I don't think anyone else felt it, so I kept it private. But it was real.

Tanguy turned in the direction of the youth leaders' cabins.

"I must go now. Thank you for listening to my story. I know that you really heard me.

"And now I'm looking forward to meeting with you, Kayleigh and the whole filmmaking team tomorrow morning, right after breakfast. I think, with understanding, we can sort this. With understanding, anything can be sorted."

I believed him, totally. Being able to understand people had gone from a nice idea in a school essay to a daily challenge – and now I was about to face my biggest one tomorrow. Thinking of meeting with Kayleigh and 'her team' gave me a stomach full of nerves, like fluttering bats.

I had to smile, though. When I was nine, I won my first school spelling bee final by spelling 'trepidatious', and the semi-final by spelling 'apprehensive' – I had to also demonstrate I understood their meaning by using them in a sentence. Well, I thought how much easier it would be to do that now, because Kayleigh had given those two words a whole new meaning for me. I was feeling trepidatious, apprehensive and all stops in between.

☆ ☆ ☆ ☆ ☆

Natsuki and I stayed on the bench for almost an hour, chatting away and munching on snacks. Our hearts were still full with Tanguy's story. It left us with a vision of a very different world – a next generation bringing change.

As we set ourselves up in the main hall again to sketch more plans for our video, we agreed that we'd include some kind of tribute to his story.

Tanguy wasn't trying to teach or persuade or impress. He wasn't looking for sympathy. He was a living example of how understanding can heal.

And he'd showed me why home is such a vital place to find.

A CHANGE OF CLIMATE

A Change Of Climate

When I finally slumped into bed that night, I almost leapt straight out again. I felt all these creepy-crawlies running around in my sheets and between my fingers and toes. Startled, I threw off my duvet and found myself surrounded by an army of ants, beetles and spiders crawling all over the bed... and me.

I immediately pictured Helena's face. I'm not sure how, but I absolutely knew that she'd done it. How childish was that? But if she had meant to frighten me, then she'd completely failed. What she didn't know was that I'd been collecting all kinds of insects from the park since I was seven. I was fascinated watching ladybirds eat aphids, bees pollinating and dragonflies hovering above ponds ready to gobble up mosquitoes. Mr Hardwick told me that humans couldn't survive without insects.

Quietly, so I wouldn't wake up the cabin, I carefully scooped up every insect I could and put them into an empty jam jar, covering it with a cloth to let them breathe. Then I hatched a little plan and kept giggling about it, trying not to wake up Skye – she was snoring, so that helped.

In the shower the next morning, I had to remind myself that time was slipping away fast – only three days to Presentation Day. "Just don't panic!" I roared out loud, hoping no one could hear me. Everything was hanging on today.

I'd never seen Maia lose her cool. One of her sayings was, 'Calmness is a state of mind'. Now that was going to be difficult. So I decided to plait my hair differently to try to calm myself down. One Dutch braided bun was the perfect remedy.

I told Natsuki I'd see her at breakfast, and then darted outside and bumped straight into Sarah. I asked her where Helena's cabin was as I had a little gift to give her. Sarah pointed to the cabin furthest away, but as I ran towards it, I spotted Helena walking along the path to the main hall. I knew she'd seen me because she deliberately turned her head away and began to speed up.

I rushed up to her and held out the jar full of insects, now with ants escaping. "I think you left these in my bed, Helena. They're very cute, but I don't actually need them."

Thrusting the jar into her hand, I casually walked off, leaving her in complete confusion and rooted to the spot. When I was far enough away, a loud burst of laughter erupted out of me… more in relief than anything else. The whole scene was so funny, as Helena had actually turned bright red as soon as she'd seen the jar. My instinct told me it was her… so was I being clairvoyant or something?

I had more to tick off my 'to-do list' before breakfast. Taka! I'd been missing her, although we'd sent texts and left notes with funny drawings in each other's cabins. She was obviously loving being in a band, although on one note she'd listed two big hissy fits which had kicked off between them, to do with 'musical and creative differences'. No surprises there.

I ran to her cabin to update her on my own dramas. Taka enjoyed sleeping in late, and I had to wake her up gently and then almost drag her out of bed. She was beyond grumpy until I started telling her my news and the latest bit about the insects.

"What? No. Okay, Leah. Let me have a quick shower and, after breakfast, I'm coming with you to your team meeting. No worries. I'll tell the band I'll join them later… with no drummer, they'll soon realise that they're going to fall apart without me!"

Taka's support meant so much. It was like being lifted out of a swamp and onto solid ground. What a friend. Who'd want to pick a fight with her?

Next up, check on Aiden. I dashed straight over to his cabin, but it was empty. I assumed he'd be nearby, but not a sign. Was he lost somewhere?

I was in trouble now. I should have paid more attention to him. I ran from cabin to cabin and into the forest, still searching. Nothing. I began to panic. No. Stay calm. Remember…

I needed to find one of the youth leaders immediately, to see if they knew where he was. I hurried over to the main hall, wondering why I hadn't gone straight there to check in the first place. As I burst in through the main doors, there was Aiden happily helping to lay the tables for breakfast. I sprinted over to him and hugged him so tightly he got annoyed.

"Aiden, Aiden. Is everything okay?"

"Why, what's the matter?" he replied, trying to shake me off.

"Well, I thought you had… I mean… don't worry…"

"I'm not worried at all. But you look really anxious… and panicky." Aiden was so irritatingly perceptive sometimes. He probably thought that I was being 'way too emotional' again and this time he was definitely right.

"It's okay, Aiden. All good. As long as you're happy, I'm happy,"

I babbled, sounding exactly like my mum and uncle rolled into one. Aiden ignored me and carried on laying the tables as the main hall started to fill up.

My parents always expect me to look out for my little brother, and I do this naturally anyway. I knew he had my back too. Mum once told me the story of when she'd heard him swear at our neighbour's teenage son because he'd been badmouthing me behind my back. My hero! I wondered how he would react if he knew how Kayleigh and Helena had been treating me. But I didn't want to trouble him.

Aiden joined up with his science group for breakfast, while Taka, Natsuki and I sat together near the front, where all the youth leaders were loudly chatting away. I'd already checked with Tanguy about Taka joining today's meeting and he'd agreed, as long as she kept everything confidential.

I noticed Kayleigh and the rest of 'her team' huddled together near the back. They were probably speaking in hushed tones, plotting how to get me kicked out of the team ASAP. The thought of that pierced like a sharp wound.

Breakfast was whizzing past and I wasn't sure that we had a plan or any strategy for the meeting. We were just angry. Then a phrase from my essay appeared and nudged me in a totally different direction.

"You know, instead of getting angry with Kayleigh, let's first try to understand where she's coming from," I proposed, sounding unusually calm.

"What! How's that going to work?" Taka asked, confused that I'd changed my tune.

"The thing is, there's something about 'home' which Helena, and especially Kayleigh, react badly to," I explained.

"Not sure why that's important. They're out of order, whatever the reason."

"But if we could listen first and try to understand them, then maybe we'll find a way to work things out together... instead of taking the easy way out."

"What easy way out?"

"Well, ranting on at each other... and then becoming enemies. As my dad says, there's no point in creating enemies. The first person that hurts is always you."

Taka looked thoughtful.

"Okay. I suppose. Yeah. In fact, you know that my parents have been at each other's throats a lot. Well, Zainab is the family mediator who's helping them. I've met her a couple of times and she's very patient. She explained to me that the first step in resolving a conflict is to not judge other people — we never know what they're really going through."

Natsuki had been listening closely. "Yes. We listen first, not judge. Let's try to understand why Kayleigh does not like our idea of 'home' very much. Then we tell her why we love 'home' very much!"

She summed it up so well. Scorpios do. It was also our best plan.

Natsuki had spoken before about 'choosing how you feel', and it made me think about choosing how I want to be. And I didn't want to be like Kayleigh.

I didn't want to be like anyone else either, not even Taka. I just wanted to be Leah.

☆ ☆ ☆ ☆ ☆

We ended up wolfing down our egg and beans on toast as our meeting was starting in five minutes. I could almost hear my heart begin thumping away like the 'boom-boom-boom' sound of Taka's bass drum.

As we hurried towards the gym, I remembered this popular scene from a famous old movie called 'High Noon'. My dad obsesses over these black-and-white Westerns, and he once got me to sit through the whole of this very boring one. Except that there's an exciting scene, the climax, where the hero coolly waits for his moment to strike in the final showdown. I couldn't help thinking that this meeting was going to be similar.

But then I thought 'no'. That would be a violent image to have in my mind. I didn't want that. Anyway, I wasn't trying to be a hero.

☆ ☆ ☆ ☆ ☆

Sitting next to Tanguy was someone new.

"Let's firstly welcome Femi. She decided yesterday to move from the app design team to ours. She's first class at coding and has already helped establish her brother's new tech company in Cairo, where she lives with her family. And she loves films! Welcome."

"Thank you. I'm super-excited to be helping make this film with you," Femi enthused.

"Okay. That's cool. And a warm welcome also to Taka, one of the musicians, who's a guest for this morning's session." Both Kayleigh and Helena stared suspiciously at her – they must have seen us together before.

"Now, including today, you've only got three days left to finish these two films for Presentation Day. I know that both teams have drafted lots of good ideas and plans, but you haven't even started filming, formatting or sequencing anything yet. So, to be frank, at the moment, it looks virtually impossible.

"What makes it even more challenging is the conflict going on here which you're all aware of – including Femi and Taka, who I had to inform, of course. If you can't work through it, you won't even have one film to show. More importantly, you won't have built any teamwork, which was the first task.

"So, please make an effort to listen openly to each other... and not be so quick to react. I know it's not easy. I struggled with this in the training they gave us as youth leaders in 'how to listen'. But I learnt that when I don't really listen, I can't even understand myself, let alone anyone else."

We all went quiet. The words 'silent' and 'listen' danced into my mind.

"So… what do you think is causing this dispute?" Tanguy asked.

Kayleigh stood up straight away and looked around the circle. Then, pointing her finger accusingly at me, she growled, "It's simple. She's the problem. She's annoyingly selfish and acting like a baby, wanting to do some stupid film about 'home', when we're facing a climate crisis. I don't know why she can't just be part of the whole group. She's ruining it for all of us. And anyway, she's too young to do a filmmaking project. She should be doing dance or pottery."

My first reaction was, 'how dare you?', but I was too shocked to respond. It was awful. I won't express the rest of what I felt, because there's no point in writing down a long list of swear words.

Helena stood up next to Kayleigh. She pursed her lips as her forehead wrinkled angrily. "Leah is a nasty little girl. Look at this," she spat out, holding up the jar of insects. "She slipped all of these into my bed to scare me. Well, it hasn't. I'm stronger than her."

Now I was livid. Taka looked horrified and ready to act. I knew we were meant to be listening and not reacting, but I can't stand lying or unfairness. That was it. Enough. I jumped up in an outburst of rage, shouting, "She's lying. She's lying. *She* put them in *my* bed. She…"

I think that astonished everyone, especially me. I'd only ever shouted that boldly before to the crowd standing around my brother like statues while he was getting beaten up. But I knew that despite the lies, I had to control my temper. Anger against anger just makes more anger, my dad often says. Remember the Code of Five, I told myself. I did this time, and it helped cool me down a few degrees.

I could sense Helena's brain whirring away and calculating her next move. I was not going to provoke her again.

Tanguy had crossed his arms and legs, looking blank, like he didn't know what to say or do next. But then he put his hands firmly on his knees as a fierce look of determination spread across his face. He told the three of us to sit down, which we reluctantly did.

We waited in silence for a minute that seemed more like an hour. It was agony. Tanguy made direct eye contact with each of us.

"We're going to try a meditation," he said.

I watched Kayleigh rolling her eyes as Rhys and Joe started giggling. I was caught, though.

"Is meditation like yoga? Don't we need a special mat?" Antonio asked.

"Meditation is the art and science of being still and present in the moment. It's a natural way of easing stresses and building inner strength," Tanguy explained.

I'm not sure if Antonio got that, but he uncrossed his arms and looked ready to give it a go. Kayleigh looked sulky, but at least not fuming anymore.

"Everyone, stand up, please. Walk towards one of the windows and shake out all the tensions in your muscles. Really shake… arms, legs, shoulders, hips. Enjoy it." By the amount of shaking going on, there was obviously heaps of tension to release.

"Now walk back to your chair, in slow motion, and sit down."

It was amazing to watch everyone pacing across the gym as if we were all wading through treacle. A soft, fuzzy feeling spread.

"Okay. Try to sit up straight, relaxing your shoulders. Take three deep in-breaths, exhaling long and slowly each time.

"Continue breathing gently, smoothly, while you sense the ebb and the flow, the movement of air from inside to outside… and that natural pause, after the out-breath and before your next in-breath."

The atmosphere in the room changed. I felt slowed down, lighter.

"Now, try to picture a pale, sky-blue colour in your mind. When you have that colour, please stand up and follow me in this self-healing movement."

We pictured the colour and then watched Tanguy intently. He was raising his hands very slowly, from being stretched out to his side to reaching right up above his head while breathing in. His palms touched, and he closed his eyes. After a couple of seconds, he brought his hands carefully down each side in a smooth arc, while exhaling all the air in his lungs.

We followed these movements three times, as tensions eased away.

"Good. Now choose one quality which you most need – a quality which you want to bring into this meeting. It could be honesty, resilience or care, for example. You choose. Then close your eyes and meditate on that quality, in silence, for two minutes.

"Sense how your body feels and what emotions or pictures arise in you."

I had to concentrate really hard until it became clear; the quality which I chose to meditate on was 'patience'. I so needed more of that… maybe we all did. I closed my eyes, listened to my breathing, and sensed my mind opening up like a passion flower in the sun.

I loved every second of this exercise. It soothed the heat and anguish, and everyone was looking more chilled now. We all sat down quietly.

"I hope you enjoyed the meditation. I definitely did," said Tanguy. "And perhaps now that we've all calmed down and come back to ourselves, we can take another step forward together.

"Let's move from meditation to mediation now. Because I think it's important to find a solution here by understanding each other's realities. What I mean is… well, let me give you an example.

"Imagine that you're all looking out at a big city, say London, from one window in a towering skyscraper. But the windows that you're each looking out of are on completely different floors. Some of you are looking out of a twentieth-floor window, where you can see blue skies and across the whole sprawling metropolis. Some of you are looking out of the ninth-floor window, where you can only see into the offices of the building opposite. While some are looking out of a ground-floor window, only able to see traffic jams and crowds of people bustling about. Same city, very different views.

"The higher up you go, the greater the overview and the more you can see. So, let's go high."

He turned to face Kayleigh and me. Only Rhys was sitting between us now.

"It's obvious how passionately you both feel about the films you want to make. For you, Kayleigh, climate change is the most important issue of our times. And for you, Leah, you feel inspired to explore 'What is home?'. So I'm going to ask what these themes mean to you. But first, are you both willing to listen to each other?"

Everyone held their breath. I glanced at Kayleigh, she squinted at Tanguy and he sat still, waiting. Eventually, we both gave a reserved nod.

"Okay. Let's start with you, Kayleigh. What does climate change mean for you?"

She didn't hesitate for a second.

"It's more about the climate crisis than climate change. It affects every single person wherever they live. Our planet is hurting and having difficulty breathing because her skies, land and waters are suffocating from our pollution... our industries, wars, the lifestyles we expect and demand. We are 100% causing this crisis," she emphasised.

"We've surrounded this earth with our rubbish, our clouds of poison... and over the last two centuries, the heat from the sun has increasingly got trapped. We've given ourselves and the planet the worst fever since life here began. You can't take from nature without giving back. And we just take.

"I think we're facing extinction – for real. You might not like that word, so check the science. Check out what the sixth mass extinction means.

"And it's us, and the next generation, who will inherit the hell that this paradise is being made into. We only have this one planet, so the climate crisis is the most important issue. And that's why I want to make this film."

Kayleigh's voice was trembling by the end and she couldn't go on. I may not have liked her, but I loved what she said. It was powerful and authentic. Everyone was captivated.

Tanguy was following every word.

"So, you're saying, Kayleigh, that unless there is more urgent action on climate change, unless we treat it as a crisis, it will be impossible to live on this planet. You're saying that we have no other home?"

"Well... yes," she said, nodding uncertainly. She seemed reluctant to call the planet our home, but she couldn't deny it and didn't push back.

We were now standing at the crossroads of our conflict, and I had no idea which path we'd be taking.

A silence echoed around the gym. Everyone was waiting.

"So, Leah, why do you want to make a film about 'home'?"

I closed my eyes and tried to go deep inside myself. What did 'home' really mean to me? This was about much more than a film.

"I know people think that where they live is their home. Of course. I live in London, England, part of the UK, part of the world. But then our world, our planet, is also part of a solar system, part of a galaxy, part of a universe. It's all connected, isn't it?

"So when I see the moon or stargaze, I'm looking into the universe… that's our greater home. Does that make sense?"

More silence.

"My friend Maia once explained to me that what's out there is also down here. 'As above, so below', she'd said. Like, there's oxygen up there and we breathe it down here… and there's iron up there, but also here in our blood…"

I felt like I was entering a dream state, and everyone was probably thinking I'd totally lost the plot. Yet, when I opened my eyes, I saw everyone looking intently back at me, even Kayleigh and Helena.

"So I think everything's connected. Maybe everything's inside everything else, like those 'nesting dolls'. There's our small home here on earth… and we live inside a much bigger home out there."

"Right. Mmm… I think I'm following you so far. But what will be the message of your film, then?" asked Tanguy, narrowing his eyes as he rubbed his chin.

"Well, if we don't understand that home isn't just our local address, how can we feel a part of the world or a part of the whole universe?

"And if we don't treat the planet as our home, how can we protect her?

"If we can't protect her, we have no home."

✫ ✫ ✫ ✫ ✫

This was the first time I'd really understood why I was so passionate about making this film. And this was the first time I'd been able to express it.

Tanguy waited.

"Right, yes.

"I think you're saying, Leah, that it's important to see the universe as our home, and that this world here is a small part of it. And you're also saying that if we don't take care of this planet as we would our own home, then we'll use her up until we break her completely."

"Yes. Those are your words, but that's what I'm saying."

At that moment, I was astonished to see these shimmering bands of ultra-violet appear in the atmosphere. I'd seen them a few times before at night, suspended from my bedroom ceiling. I'd no idea what they were.

Now they crossed the room, swift as ripples across a lake. I could breathe them in and they filled me with wellbeing. Probably no one else saw these sorts of glowing wavebands, and for sure no one would believe me if I'd have mentioned anything. But it didn't matter. Tanguy seemed to be leading us to a breakthrough.

He paced over to one of the windows and looked out into the distance. After he'd come back to his chair, he scanned our faces… searching, observing. I found myself doing the same. We were all gripped.

Tanguy now focused on Kayleigh and me.

"Thank you both for listening to each other. It shows respect, and that's at the core of all teamwork," he noted, sitting upright in his chair.

"You know, I was up most of the night wondering how I could help you solve this argument. Because it's not about some silly camera, is it?

"And while listening to you both, fireworks were sparking off in me. It was amazing. Neither of you have noticed it yet, but you're actually working on the same film, for the same reason!"

He emphasised each word and stared at us expectantly, waiting for it to sink in.

"I don't think I want to do the same film as her," Kayleigh replied, her lips pointing downwards as if she'd bitten into a raw lemon. For the first time, however, I felt for her. Whatever she'd been through, she clearly struggled to trust anyone.

"That's fair enough, Kayleigh, but it's not about that," said Tanguy, patiently. "It's about you both being passionate about exactly the same things – but in different ways."

"Are you saying that the climate crisis and home are directly connected?" I asked.

"Of course... although I've only just understood the connection myself. So, please bear with me," he encouraged, smiling.

"What I'm trying to say is that the climate change which needs to happen first, before all these dark problems can be solved, is the climate in each person... in the home that each person is; the climate in me, in you and in the whole human race.

"Don't you think that growing trust, tolerance and respect would produce a radical change of climate? I believe it would, and then the deep healing could begin... when we respect this earth as our home."

After a few mumbled yeses, everyone started searching around to see who'd actually got it. But Tanguy had caught a very big fish, and he wasn't going to let go.

"Don't you think that there would be a massive change in climate if we could find the courage and strength within to make these changes in our mindset and, therefore, in our lifestyles?

"Because I don't believe that all the solutions being promised by governments and leaders will ever change the climate of mistrust and entitlement among them or in society. And if that climate doesn't change, then nothing else will... nothing."

No one moved. This resonated. It was a much-needed reality check.

Kayleigh jerked noisily to her feet, and I quickly shrunk back into my chair. She was taller than me and had a harsh voice that could cut right through you.

"I do get what you're saying about the climate. It makes me incredibly anxious. And I've never thought about a change of climate inside people first. You're right. I agree, totally.

"But when you start talking about home, I don't think you know what you're talking about. It's total rubbish."

I thought it was insulting to talk to a youth leader like that, especially someone as kind-hearted as Tanguy. He seemed completely unfazed, though.

"What do you mean?" he asked.

"You have parents, don't you?"

"Yes, but I haven't been with them for nearly ten years."

"Yeah, but they're out there, aren't they? You can speak to them or fly back home one day. I can't. I..."

Kayleigh was choking up. She trailed her fingers down her cheeks and then rubbed her eyes like she was trying to force back the tears. Her tougher-than-anyone-else image shattered. She sniffed and wheezed, pressing her hands to her mouth like she was praying.

"Look, none of you get it, do you?" She looked around at all of us, pacing the circle of chairs. "You talk about home. What do you know?" she threw at me. "I never had one... my mum put me up for adoption when I was three and I never saw her again. It hurt so badly... like someone stabbing at my heart, for months, years. I don't even remember who my dad was... no idea if either of them is still alive. I so don't care anymore, but...

"All I've known is children's care homes and foster parents, that's it. The rest… usual trouble. So don't talk to me about home – what home?"

Kayleigh sat down and scraped her chair forward. She didn't cry at all. Instead, she grimaced and folded her arms tightly in front, like she was protecting herself with body armour. I glanced at Taka and Natsuki. We finally understood why Kayleigh hated the idea of home so much.

Then something sparked Natsuki urgently.

"I am… so sorry to hear what has happened, Kayleigh. I don't know what is life without home. It must be very hard. No peace.

"Some of my family had to move when Fukushima nuclear accident happened. I was six years old. They came to stay with us in Kyoto – now for many years. We make a good new home for them, inside ours. But it will never be home for them. They want their own.

"Now I learn a new thing from Mr Tanguy – home starts inside. There is home inside me, you, everyone. We can change climate inside us… make peace, heal ourselves. Then we help to heal the climate on the planet."

A warm atmosphere of wellbeing permeated the room. Maybe her speaking about healing had actually brought some in. It reminded me of Maia saying, "To think it is to create it."

Tanguy smiled at Natsuki in agreement and then turned to face Kayleigh.

"I've felt this pain and anger too. It cuts deep. It still hurts.

"When I was travelling north across Africa, I spoke to my uncle many times about these feelings. He tried to show me that I am not my pain, I am not my anger. I can choose differently. And I chose to not be defined by how badly people have treated me. I want to be free of that. I will define who I am."

No one except Natsuki and I had heard any of Tanguy's story. We were in awe about how his experience had strengthened him. The soft, reassuring tone of his voice seemed to dissolve the screeching sound of the conflict in me.

He smiled knowingly at Kayleigh. She unfolded her arms gently into her lap... the hardness was melting. I looked around me. The team began to look inspired, as if the vision of our project had flooded back in. A few seconds later, I surprised myself by walking over to Kayleigh with an air of confidence. I crouched by her chair.

"Kayleigh. I'm sorry for being insensitive. I didn't know your story. And now you've told us why you want to make this film, I think Tanguy's right. We do share the same passion and reasons. So, let's do this together. One film. One team.

"We must feature climate change, beginning at home, in each of us... showing that we need to treat the planet as our home too, before it's too late.

"I don't know if people will ever change their lifestyles. I don't understand why change seems so difficult. It can happen, though. Let's try to find a way to speak to the world through our film."

It was as if there were only Kayleigh and me in the gym. She'd gone quiet, but her eyes were following mine.

Then it all went crazy. "Yes, we can do this!" Femi cried out. "We can show how things can change." Then Darweshi and Antonio started cheering, while Rhys jumped up and down.

As I stood up, Tanguy dashed over to shake my hand... so unlike him. It was awkward, and we both laughed. Then Helena approached me shyly and actually apologised in front of everyone for the insects. That took real courage.

It all felt so hopeful, until it didn't. In our noisy enthusiasm, we'd lost sight of Kayleigh. She'd broken down, bent over in a corner, head in hands, crying her heart out. I'd never seen anyone cry like that. It was like the floodgates of years of hurt had been smashed open.

I wanted to wrap my arms around her, but I could only look on with sadness. For a few seconds, the only sound in the gym was Kayleigh weeping. No one knew what to do, until Femi walked over to console her.

I watched her gaze at Kayleigh with such compassion as she placed a hand tenderly on her shoulder. She looked up briefly and, although Femi never uttered a word, it seemed to calm Kayleigh down.

Tanguy had been waiting and watching, and now he went over and knelt down by Kayleigh's side. After a short while, he carefully pulled her to her feet and led her out of the gym. We all went back to our chairs, wondering what to do next. Antonio and Joe looked confused and worried, but Rhys was clearly ready for action.

"Can we work together now? Can we please start filming?" he asked.

No one answered, so Femi quietly said, "Yes, Rhys. Very soon."

We began glancing towards the entrance, anxiously waiting for Tanguy and Kayleigh to return.

When the door finally flung open, and they came in, all the nervous fidgeting stopped instantly. They stood literally shoulder to shoulder, which I think gave Kayleigh not only physical support but emotional too. They sat down together on the edge of a table.

"We've had a good talk… shared a couple of private stories about our past… and we're back in the present. The past is past. We're ready to move on now and make this film," Tanguy said, touching Kayleigh's shoulder with his. Kayleigh's face softened. She walked back to her chair and opened her laptop.

Suddenly, Taka got up. I realised that I'd been so engrossed in all the drama, that I hadn't even glanced across to check her expression as I often did, to read what she was feeling. It looked like she was juggling her thoughts, wondering which one to share.

"You know, what you've just said, Tanguy, reminds me of a conversation I once had with my grandad. It was about his life in the army, which sort of became his home after his parents died.

"He talked to me about how easily the past can bury the future. He told me stories about the thousands and thousands of people who had died in wars because of complete stupidities… wars that had started because of a stray dog, a bucket, pastry, and someone's ear! Yeah, right… I didn't believe him either. So I googled it right there and discovered even more stupid things which trigger wars.

"He explained that the real reasons for those wars were to do with the past; that some nations have a very bloody history, and if people can't let it go, they pass it on from generation to generation. The hurt and anger are just under the surface and only need a little spark to set off a wildfire of violence.

"That's why I'm really grateful I could come here today, because it's made me think about all the times when I become insecure or get hurt, and I only need a tiny trigger to kick off. I must try to control that! It's a bit like the bust-up here about a stupid camera… and now we've seen that it was never about that."

I'd never heard Taka speak out like that before. And although Kayleigh stayed silent, dabbing her puffy eyes with a tissue, she was now listening closely… and so was everyone in the team. I wished we'd been videoing it all.

"You're right, Taka," said Tanguy. "I so wish that we weren't still living in a world where the trauma of the past so often shadows our present… where war is accepted as a way to resolve issues. Haven't we learnt anything?

"But think about it. Perhaps it can change with our generation. If we can overcome this little fight together, and I believe we just have, then we can overcome much bigger things together too. With understanding, anything can be sorted."

I loved his positive energy. And he and Taka had just helped me take understanding people to a new level! If only I could write another essay for Mr Eaton.

I had to pinch myself to realise that I was still at a summer camp, and that all these big challenges and insights, meditations and mediations, were absolutely not on Kamlesh and Emilia's neat little activities schedule.

Tanguy's energy had filled the gym, which now felt more like a silent temple somewhere in the middle of nowhere. He got up from the table as if he was about to leave, but something stopped him.

"After these last few days, I believe that each of us has grown up a lot. Look around the room. You got angry and fought with each other, but felt the same passion for this film. You've ended up listening and treating each other with respect.

"You're now ready to be a real team and produce the most brilliant film for Presentation Day. One film, one team, as Leah said.

"It will be a film with a powerful message. We will show it to your families, your friends, to the whole camp. We will show it to the world."

As soon as Tanguy finished, without anyone saying a word, one by one, we all spontaneously rose to our feet. We didn't cheer and we didn't high-five. We were simply ready.

I looked across at Kayleigh, now standing strong. She'd fixed her steely gaze on Tanguy. Anyone watching might have thought that they were trying to outstare each other. They weren't.

"Yes, Tanguy," Kayleigh suddenly declared. "We will show it to the world."

WINDOW TWELVE

LET THE NEED LEAD

HOME

THE GREAT UNKNOWN

MT TRUTH

INSPIRING

DESERT OF DESPAIR

THE CRYSTAL CAVES

THE ROCKS OF COURAGE

THE RIVER OF HOPE

MT CLARITY

THE TANGLED WOODS

THE BRIDGE OF UNDERSTANDING

THE SWAMP OF CONFLICT

THE RAVINE OF WORRY

ARCHWAY OF CALM

Let The Need Lead

W hat's going on?" I shouted at Natsuki, to be heard above the rowdy lunchtime chatter. Bursts of nervous laughter were echoing off the walls of the main hall.

"Pressure is on! Every team wants to be the best." Natsuki always had a clever way of getting straight to the point, like my Scorpio uncle.

"Ah. Of course. Nerves are jangling!" I giggled, rattling a fork around an empty glass to demonstrate.

"Yes. Nerves. Each project group has only two and a half days to get their presentations finished."

"With an audience of over 150 coming, that's scary."

"People are now very competitive. Everyone looking over their shoulder to see what other groups are doing."

"Well, our group hasn't even properly begun. We're way behind. But after this morning, it feels hopeful."

"Yes. Mr Tanguy understands people."

"Yeah, he cares. He's like a mediator who gave a talk last term at our school. He showed us ways to resolve conflicts through peer mediation."

"What is peer mediation?"

"It's like young people helping other young people to work through their issues. Our school now has eight teenage mediators – I'd like to be one in the future. Anyway, I can ask Maia."

We had to be back in the gym in around ten minutes, which was more than enough time to devour a brownie with an unbelievably sweet dollop of cream. We were going to meet with Tanguy for half an hour and then it was over to us.

With my last spoonful of brownie, I caught a glimpse of Taka heading towards the main exit with her band. I told Natsuki I'd see her in the gym and rushed over to catch Taka before she left.

"Hey, Leah! Wow, the session this morning was so moving… and Tanguy's such an amazing youth leader. I hope you can crack on now."

"Yeah. I hope so too. It's still a bit, er… volatile, though. I think that's the word. But I wanted to say that your grandad's story really helped us. He must have been such a special man."

"He was. I'm glad it helped."

"And thanks so much for being there for me," I said, giving her a little hug.

"Of course. We're best friends, Leah. That's what friends do," said Taka, squeezing my arm.

I glowed with pride. Being someone's best friend in the world is the greatest feeling ever.

"Anyway… need to catch up with my bandmates. They've been begging for me to come back… I knew they would!" With a wink and a wave, she was off.

Just before leaving the hall, I went quickly over to see Aiden at the science group's table, which had test tubes, thick textbooks, and plates of lunch spilling over with double portions of chips.

"If we use water, soap and vinegar, then we only need to find some baking soda," said a serious-looking boy as he dunked a chip in a splodge of ketchup.

"Yeah, but we want something that explodes, not something that can only fizz," piped up a girl in a long peak baseball cap.

"Look at what it says here!" said another boy in a bright red T-shirt with the saying, 'I'm an Alien. It's in my DNA', written in big black letters. He proudly held up a book called, 'The Top 20 Exploding Science Experiments of All Time'.

"I can't wait to see your best-ever exploding presentation!" I winked, putting my hand on Aiden's shoulder. Aiden looked embarrassed and no one laughed. Science was obviously serious business for my brother and his mates. The truth was, I wasn't only looking forward to seeing their project, I was also proud of my brother for having made new friends.

Before I left, Aiden turned his head to the side and whispered, "Have you spoken with Mum and Dad this week?"

"With Mum. Just once."

"Oh. I've been speaking to one or both of them… most mornings before breakfast."

"Aha, right…" I mumbled, as a pang of guilt rattled through me for not having called more often. "So, what did they say?"

"Mum said that they were both very pleased we're enjoying ourselves and meeting people from around the world."

"That's good. She made a joke with me about them not being helicopter parents. She told me she trusts us to look out for each other."

"Good. Okay," replied Aiden abruptly, as he turned around to continue discussing experiments with his scientific buddies.

✩ ✩ ✩ ✩ ✩

Tanguy had set up the tables in a circle, which felt much better than the usual rectangle. In a circle, things somehow flow and you can't hide.

"Okay. Let's make a fresh start together," said Tanguy, keen to get our filmmaking project speeding down the runway.

"I know that we all want to get cracking, but I have an important question first. What is the best kind of leader?"

Femi put her hand up immediately.

She was crisply dressed in a white T-shirt and faded jeans with a rope-like red belt. Her shiny black hair was styled into a stunning fishtail braid.

"The best leaders set a good example by how they live. That's it. If you can't lead by example, you can't lead," she said confidently. She'd clearly thought this through.

"Er... exactly, Femi." Tanguy seemed impressed.

Femi continued, "I was once in a lesson where the teacher gave a talk on the importance of showing respect and not judging people. I totally agreed with him, but he never showed me any respect – that's not leadership."

Tanguy nodded. There was a long pause. At that point, I wasn't sure where Tanguy was going with all this.

"Okay, so before we start, I've got a great exercise for you," he enthused, striding over to the whiteboard.

He drew three big stick figures and above each of their heads he put a question mark. Then, under the first stick figure, he wrote, 'The Football Club', under the second, 'The Architect', and under the third, 'The Builders'.

"So, here's a short story and a question.

"Say that the big football club, Brighton – their stadium's along the coast from here – have an exciting vision for all young people in this area. They want to fund a brand-new, state-of-the-art sports centre. So they hire an architect and try to find the best builders.

"Who is the leader of this project? Is it the football club who are paying for the new sports centre? Is it the architect who is designing it, or the builders who will construct it?" Tanguy questioned, excitedly tapping each of the three stick figures in turn. "Which of the three?"

Most of us pointed to 'The Football Club', as they were the ones paying for the project. But some pointed to 'The Architect' as they lead the project with their design. Only Rhys said it was 'The Builders'.

"It's obvious. Without them, nothing at all is going to happen, is it?" Rhys folded his arms, looking smug and satisfied that he was the only one who'd got it right – I could see why he and my brother had become friends.

Tanguy smiled playfully. "Well, it's none of them!" he exclaimed. I thought he was about to celebrate catching us all out, like a striker who's just nutmegged the goalkeeper from a tight angle.

"The football club, architect and builders must each take a lead in the project of course, but…" He was teasing us now, and I was confused… surely one of those three takes the overall lead?

Tanguy held us in suspense for what seemed like ages until he finally delivered his point. "It's the need of the youth which leads the project… or at least it should be. The sports facility is for them, isn't it? So the need of the youth leads."

I think we were still with him, just about.

"Sooo," he breathed out as if he was going to reveal a hidden secret. "Let the need lead… yes? I'll write that on the board."

LET THE NEED LEAD

"As youth leaders, we're always checking the needs at the start of every day. What does the whole camp need? What do specific individuals need? What equipment do the project groups need? Then we can organise ourselves to meet those needs. Yes?"

Most people nodded or said 'yes', except me, of course.

"I'm sorry, Tanguy. I get what you're saying, but I can't see where you're going with this."

"Well, before you start making your film, you must be very clear about what the needs are. Can anyone say?"

Femi stepped forward again.

"The need is to build good teamwork in making a film for Presentation Day, choosing a topic we're all passionate about. Then to share our message with everyone coming. For our project, we have two main themes: 'the climate crisis' and 'what is home?'. So far, we already see the direct connection.

"We now understand that you can be at home inside yourself and change your own climate. This needs to happen first if we're going to rescue this planet."

We all looked at Femi, quite stunned – even Tanguy.

"Wow! That's so lucid, Femi. You summarised the need brilliantly. Thank you."

Tanguy began writing enthusiastically on the board again.

Good Teamwork:
Step 1: Identify the need and let it lead.
Step 2: Find out who's best at doing what.
Step 3: Support and make space for people to try new things.
Step 4: Listen and communicate – in that order.
Step 5: Be curious. Question everything, including yourself.
Step 6: Enjoy the challenges – it's the only way you'll grow.

"I worked this out during camp last year – I hope you find it helpful."

I guessed that this could be Tanguy's Code of Six about teamwork. Smart.

"Okay. Shall we vote now for the best person to be project leader? I appreciate that you're still getting to know each other's abilities… but who do you think might be best to coordinate the research, the filmmaking and the production?"

That put each of us on the spot, and I noticed a few people squirming in their chairs. But I began to see now where Tanguy was going with this. If we all ran around frantically just doing our own thing with this project, then it would end up like the last cake I made – undercooked, over-sweetened and falling apart at the edges.

After half a minute of mumbling and muttering, Darweshi declared, "I vote for Femi," and a big 'yes' rang out.

Tanguy added his vote. "I think that's a wise choice… you've got an excellent feel for what this project needs, Femi.

"You told me yesterday that you've had some experience with editing and animating videos – that's going to help a lot. So, are you okay with being project leader for these crucial two and a half days? I mean, they have voted for you…"

Femi nodded her agreement and gave the hint of a smile as she bowed her head, looking slightly embarrassed.

"Okay, that's great. So, Femi… how best to organise this team to get the project moving?"

Femi didn't hesitate.

"I'd suggest that Kayleigh heads up a group to focus on the climate crisis – she seems the best informed. And then I'd suggest that Leah leads a group focused on 'home', as she's taken the initiative in that.

"But both groups need to stay connected. We need to make all the pieces fit together to create the biggest impact with the audience."

Natsuki and I both raised our eyebrows in amazement and there were a few 'wows' from the team. Femi was a natural, inspirational leader. So organised too. I had to ask her if she was a Virgo.

"You sorted that out far more efficiently than I could have done, Femi!" gushed Tanguy, still astonished by how quickly she'd taken the lead.

"Kayleigh, Leah… are you happy leading the two themes?" asked Tanguy. We both smiled at the same time. I was really chuffed that Femi had put me forward as a group leader.

"And how will you project manage this, Femi?"

"Well, I'm keen to coordinate it all – filming, editing, sequencing, voiceovers and any photographs or music the team wants to use," she said, as if she'd been planning this for days. Maybe she had. This was starting to look good.

"Brilliant. You're ready for takeoff then. Just remember to manage your expectations."

"What do you mean, Tanguy?" I asked.

"Don't expect it all to go smoothly!" he said, winking, as he spun swiftly towards the door and left us to it.

I loved Tanguy's natural sense of humour and humility; it encouraged everyone to speak their minds. His free spirit promoted ours.

☆ ☆ ☆ ☆ ☆

"Okay, here's what I'm going to suggest," said Femi, in a friendly but firm tone.

"First, let's decide on the two focus groupings. I'm not talking about who wants to be in Kayleigh's group or Leah's group. We are one team now.

"I'm talking about the film, and which focus you believe you can contribute best to."

Well, that got decided without any dramas. Helena, Darweshi and Joe chose the climate, and Natsuki, Rhys and Antonio chose to join me with home. Four in each group felt right. And our group had now doubled in size, so I was doubly excited about that!

"Good. So, where do you want to work?" asked Femi.

"The library," replied Kayleigh decisively. I didn't expect that. Although the library had the best internet connection and reference books, I really thought that Kayleigh would've wanted the bigger space of the gym and to be closest to the camera and equipment. I probably had a very narrow view of her.

"Okay, good. So the 'home group' have got the gym.

"Now, before you get started, could you each explain what your aims are for the film so that your content matches?"

"Sure," said Kayleigh. "Our message will focus on the devastating impact of human behaviour on our planet. We'll be presenting vital issues to do with levels of consumption, the 'throw-away society' and how some governments and global corporations use 'creative accounting', meaningless targets and ads to fool everyone into believing that they're treating this as a crisis."

Her message was very close to my heart, and wow, she really knew her stuff. I found it a bit intimidating though – she sounded so professional, and I had to go next. I pulled back my shoulders and clasped my hands.

"We're going to explore 'what is home?' with video clips and interviews. We'll try to show the bigger picture of why a home is essential for all forms of life in the universe, including human beings. We'll find examples of rewilding projects around the world which show that when people respect each other and respect the planet as their home, the climate naturally improves. That's where both groups connect."

Kayleigh raised an eyebrow quizzically and seemed genuinely interested in what I'd explained... like she couldn't disagree with it. I had to remind myself how much things had moved on in two days – especially between Kayleigh and me.

"Great, thank you," Femi responded. "I can see why Tanguy

said that you're both working on the same film, for the same reason. Can you see it now?"

She left that question hanging in the air... until Kayleigh grabbed it.

"I'm not sure, Femi. Not sure. I guess we can give it a try."

"I agree. Let's work on it," I said, sensing the fine balances.

"Good. Thank you both for being so honest," smiled Femi, with hope in her eyes. "I'm going to be working at this end of the gym, where I can log and collate all the raw footage, images and sound, and prepare for post-production.

"So, please let me have any videos, photos, music or voiceovers as soon as you're ready. I'll drop in on each group from time to time and see where I can help.

"And look, we really don't have much time anymore. So less talk now and more action. Let's see if we can turn our message into a powerful film."

Kayleigh and the climate group left in a hurry. We set up at the other end of the gym to Femi, who'd kept all the filming equipment right by the side of her table. She obviously intended to stop any camera wars from breaking out.

WINDOW THIRTEEN

THE BIGGER PICTURE

The Bigger Picture

"So what's your idea?" asked Rhys eagerly.

I proudly placed on the table the big pad that Natsuki and I had been working on and opened it up. At the time, we thought our sketches were an ingenious plan. Now they looked a bit of a mess. It was like we'd gathered ingredients for a delicious dinner, but forgotten the recipe. I stalled for time.

"Well, the thing is, ermm…" I cleared my throat as Rhys and Antonio stared at our scribbles, their eyes glazing over.

"Is this it? It looks more like graffiti than a plan," moaned Rhys. Antonio was frowning – he probably couldn't believe it either.

"We only made sketches. Now that we need them, they make no sense. Sorry," sighed Natsuki, scrunching up her face in frustration.

I opened my tablet as if I had a fancy PowerPoint presentation ready. They waited. And waited.

"Well, come on. Where's your plan?" Rhys complained.

I was about to turn the tables and ask them for their ideas when… whoosh, ping! Like lightning, a brainwave crackled through me from my braids to my trainers. I jumped up and stood excitedly by the whiteboard.

"Okay, so here's my idea," I announced, desperately struggling to work out how I was going to do this.

I grabbed a green marker pen and began drawing three scrawly pictures on the board. As I was furiously sketching away, I could feel their impatient stares like needles on my back.

"Okay. Each of these pictures represents different ways to think about home.

"This first picture I've drawn is of a happy person – let's call him Sean. He's at home in himself."

'Oops' I thought. That was a big mistake. How come I blurted out Sean's name... and did they know him? I blushed, my hands getting sweaty already. I caught Natsuki's eyes shining back at me.

I gripped the marker tighter and moved on swiftly. "Yes. So this is someone who feels at home, inside. He looks confident, peaceful, and pleased to just be himself. I can't draw all of that on a stick figure, but you know what I mean." I paused to catch my breath.

"This second picture is meant to be of, say, Antonio in his hometown in Spain, with his family. Your birthplace, or where you now live, is another kind of home.

"Then I've drawn here a few animals and the names of their homes: a lion's den, a rabbit's warren, a badger's sett, a beehive... fascinating places. That's where they live. It's home for them."

As I was imagining the fourth picture I wanted to draw, Natsuki jumped up and neatly drew a person standing on top of the planet.

"That's it, Natsuki! How weird. That's exactly the picture I was thinking about – the one we did in the main hall. We must be telepathic!"

Another example of tuning forks, I thought; sounds, pictures and ideas travelling instantly, from person to person… much faster than any internet speed.

I refocused.

"Ah! I know. There needs to be a vital question underneath the planet: 'Do you think of this as your home?'"

"That's such a cool question, Leah. I can draw a much better picture though, and we can use it in the film with a voiceover of me asking the question," Rhys boasted, glowing at the prospect of having a starring role in the film.

"Er… we'll see, Rhys… could be…"

The final picture seemed to draw itself – I didn't even have to think about it.

"This is meant to show our solar system, inside our Milky Way galaxy… and those little spirals everywhere are meant to represent some of the billions of other galaxies in the universe.

"The universe is our biggest home, isn't it? It's the place where we live, where animals live… it's home for the planet herself and for all those galaxies and space… for everything, right?"

I was on a roll here, and I could see the whole film starting to unravel in clear images and vivid colours in my mind.

I put my marker pen down, holding my breath as I turned around anxiously to see if they were on board.

"Well, your pictures are a mess, Leah, but your idea is brilliant and original. Who would ever think about home in all these different ways?" said Antonio, looking encouraged that we were finally making progress.

"I love your idea – really, Leah," said Natsuki, warmly.

"But how will any of this go into a film?" asked Antonio.

"Well, I'm not sure. I haven't got that far."

"I know!" Rhys cried out, rushing up to the whiteboard and wiping it clean in his enthusiasm. "We can start with a picture of space…. that Hubble telescope picture of thousands of galaxies. The bigger picture.

"Then we zoom in on a fantastic photo of our spiral galaxy, which I've already got on my phone. Then, zooming in further, we see our beautiful blue planet floating and spinning in space."

"Can we show the magnetosphere too?" asked Antonio.

"The what?!" We were clueless.

"It's the Earth's magnetic field; it protects us," replied Antonio as if this were a fact which everyone should have learnt by now.

He strolled up to the whiteboard and drew a small picture of our planet, with these big coloured rings of radiation arcing out of the North and South Poles and surrounding the earth.

"Wow. This magneto thing looks like a force field around a space ship… or the energy field around a person," I said, imagining.

"What? What energy field?" Rhys challenged me, creasing his forehead in confusion.

"Well, there's much more unseen about a human than seen," I answered, remembering a phrase that Maia had used.

"You're weird," said Rhys.

"Please, don't call me that."

"Well, you say totally weird things sometimes."

"Look, Rhys. It may sound weird to you… but there are things in us and around us that we don't see."

"I can see you. What else is there? You are weird."

"You can't see my thoughts, my feelings, my reasons, my worries... can you? You can't put love under a microscope and measure it. We're full of energies. Energy is everywhere, even if you don't see it."

Rhys had no reply, and I backed off. This wasn't the time to discuss things I'd only spoken with Maia about. She'd described the aura, an energy field around each of us, which sounded weird to me at the time... until I started to see and feel things. Anyway, for another time, I thought.

"What does this magneto thing around the planet protect us from?" I asked Antonio.

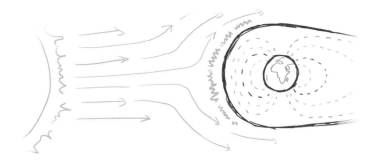

"The solar wind. Without it, I don't think we could survive the radiation from the sun for one minute."

"I wonder if people realise that it's there, like a roof over our home. It's amazing."

I was in awe at what we were discovering together. Images and scenes were now linking up. The film was taking shape.

Then a voice boomed over from the other side of the gym. We'd forgotten all about Femi. "Why don't you send someone over to the library... exchange ideas... see if they want to suggest anything?"

I bit on one of my fingernails, worried now that both groups might be heading off in totally different directions. How would our plans tie in with theirs?

Antonio immediately volunteered to go across to the library. In the meantime, Natsuki and Rhys were straight into their phones, scrolling away for photographs, video clips and facts.

Fifteen minutes later, Antonio strode briskly back into the gym. He was on a mission.

"I told them all about our ideas, and they didn't get it. But when I mentioned the magnetosphere, Kayleigh got really excited and said, "Get some pictures of 'space junk'." I pretended to know what that was and told her, "No problem." So, I'm sorry... but what exactly is 'space junk'?"

"Well, I did a school project on the main types of pollution and actually focused on space junk," I said, proudly. "Often people aren't aware that there are thousands of pieces of debris from satellites, and other stuff we've dumped, orbiting this planet and flying faster than bullets."

"Ah. 'Basura espacial!'" sighed Antonio, slapping the table. "I didn't know the English for it."

I glanced across at Natsuki with my mouth gaping open, wondering if she was thinking the same as me... that we'd discovered another link between home and the climate crisis. I had to speak out.

"You couldn't live in your home if it was full of junk, could you? Well, we've filled the planet and its atmosphere with all the toxic rubbish we don't want, and it's created a climate crisis.

"Maybe cramming our landfills, minds and bodies with junk 'food' is part of it too. If we took care of our planet as we do our home, would we fill it with toxic rubbish every second of every day?" I asked.

An image of trillions of particles of plastics floating in the oceans came into my head, and I trembled inside, feeling sick. We had to speak out about this too.

"I think, in our film, we must show how we are damaging ourselves. Because we hardly treat anything as a home, not even our own bodies."

Femi heard me from the other end of the gym and dashed towards us.

"That's such a powerful statement, Leah. Can you write and record that? Then we could use it as a voiceover."

Hearing this from Femi... well, I was flying high.

She went back to her desk and slid her computer into a laptop sleeve. "I'm going to suggest that both groups do as much as they can today. You've still got about an hour and a half before dinner. Then we can all meet after breakfast tomorrow to collate our ideas and combine the photos and video clips. I'm going to the library now to tell the rest of the team and see how they're doing."

I watched as Femi gathered her things and placed them tidily, one by one, into the many pockets of her sky-blue canvas backpack. There was something special about her efficiency and calmness that made me admire her. She didn't judge anyone and I think she'd won the respect of the whole team without even trying to.

"Thank you so much," I said to Femi before she left. "It's amazing to watch how you build teamwork."

Femi's face lit up. "I'm just trying to let the need lead," she said, winking. She'd really got the point Tanguy was making earlier on.

✫ ✫ ✫ ✫ ✫

That evening after dinner, Taka and Aiden came over to our cabin to hang out with Natsuki and me. As soon as we sat down on the steps, Taka was onto us. "I want a blow-by-blow account of what happened in your team after I left. Has the peace deal lasted?"

"Yes. I think so," smiled Natsuki. "Femi is the team leader now. We like her. She is helping us work together. And Leah has a very good plan. Kayleigh too."

"Yeah, with Tanguy and Femi's help, we're using our differences to be more creative. I'm starting to feel proud of us as a team," I said hopefully.

"Well, I feel proud that you and Natsuki both stood up for what you believed in… even when you were in the minority," said Taka. That was so good to hear.

We then asked Taka and Aiden about their project groups, and Taka couldn't stop giggling.

"I had a bit of a bust-up with Josh, the lead singer in the band," she said, with a hint of mischief. "I argued that he was singing out of tune on one recording, but he snapped back claiming that my sense of rhythm kept going off the rails in the last ten seconds of each chorus.

"So, the bass guitarist suggested we each listen back to the recording, after which he pointed out that we were both right! We all fell about laughing and decided that although we needed to be more in tune, we weren't going to take ourselves too seriously." No chance of that with Taka around, I thought.

Aiden updated us on the science team and their various exploding experiments for Presentation Day – they were absolutely loving it.

"But when our youth leader, Raj, came in and saw what we were doing, he totally freaked out! He said that at Presentation Day, our experiments would be a fire hazard and a health hazard, and could get the whole camp into big trouble. We were gutted.

"So, now we have a new safely exploding experiment to show

and it has a big message. I can't tell you what it is, though. It's top secret until Saturday."

"We also have a lot of science in our project," replied Natsuki encouragingly.

"Well, you might need the experiment which we're going to show," said Aiden, half giving away his secret.

Just as Taka and Aiden were leaving, a group of boys passed us on the way to their cabin. I can't remember exactly how many there were, because I only had eyes for one of them. I'd really missed Sean.

When he saw me, he raised his hand up as if to say 'hi'. He didn't actually say 'hi', but I think it was as good as a 'hi'… just without saying it. Anyway, I really don't want to obsess about it…

☆ ☆ ☆ ☆ ☆

"Can each group please report on their progress. We need to make the two halves into a whole," Femi stated, as everyone sat there looking full up. We'd each had a big, cooked breakfast with home-baked blueberry muffins. It was meant to be one muffin per person, but I noticed a few pockets bulging with extras.

Kayleigh spoke up first.

"Well, we've got video clips, photos and research which show the magnitude of the climate crisis around the world. It's shocking and incredibly sad when you see this much evidence.

"Darweshi and Joe focused on how human behaviour in the last 200 years has been increasingly destroying the environment. So we've added some data to do with the explosive growth in intensive farming, transport and consumerism, as well as statistics on overfishing, deforestation and all forms of pollution. This shows the direct link between modern lifestyles and their harmful impact on our planet – it's truly terrifying."

"Yes. It is. Thank you, Kayleigh. That sounds compelling. It's so important that this message comes across in our film. Excellent," said Femi.

She then turned to me. "So, Leah, how has your half of the team got on?"

"Well… we've been collecting pictures of the different kinds of homes which exist. We're trying to show how crucial it is to recognise and protect them: from whole eco-systems like rivers and lakes which are home to thousands of different species, to the natural habitat or home of a single animal.

"We've got high-definition photos showing how beautiful and unique these homes actually are, like the nests of the horned coot – these birds carry pebbles from the shore to shallow waters where they build an island which can weigh one and a half tonnes!

"We went a bit wild piecing together a collage showing how every constellation, star, planet and moon in our Milky Way galaxy are connected in some way.

"Then, we focused on how humans and every form of life on earth is connected; how we could protect our world if we decided to think of it as our home and keep it safe. That's a complete change of attitude, and it's one of our key messages.

"Finally, we're looking for a clip to do with making a home inside yourself… I mean, like a safe space deep inside. A place where no one can hurt you, and you hurt no one.

"It's really tough to show this, but we're thinking of doing a video of Natsuki explaining how the meditation with Tanguy made her feel at home in herself."

Femi seemed to swell with pride. "That sounds so interesting. You're bringing such an original perspective. I'm sure it's not been easy."

Her comments meant so much to me, and I noticed our group

were sitting on the edge of their chairs. Kayleigh and Helena, however, seemed bored, and Darweshi and Joe were fiddling with their phones under the table. Trouble was brewing.

Sensing this, Femi asked, "Can you all now see how these two themes connect... how they represent two sides of a crucial message?"

"No, not really," sniffed Kayleigh, sounding irritated by the question. Femi held back from responding, and Kayleigh sat up in her chair and pressed on.

"Look, we're focusing on a crisis, right now. No one can escape it. Yeah, I get that treating the planet as our home is important. But our message is, well... this is a fight, with protests and marches and..."

The tension was rising.

Suddenly, we each turned to watch the gym door as it began to creak open. In walked Tanguy. We were relieved to see him. He was smiling away and looking casual in denim khaki shorts and a turquoise T-shirt with the words, 'Je me sens bien dans ma peau', which he later told us meant, 'I feel good in my own skin'. Tanguy spoke fluent French, which made him even more cool.

In front of everyone, Femi updated Tanguy on the positive progress of both parts of the team. She was also very honest. Without making a big deal of it, she described the difficult moment which he had walked into.

"Sounds very healthy to me," Tanguy reassured us. "Does anyone want to say how these two halves can join together now?"

Kayleigh clearly hadn't finished. "I don't know. Maybe we should have two films..."

I watched Tanguy intently. His face seemed to be tensing up, yet his gaze was soft.

"You know, through experience and the challenges we all face, we can develop a powerful instinct. It's good to listen to it. And I may be wrong, Kayleigh, but my instinct says that there's something about making this film which you haven't told us yet…"

"You may be right."

"Can you share what it is?"

I saw a few of her tears come and go.

"It's… well, this climate crisis is much more of a personal issue than any of you realise."

"How do you mean?"

"Well, the crisis is happening across this planet and it's destroying people's lives… real people. I mean… you've no idea, really, no idea."

She tightened her lips, leaned forward and folded her arms, grabbing each elbow like it was holding her up. Whatever Kayleigh was building up to say, she was steeling herself to not lose control.

"I lost someone to this crisis. The only human being who really meant something to me. It was… his name was Callum.

"When I was ten, the children's home I was in found me my third and best foster family. It was the best because there was a boy there of my age who they were also fostering. Me and Callum had the same attitude about everything: adults, school, gangs, clothes, football.

"He loved his football. He used to kick a ball around the house, the garden and in the school playground at every break. When he was eleven, he got into the under-12 football team representing the school. It was his proudest moment.

"But Callum had asthma, and the playground was right by a main road. He'd spent years running around there and breathing in air pollution at dangerous levels, and had been to the doctor loads of times. But the doctor kept prescribing him stronger inhalers, steroids and stuff. He only got worse.

201

"On his twelfth birthday, we were having an amazing party with a few of his friends in the back garden where we lived. We spent all afternoon playing football and having races. I'd never seen him so happy.

"All of a sudden, in the middle of a game, he slumped to the ground. He could hardly breathe. He was having a severe asthma attack, so bad that they had to call for an ambulance and he was rushed to hospital.

"He was taken straight into intensive care. And he never came out again."

Kayleigh's face turned ghostly – she never blinked. Some of us couldn't hold back the tears. Seconds sped past. I felt numbed, but wanted to speak out.

"This might sound clumsy, Kayleigh... but listening to your story... it's heartbreaking. I feel sad that Callum had to suffer so much, and that his life was stolen from him. I can't imagine what it must be like to lose your best friend. No words can describe that.

"I also want to apologise... to say sorry for having judged you. I didn't appreciate your passion and reasons for wanting this climate crisis sorted. No one should ever have to suffer in the way that Callum did."

I walked over to Kayleigh and simply said sorry again, as I touched her arm lightly. She didn't respond at first, but then looked up at me helplessly. Her eyes seemed empty – yet slowly, a little fire began to flicker behind them.

Helena whispered across the table, "I get you, Kayleigh. I believe Callum would be proud of what you're doing. We are."

"Yes. We are," several of us chimed in.

Tanguy stood beside her. I felt this surge of belief and compassion coming from him. Kayleigh must have felt it too, because she rose to her feet as he held out his hand.

"I hope you feel the warmth of support around you here, Kayleigh.

"Perhaps this project seems trivial considering the tragic story you've just shared, but I believe it becomes even more significant now."

Femi was on the same wavelength. "Tanguy's right. We have an opportunity here to do much more than a summer camp project.

"We can weave our stories and passions, and send an urgent message to the world. That's why we need the two messages and the two groups to make a whole. They belong together.

"You know, it's so clear to me now that home is the climate we make, and the climate we can change. And that begins here, now, with us.

"This could be the first of several films that we produce, bringing some gritty understanding and hope to people in these crazy times… especially for our generation who stand to lose the most."

Femi sounded like an ambassador for all the youth around the world.

Kayleigh's mood lightened, like a dark veil had been lifted. She looked ready to fight on, and so was the team.

Tanguy seized the moment. "Kayleigh, would you be okay if we made a specific mention of Callum in the film? Not to add drama, but to add reality."

"Yeah. But I'll do that part on my own."

"Got it, Kayleigh. I know it's not easy to share something so raw and personal. Callum's story has made the life-or-death situation we are in very real. I'm so pleased you've agreed to share it in the film. It may help others face the truth."

Femi cut in. "This makes completing our film more urgent now.

"So, I suggest we set up the tables in a circle again and write on the whiteboard each of the elements that we're going to show in our film. Then we can put them in sequence. It's going to be extremely tough to finish this film in less than two days, but..."

"... we can do it," said Tanguy, completing her sentence. "I'll stay with you for another half an hour and then leave you to press on. You can do this, can't you?"

Our actions were our answer, for as soon as Tanguy had finished his sentence, all of us rallied around setting up the tables, doing final plans on the whiteboard and starting to sequence the whole film presentation.

I felt this unusual force in myself and in the spirit of everyone there. We were more than ready. We had finally become a team.

YOUR EYES ONLY SEE WHAT YOU'VE TAUGHT THEM TO SEE

Your Eyes Only See What You've Taught Them To See

Tanguy left the room, and Femi was on edge. "Let's do a time check now." Her tone of voice sounded sharper. The pressure was getting to all of us.

"We've only got a couple of hours before lunch, and maybe five afterwards. Can we bring back sandwiches and have a working lunch here?" Femi didn't wait for an answer. She was sprinting towards the finishing line and trying to keep us on track.

"We don't have enough content for the film and we've also got all the voiceovers to do. It's going to take hours to edit the videos, photographs and sound into a final cut for the film presentation. We have the whole of Friday... so I believe we can probably do it."

Femi didn't sound convincing. I can usually tell when someone is doubting themselves because that's often me.

It was a hectic morning and chaotic afternoon. There was the constant racket of people screeching chairs in and out, running from one end of the circle of tables to the other, internet videos suddenly breaking out into news reports and bursts of music.

Helena had found a video highlighting the environmental destruction of rainforests around the world. There was a part showing how the natural habitats of orangutans in Sumatra were rapidly disappearing. As they were editing it, you could hear the piercing buzz of chainsaws and men shouting orders. It sounded like a war zone.

Meanwhile, Femi was focused on logging and assembling the material to be ready for the first rough cut. After a couple of hours, she made a brief announcement over the hubbub.

"The quality of what you've given me is brilliant, but there are too many photos, not enough video and two sections which don't yet have any music or narrating," she explained, urging us on.

Natsuki and I immediately began volleying new ideas back and forth like quick-fire tennis at the net. At one point, I swivelled around lazily on my chair and was suddenly looking straight at the stack of filming equipment still placed within arm's length of Femi's table. And at the top of the stack, there it was – the professional video camera, sitting like the 'must-eat' cherry on a cake. The camera!

"Do you see that?" I asked. Natsuki stared back at me as if I was going doolally. "We had all those fights over that equipment and now it's been sitting there for days gathering dust. No one's touched it."

Natsuki took a long hard look at the camera and then grinned back at me.

"Okay, good. Now we're thinking exactly the same thing," I said. This wasn't clairvoyance, this was staring us in the face.

"What do you want to film?" whispered Natsuki.

"I've got an idea. Come with me."

I walked swiftly over to Femi's desk, with Natsuki following close behind.

"Femi, sorry to interrupt you. After dinner, do you think we can take the camera and equipment into the forest?"

"You want to film tonight?"

"Well, you said that we need more footage and… we haven't worked it all out yet, but it's to do with filming different homes on the planet. We can record live."

"Homes on the planet, at night?"

"Yes. Trust me, please. We need to go straight out into the forest, rather than sitting around talking about it or just downloading more videos from the internet," I insisted, moving towards the camera.

"Mmm… okay," said Femi, warming to the idea. "I think I know how to do this. It's best if you both sit down now. We must be careful here. That camera has an unfortunate history, hasn't it? And we don't want to go there again."

Femi sounded like she had a cunning little plan. She tapped her glass loudly a few times with a pen to get everyone's attention.

"Excuse me! Hello! I want to ask a brief question. We have to hand the filmmaking equipment back tomorrow afternoon. I guess no one needs it now…?"

I could just about make out the sliver of a smile on Femi's lips.

Having given it about four seconds, my hand shot up. "Well, I guess if no one else wants it, Natsuki and I could try doing some filming after dinner – some original footage to add to the internet clips."

"Filming what?" asked Antonio with interest.

"Things in their homes. I mean, like… a deer in the forest or a star in the sky… oh, I can't explain it all…"

Fortunately, Femi stepped right in.

"Does anyone else want to take the camera?" she asked tentatively.

No one answered and when I glanced across at Kayleigh, I was relieved to see that she was more interested in carrying on her conversation with Darweshi in front of his computer.

"Okay, well, does anyone want to join Leah and Natsuki this evening?"

I was amazed to watch not only Antonio and Rhys raising their hands, but Helena too. I clenched my right hand into a fist under the table and whispered to myself, "Yesss!" Natsuki heard me and whispered back, "Hai!" What a team.

☆ ☆ ☆ ☆ ☆

After dinner, Tanguy gave us the keys to the gym. As soon as we entered, Helena and Antonio both made a grab for the camera.

"Er… well, hold on!" I said, urgently. "Why don't you take the camera, Helena… and if you can carry that tripod, Antonio, then the rest of us can bring the lighting and the other gear." No one flinched. Problem solved.

Suggesting Helena take the camera was deliberate. I wanted to improve my relationship with her. I thought that she'd already made the first move by deciding to join us. Maybe, for all of us now, making the film was more important than taking sides.

We skipped and hopped towards the forest like children, absorbing the colourful sights, sounds and aromas of summer. It was a warm, sweaty evening, and the sun had nearly gone down. By the time we got deeper into the forest, it was difficult to see the way ahead, so we all got out our torches – Natsuki's LED metal one shone the furthest into the distance. A wonderful sense of adventure was in the air.

"A bit further and we'll reach a clearing I've already been to. Once we've set up the lighting equipment, we'll be able to film some of the natural habitats of creatures that live there," I said, quickly trying to remember the plan I'd scribbled on a pink sticky note that I'd left in the gym.

Then I spotted some insects on the move and pointed my torch.

"Helena, can you see that little army of ants crawling up the bark of that beech tree there? And look, there's an amazing stag beetle. Do you think you could film them?"

Helena seemed puzzled. "Why? I haven't got a clue what you're on about… but… awwww, look at that little cutie!" We all turned to see, and there it was – a hedgehog near the foot of an oak tree. It became a spiky ball as soon as we moved closer. Helena pointed the camera – she was on board now! But then…

"I think I've gone through all the steps Tanguy described, but it's not working! And even if it did, I'm sure you need to find a special night setting control or something. We didn't even bring that instructions booklet. We can't use it," grumbled Helena, frustrated. She glared at me like it was my fault.

"Don't worry. Let me think for a minute…"

Antonio cut in as if he'd been waiting for this moment. He took a couple of casual steps forward.

"Before I flew to London, I made a short film about wolves. We live in Antequera, not far from Málaga, and there's a very special wolf park nearby called, 'Parque de los Lobos'. There are four kinds of wolves which live there, almost wild, and I filmed them to understand the complex way in which they organise themselves as families. They're born to hunt as a team," he explained, looking very pleased with himself.

"And your point is?" snapped Helena impatiently.

"Well, I used the same video camera as this one, only the one I had was an older model. I just need to check the batteries and find the right settings on this one."

With Helena peering over his shoulder, Antonio set the controls and adjusted the lens like a professional. "It's quite simple. You just go through the settings carefully. We're almost ready," he stated proudly, as Helena broke into a little giggle. She seemed to have these sudden changes of mood, but Antonio wasn't fazed. In fact, the two of them kept standing very close to each other. Mmm.

"Can you help me set up the tripod, please? And can we have some lighting over there?" Antonio asked politely, as Helena grabbed the lights and Rhys followed with the tripod.

"Great. No time to waste!" I said, with a nervy smile. "Let's begin by filming anything on the forest floor, in the undergrowth, up the trees… anything that moves. Then we can try to track where it's coming from, where its home is."

Within half an hour, we already had some great footage: a close-up of that army of ants crawling out of a crack in the bark of a tree, a spider trapping a big fly, the hedgehog plodding along and this tiny night bird making beautiful flute sounds, which Natsuki recorded. We all loved it, even Helena. She was actually fine to work with, as long as there was a plan which was going according to plan!

"Okay, I think it's time to gaze up and observe the night sky," I said, with a thrill that fizzed through to my fingertips. I was now getting closer to my original idea, and there was a sense of awe rising up in me… the same as I'd felt on that special 'stardust night' in the park. A sense of complete wonder.

Before anyone knew what to film next, Natsuki was suddenly pointing up with great excitement. "Look! That, there. See!" she exclaimed, looking very at home in the skies, like me. And surprisingly, so was someone else…

"It's called Cassiopeia, named after a queen. It looks just like the letter 'W'… isn't that incredible?" marvelled Helena, turning to Natsuki and tracing the letter 'W' in the air to show her.

"Where I come from, in Møn, southern Denmark, the sky is so black at night that we sometimes spend hours stargazing from the balcony." Helena was on a roll.

"Now look... up there!" Natsuki called out, pointing to a very familiar constellation that no one could remember the name of.

Helena smiled knowingly. "It's called the Great Bear. It looks like a plough. If you focus on those two stars at the end of the plough's blade and then track straight up, you'll see that they're pointing to the Pole Star. The Pole Star shows where north is, and it's what sailors used to get their directions from and..." Helena trailed off. She'd tilted her head a little, as her jaw slowly dropped open in amazement. We tried to trace her line of sight.

"There it is! Can you see that triangle of stars? Look!" she urged, her eyes opening wider.

We couldn't see it at all. "It's there! If you look again at the Great Bear... well, those two stars near the handle... they point almost directly to that bright star Deneb. Can you see it now? If you can, you'll notice how it forms a triangle with two other stars – that one and that one... Vega and Altair. It's called the Summer Triangle. Isn't it beautiful? It's like a portal into the whole galaxy," she sighed, spellbound.

Apart from Helena herself, I think I was the only one who could make out this triangle of stars, because everyone else was straining to see.

A strange feeling came over me... a sense that this might have been the portal I'd gone through when I travelled the skies that night. Is this what you pass through when you die?

My attention began drifting away towards my big question... until... "Don't miss this," whispered Rhys, cupping his hand to his mouth. He was pointing his torch towards a stunning white owl on a branch a few metres away. He hushed us, pressing his finger firmly to his lips.

"Shhh. Quiet. Antonio, can you film it? It's about to take off," he mouthed, making desperate little hand signs for each word. No one dared breathe.

Antonio managed to film the owl just as it spread its huge, rounded wings to glide up into the night. We gasped in awe. Beauty in motion.

It was starting to get cold now, and we still hadn't filmed any of the stars. So I asked Antonio if he could photograph the Summer Triangle, plus a constellation or two. "I'll try my best, but I need to adjust the shutter speed and aperture… I'm not sure if anything is going to come out. Can you help me, Helena?" Surprise, surprise, she leapt at the chance.

We were soon heading back to the gym in good spirits. Seconds after entering, Antonio excitedly showed us footage of the owl gracefully taking flight.

"It's a barn owl," said Rhys, who obviously knew quite a bit about birds.

Antonio was enthralled. "I'd no idea that its body was so big and white and its wingspan so wide."

We then swiped through all the shots we'd taken; most of the images were sharp and looked stunning. The night sky ones were a bit blurred though, but there was one lovely photo of the Summer Triangle and two of Cassiopeia which we could use.

Huddling around Antonio and watching replays of the filming and all the images got us so inspired about our project… although we had no idea how we were going to incorporate everything into the main film.

As we ambled back to our cabins, I found myself looking

inquisitively at Rhys and Antonio, who up until a couple of days ago had both been fairly quiet. I realised that just because someone hardly ever speaks, it doesn't mean that they don't have something important to say.

I knew now how quick and easy it was to judge other people, which I'd done with Kayleigh and Helena. I was still too impatient and critical – faults which Taka had told me about before. But I wasn't listening then.

I guess it's true what my uncle says: it's much easier to see the faults in other people than to see your own. I gave myself a bit of a telling off for that – it's one thing for me to write a top-of-the-class essay about understanding people, and another thing to actually put it into practice.

These sorts of new thoughts continued streaming through my mind as I lay awake that night. For the first time in my life, I realised that I wanted to become much more aware of myself.

Something was changing, deep inside me.

AN UNUSUAL WORKOUT
IN THE GYM

An Unusual Workout In The Gym

Early the next morning, I walked out to my special place in the forest to do the meditation Tanguy had shown us. I took my trainers off and sensed the moist earth with my bare feet. I stretched out and upwards, trying to remember the sequence of movements and breathing. After a couple of minutes, it clicked, and as I meditated again on the quality of patience, I felt every muscle in my body relax, especially across my shoulders.

I wanted to stay longer in that peaceful state of mind, but I'd be late for breakfast, so I sped off barefoot to the main hall. Approaching the entrance, however, I slipped on my trainers and decided to take my last few steps in slow motion. It left me feeling like a supercharged battery.

The whole filmmaking team sat together on both sides of a long table, chatting and munching away happily. It was a first. I deliberately sat opposite Kayleigh, wanting to find a way to build bridges.

"I heard you found a shocking video, showing hidden nano-particles of plastics in fish," I commented.

"Yeah, plus the damage it does to their brains. Unbelievable. We also have a video taken in a lab that backs up Callum's story; it shows nanoparticles of car diesel fuel exhaust in the air. In cities, we're breathing this stuff in. It can go straight into your bloodstream and make you really sick... even kill you eventually. It's totally insane," raged Kayleigh, banging the edge of the table and shaking her head.

"I agree. It's a crisis, and it doesn't have to be that way."

"Yeah. It's almost too late..."

We both paused. I offered her a chunk of my brownie and she grabbed it, half smiling.

She was genuinely interested in the filming we'd done last night, and that brought us naturally on to chatting about the structure of the whole film.

I'm not an expert on body language, but when she slanted her body to move in closer to speak, opening her hands onto the table, I felt a glimmer of warmth and respect come my way.

Within an hour, we were all jabbering away back at the gym, where Femi was busy completing a schedule on the whiteboard. We only had today to finish everything.

"Hi, everyone. I hope you slept well and had sweet dreams about Presentation Day tomorrow!" chirped Femi, sliding snugly back into her chair. "I've collated all the material we've got, so let's draft out the order of our story. How will it begin?"

As we each sparked off with ideas, Femi began placing all the content in sequence. The whole plot was coming together now like we were on fast forward.

With help from Antonio, Darweshi and Joe, who were all pretty techy, Femi began transferring the content into a video editing program. Meanwhile, Helena had her earphones clamped on as she sorted through the selections of background music. The rest of us worked on preparing to film a couple of scenes with the camera, plus recording voiceovers for key moments – we wanted to let the images do the talking, but we also wanted to share the message behind each of them.

We slogged away non-stop for hours, including Antonio and Helena filming Natsuki doing the meditation in the forest. By late afternoon, Femi stood up and announced that she was finally ready to show us a rough cut of the film, to get our feedback before going any further. We all crammed together around her laptop, unable to contain our excitement. This would be the first time any of us, including Femi, would be seeing an edited draft of the entire film.

Four and a half minutes sped past and no one's attention wandered a millimetre from Femi's screen. As the music faded at the end, we looked around expectantly, trying to read each other's first reactions. That wasn't hard. We were stunned. The tentative glances quickly turned into yelps of delight and leaps in the air. Soon after, we crowded around Femi like a rugby scrum for a spontaneous team hug. She'd done an amazing job.

"It's come together really well, hasn't it? Well done, you lot!" enthused Femi, her face glowing and eyes on fire. "I'm so happy… but… we're only halfway there. There's lots more sequencing, editing and fine-tuning to do."

Although I could still sense nerves rattling underneath the surface, we were really starting to enjoy working together as a team… which was going to make it difficult for me now. I wanted to add something different without throwing a bucket of cold water over everyone's enthusiasm.

I was wriggling uncomfortably in my chair and pulling on my ponytail until I couldn't hold back any longer.

"Er… I want to suggest a little edit."

Heads turned. The spotlight was on me.

"The thing is… there's a part in our film where we say that governments need to act now, urgently."

"Well, what's wrong with that? They do need to act urgently, don't they?" huffed Kayleigh, almost shouting at me in disbelief.

"Yes, of course. But people have been pointing fingers at governments for so many years and yet what's really changed? Tanguy mentioned this on Wednesday."

"What are you trying to say, Leah?" Femi questioned pointedly.

"Well, I was on the computer in the library yesterday, and I found this video from 1992 of Severn, a 12-year-old Canadian girl, passionately addressing world leaders about the planet and the environment. It almost made me cry to see the distress on her face and hear her worries about the future. And she was younger than most of us here.

"Everyone applauded her, made fantastic promises and did nothing. Since then, Greta and many others have been out there bravely campaigning and leading by example. But if politicians are listening and acting, then why is the crisis getting so much worse?"

I hesitated for a few seconds, anticipating an argument. But a supporter came out of the blue.

"Yeah, I get that," agreed Kayleigh. "It is getting worse. And I'm so sick of hearing 'net-zero carbon emissions' blah-blah from people who don't even know what it means. And anyway, everything's still rocketing up – CO_2 and methane levels, extreme temperatures, natural disasters. I mean, aren't people absolutely terrified watching the polar ice caps melting, really?

"All this will only get worse unless the target is to go 'climate positive'. Without reaching that target, I don't believe we're going to have a future." Kayleigh's face had turned to thunder.

"So, how can we get there?" I asked.

"Almost every person alive can change their lifestyle, from today… reducing their consumption, reusing and recycling more, wasting less, supporting sustainable farming and only buying cruelty-free products which are also friendly to the environment… and so much more.

"You know, the planet naturally recycles everything it produces 100%. So, every single manufactured product should be 100% recyclable. Every single product," she emphasised.

"I so agree, Kayleigh. I had a similar thought yesterday. And also… well, I think that every leader on the planet needs to reduce their carbon footprint by 50% now… right now. That's the only way they can call themselves a leader in this crisis and be respected. Wouldn't that totally change the climate at the next world conference?

"To be 'climate positive', our whole mindset needs to change positively first," I argued, feeling like we were both in sync. And I couldn't stop now…

"We're one human race, living on the same one planet. I mean, I'd love to see everyone come together to save this world, but if we can't learn to respect each other and be kind, will anything ever change? Adults tell me that's 'so naïve', but I think it's totally naïve to believe that so-called 'green technology' is the answer to everything.

"So I'm just saying that instead of focusing our energy into trying to convince all those governments who aren't listening, maybe we can be leaders – our generation."

I'd never worked all this out before, but it seemed so right. Kayleigh raised her eyebrows and seemed to be following me intently. Maybe she was surprised about how much I'd actually researched this.

Femi drew in a deep breath and looked at us both, laughing with relief. "You two are so on the same page! You must see it now."

Kayleigh chuckled for a second. But it seemed like one dark cloud still hung in the air. She dropped both hands heavily onto the table and then clawed her fingernails along the edge. "You know, I've got a close friend who suffers from 'climate anxiety'. Millions do, especially around our age. I do too, and I've absolutely had enough of it."

"I feel the same," I added. "And there's another anxiety… to do with feeling lost… no purpose… not seeing a future."

"I know, I get that sometimes too," Helena chipped in. "But making this film has filled me with so much hope and purpose."

"Me too," said Joe. "I want to show our film to my whole school when I get back to the States. It makes me so proud."

Although it was inspiring to hear this, I wanted to get practical.

"Kayleigh, can you help me do a minor edit on that voiceover part which blames leaders for everything?" I asked, swallowing uneasily and surprising myself at being so direct.

"It's okay, Leah. You do it," she said, with a little wink. That was all I needed – her approval. I knew it was tough for her to accept me making this edit. So that wink meant a lot to me.

Femi was now ready to move on. "Why don't we take a quick break now and then let's get this plane off the runway… Saturday's approaching fast!"

There were a few cheers of excitement as people shuffled around the room or went outside to get some fresh air. This session had been sort of… epic football training. We'd learnt how to look up and pass the ball properly to each other.

☆ ☆ ☆ ☆ ☆

As it turned out, we worked right the way through dinner, editing the music and finding new content. Everyone was tapping away furiously on various devices or dashing off to the library to do some final research. In the end, my voiceover edit only took a few practice runs to record and when I played it to Kayleigh, she gave me a big thumbs up.

No one left the gym, except Natsuki and Rhys to make sandwiches and bring them back with special permission from Kamlesh; he was delighted to hear about our little dinner workout in the gym – we were just doing a different kind of weightlifting.

"Okay, the last edits and additions you've given me are excellent… although they need to be sequenced," insisted Femi, sounding even more organised than usual. "But I must say that in the end, we've actually got too much material. That's good news, except that I hope you don't get too disappointed if you find some of your clips lying on the cutting room floor!"

A few laughs rang around the gym – I think everyone was too excited and exhausted to mind.

"So, for the opening, I've got this incredible Hubble Legacy Field image of thousands of galaxies, which Rhys uploaded to my drive. Then, Leah's given me some beautiful acoustic music for that scene, called 'Innisfallen' – whatever that is."

"It's a mystical island in Killarney, near where I was born," I said, proudly.

"Great. Thanks. Then, I've got to insert that colourful image of the magnetosphere, which Antonio sent and… Leah uploaded an unusual picture called 'the human aura'. I'm not sure what it's about, although…"

"Well, if the magnetosphere is the planet's aura, then this picture is the human's aura," I cut in, to explain. "Both are made of energy. Ours is all electricity and magnetism too. It's part of the home we live in. You couldn't move or breathe or feel without it," I said, expecting someone to throw the word 'weird' at me again.

I checked Kayleigh, Helena and Rhys's faces. No pushback. They looked cool.

"I want to know more, Leah," said Natsuki with curiosity.

"I don't know much more, but there's a lot out there on the aura," I replied.

"Mmm. Okay. I guess we could include it," said Femi, brushing her fingers lightly across her newly braided bun. She continued at speed. "Right. Then there are two images of all that horrific 'space junk' and a voiceover from Kayleigh, followed by photos of micro-plastics in nature.

"Next, I'll insert those stunning photos of the Northern Lights, which Helena's parents emailed.

"I've still got to pinpoint exactly where to put that clip of deforestation taken from a drone. Tell me where you want it afterwards, Kayleigh. And I guess, right after that, comes your painting showing the greenhouse effect?"

"You got it," said Kayleigh.

"Good. I've also got that photo of Callum from the press and, mmm... let me see what's next. Yes. I've already put in Sarah's surfing video, but I still need to include Joe's closing music from the Trust Companions. Never heard of them, but their supercool song, 'An Opportunity', is a perfect way to end the film.

"Finally, I need to sequence some short recordings of Leah, Natsuki and Helena talking about home. They really bring the film to a climax.

"Okay, that's it so far. Let's get back to work!"

Darweshi, Joe and Antonio all crowded back around Femi to help with the final tweaks, and a few hours later she closed her laptop, stood up and declared, "That's it. We're done. I'm done. I think we have our film!"

"Fantastic! We've got to watch it now!" shouted Joe, and we all whooped and whistled in agreement.

Right at that moment, Tanguy walked in. His timing was spot on.

Femi excitedly described to him what had been happening, her face changing like the weather, hands sweeping out and then clasping together to emphasise different points – she was as expressive as an actor in those silent movies.

"Wow. Your message definitely comes across, and I can see the incredible spirit you've built," said Tanguy, beaming one of his ear-to-ear smiles.

"So good to hear that. I'll play the film then," said Femi, re-opening her laptop.

"Ahhh, well, hold on… I appreciate how keen you are to see the film right now, but can I suggest you watch it with fresh eyes tomorrow morning? Then you can do any final edits live," he reasoned.

How could we possibly wait until tomorrow? It was hard to accept, but we knew Tanguy was right. Anyway, half the team were already falling asleep. And we had packing to do. Summer camp was ending tomorrow at 8:30pm.

☆ ☆ ☆ ☆ ☆

We all left the gym together, joking about the disasters which might happen with our presentation.

"The video projector is going to burst into flames the first moment we mention global warming – pshhht!" yelped Femi, making fiery sounds and throwing her hands up in the air.

"At least that'll get their attention!" quipped Joe, with a wicked smile.

It felt so good to be part of a team who could laugh and argue together, and still get a great result without anyone giving up or feeling not respected.

As we approached the cabins, we heard a few loud voices rising above some hip-hop music blaring away.

"That's Josh and his bandmates throwing an end-of-camp party," said Helena.

"Mmm. Taka never mentioned anything to me about it," I wondered out loud.

"Well, it's not really allowed, so they kept it a secret. Anyway, they only decided to do it at the last minute," said Helena, as she started heading in the direction of the music.

"Let's go!" cried Natsuki, nudging me in the ribs.

"I'm not sure. If it's not allowed… I don't want us to get into any trouble. And we need to pack and get up early," I said, sounding sensible. Except that as soon as I'd finished my sentence, I knew I wanted to go – especially as it might be my last chance to see Sean.

In the end, only Antonio, Natsuki and I joined Helena heading for Josh's cabin. All the band were there, some of the dancers I'd seen around and a few people I'd never met. Sean wasn't there, though, and my heart sank. Would I see him again?

As I went behind the cabin, I was surprised to see Taka dancing with a guy I didn't recognise. What a mover! They looked really into it and each other, but as I approached, she ran up to me and we hugged. She introduced me to Jaali, who seemed really cool apart from his soppy lovesick grin. Taka told him to wait there, so we could go for a walk and speak in private. It felt good to be the priority over Taka's potential new boyfriend.

"Can't believe you haven't told me about him!"

"Sorry Leah, with so much happening, it's never been the right moment… and you've been full-on with your team. Anyway, we only held hands yesterday… I've got so much to tell you when we get back. You know, he's in the dance crew!"

"And is he… I mean, is it…?"

"… ahhh… who knows?"

"I can't wait to hear more!"

Taka's smile reached her ears – she had heaps more to tell. "Anyway, I'm so happy we came to camp... although, you know, because I arrived late, I was afraid that people would've already made friends and no one would accept me.

"My fears kicked off the first morning, watching Anja – Miss Cutest of all time in a crop top – and her male groupie gang, hanging on to her every word," she grinned, imitating Anja stroking and swishing her hair and strutting around the main hall like a catwalk model.

"But then I checked out her followers and thought, 'You can keep them!'"

"Wow, Taka. I'd no idea you'd been feeling insecure early on... I thought it was just me!" We laughed louder than the hip-hop music. It felt good to be so honest with each other.

"Well, it was a bit difficult at first, because you'd already made friends with Natsuki. But the three of us have had so much fun, and now I'm the drummer in a band and going on long hikes with Jaali!"

We both agreed that meeting new people from around the world had built more confidence in us. We'd dared to say and do things we'd never dreamed of before. We'd also learnt a lot about ourselves, about other cultures and, of course, about boys... although we still had a few details to sort out on that topic!

When we returned, Jaali was dutifully waiting for Taka on the cabin steps. He seemed smitten.

As Natsuki and I headed back to our cabin, we had a chat about how to stay in touch.

"I'll be begging my parents, and saving up as much as I can, to fly out and visit you in Kyoto next summer."

"Yes. I want to show you special places."

It was always different speaking with Natsuki away from

the bubble of the team or the cabin we shared. We were freer. Although we were from totally different cultures, we shared the same interests and questions. We'd also gone through some challenging times together at camp and supported each other every time. There was a real connection.

I was planning to write to her about my big question after camp. Now that we were about to leave, I was getting more desperate to find an answer.

But I was starting to believe that the answer lay inside an even bigger question, which had inspired this whole film for me.

'What is home?'

SOMETHING'S MISSING

Something's Missing

At breakfast the next day, the whole hall became like an open-air marketplace. Each project team was huddled together, frantically discussing last-minute changes.

Presentation Day was due to start at 2pm – only five hours away and our team were puffing and panting to finish the last lap. We hadn't even seen the whole film yet or done the final editing. Fortunately, we were not alone.

Taka's band needed to do a final rehearsal, and Aiden's science team still hadn't agreed which experiments they were going to show. He told me that it wasn't only their experiments that were explosive, it was also an 'illogical argument' they'd had yesterday. "It's okay," he reassured me. "I wasn't involved. I just swept up the glass beakers that got smashed on the floor."

Having asked Tanguy to join us for our final session, we dashed over to the gym. Femi and Antonio had already set up the projector and screen, ready to go. Everyone went quiet as the film began to play.

When it ended, no one could speak.

We looked around at each other, and almost as one, we leapt up and down, cheering again. But after it all quietened down, I was left with an uneasy mixture of feelings… inspired, hopeful, and a bit hollow. I couldn't explain it.

Kayleigh, Helena and Natsuki all caught me frowning. "Argh. No. What's the matter this time, Leah? It's a beautiful film. And it carries such a meaningful message," pleaded Helena, her brows furrowing scarily.

"Yes, it's stunning, all of it, especially the message. But there's something missing," I insisted, holding onto my instincts. A few tired groans came my way.

Tanguy sat down next to me. "What's up, Leah? What's missing?"

"I'm not sure…"

For a few seconds, everything blurred into slow motion, and a blanket of silence covered the room. I sensed the presence would arrive, and seconds later, it did. The whole atmosphere turned electric blue.

I could just about make out the shape of the presence for the first time. It was like a little hill, rising floor to ceiling and filled with a wispy white. Wherever it had appeared from, I felt certain now that it brought healing and protection. No one else noticed, and I really didn't care anymore.

My whole body relaxed as I stood up, feeling a sudden flow of energy… like something was trying to speak through me again.

"We're made of stardust, and we're spinning through space at thousands of miles per hour. We can't be alone out here. Our film says that the universe is our greater home, and I think it's a peaceful place."

I watched Kayleigh roll her eyes as if to say, 'Here she goes again.' But this time, it didn't bother me one bit.

"So, I wonder... how to reduce the conflict going on between people and in people? To make peace and let the stardust shine. It might sound like I'm dreaming, but what I'm trying to say is that... well, I think that the greatest success in this project is that we've become a team.

"Through all our fights and difficulties, we've learnt to respect and trust each other more. If that happened across the world, then...

"So, I think this team is an amazing example of how the climate can change between people. That's what's missing. That it is possible. We've got to say that in our film."

That was it. I'd spoken freely now, and I had no idea if everyone was thinking I'd gone crazy. But no one had their heads in their computers and Antonio and Natsuki actually clapped.

Before I could sit down, I was surprised to see Kayleigh now smiling at me. For a split second, I didn't know whether that smile was genuine or mocking. I shouldn't have been so suspicious.

"You know, I couldn't stand you when we first met. You were so annoying, and I thought that your idea of 'home' was stupid and childish... and it hurt too, because of my experience in homes. Plus, you were so stubborn. But I think I get you now, Leah. You're a bit of a dreamer, like me.

"We don't have time to add anything new into the film, so why don't you do a live introduction to the audience and tell them what you've just told us?"

I stood there, so moved.

"Thank you for saying that, Kayleigh. I'd love to introduce the film. But you'd be much better than me at doing it. I've never, ever spoken in front of such a huge audience, and also... well, I believe that you'd be the best person to represent the team."

"Mmm..." mused Tanguy. "We haven't discussed who was going to introduce the film, but we need to. And I think you should both do it. That would be so cool, so authentic. What do you think, team?"

The response was a mixture of thumbs up, nods and shouted yeses.

"I'd love to do it with you," I offered.

Kayleigh hesitated. She had her elbows on the table, with both hands propping up her head and framing her expressionless face. She then narrowed her eyes and combed her black fingernails through her spiky hair. "Okay. But no one's going to tell me what to say."

"That's great to hear," smiled Femi, as she walked over and gave her a friendly hug. I'd never seen Kayleigh let anyone hug her. She closed her eyes and held on tightly.

"You'll both be excellent," beamed Tanguy. "Now, we're fast running out of time and before you all go and set up, can you decide what to call your film?"

"Well... it's simple, isn't it? I think we should call our film 'Home'," said Kayleigh, as she moved towards the door. I nearly ran over and hugged her myself, as everyone let out a noisy 'Yeahhh!'. We'd nailed it.

As we stepped outside for a break, I was feeling proud for standing up for what I believed in.

☆ ☆ ☆ ☆ ☆

The last two hours were ticking away as we did the final tweaking and hurriedly set up the projector and screen in the main hall. We'd become a beehive, and with Femi as queen bee, each of us worker bees knew exactly what waggle dance to do.

By 1:30pm each of the groups had gathered near the stage, presentations at the ready, while parents, families and friends were already streaming through the doors. I couldn't believe how many had come: over 150, including my mum and dad, who waved at Aiden and me as soon as they spotted us sitting with our teams.

Tanguy had told us earlier that two sets of parents had driven over in one car all the way from Frankfurt in Germany, and other family members had flown in from around the globe, including Darweshi's parents from Kenya, Antonio's older sister from Spain and Femi's mum from Egypt.

I felt very sorry for Natsuki though, as she had no family there... and as far as I knew, Kayleigh had no one coming either.

When all the guests were sitting down and a natural hush spread throughout the hall, Emilia and Kamlesh gave a warm welcome. They said that they didn't want to make a big speech and, unlike most adults, they actually didn't!

"Let every presentation speak for itself," began Emilia. "This year, we've been truly impressed by the high level of creativity and teamwork. And many new friendships have begun, which is really special – hopefully, they'll last well beyond camp.

"Each team member has brought their own unique character and talents to the presentations you're about to see. We know you're going to really enjoy them!" That sounded a bit cheesy, but everyone applauded.

As soon as it went quiet again, the first project group walked confidently up on stage. It was the band, and as they all strapped on their guitars and fussed around tuning up, Taka sat down firmly on her stool and gave her drum kit a full-blooded, high-speed warm-up. Wow! And although the lead singer, Josh, had great stage presence with an almost convincing rockstar pose, I think all eyes were on Taka.

Their opening song was a brilliant rock version of 'Where is the love?', followed by a rock/reggae fusion kind of song they'd composed, called, 'Edge of the Beat' – they even mixed in some cool drum and bass beatboxing! It was so catchy, and everyone spontaneously joined in the chorus: "We're goin' past the edge, edge, edge of the beat." Taka's drumming drove the song. She was in her element.

After the band left, to much applause, the dance crew stepped gracefully onto the stage in a neat line. As the music began, they criss-crossed in complex formations of waves, triangles and circles to the song 'My future'. Jaali was good, but I reckon Sean should've been the lead dancer. He was so in sync with the music… but then I wasn't paying much attention to the others.

The theatre group were next up with a funny play about fashion, followed by the team who'd invented a clever travel app, and then the website project. Everyone was loving the presentations and performances. I think they were surprised by the high level of talent.

Then the pottery group displayed these colourful, glossy mugs and original cereal bowls they'd crafted. They had painted pictures of gemstones and glitter on the outside… lovely sparkling diamonds, rubies and emeralds.

It began to dawn on me that while our team had been so engrossed in making our film and sorting out conflicts, all the other teams had been preparing these incredible presentations. They were captivating, although I must admit that a serious competitive streak flared up in me… ours had to be the best! But Maia would have had something to say about that – she was all about 'doing your best', not trying to prove you're the best.

The science group then marched on stage like an army unit on parade. Aiden looked serious as he stood calmly alongside the team – most of them were taller than him, but probably not braver! They gathered in a semi-circle behind a long table full of all sorts of neatly arranged scientific apparatus. One of the older girls stepped forward.

"Hello, everyone. My name's Yvonne. We have put together an experiment to explain how sea levels on our planet are rising."

She placed a glass bottle full of blue-coloured water on the table right in front of the audience. "Now, look please at the top of this bottle," one of the boys in the team then announced. "Do you see this straw poking up ten centimetres from the top? Look!" he said, pointing to the straw. "Now we're going to position a heat lamp right by the bottle, and you'll see the water quickly warm up inside and start to rise up to the top of the straw." Soon, it was spilling over and forming a blue puddle on the table.

They explained that this showed how global warming and ice caps melting is causing the sea to expand and sea levels to rise.

Yvonne continued, "In this last experiment, you may wonder why we are using a couple of bottles and thermometers, a balloon, vinegar, sodium bicarbonate and a heat source," she said, pointing to each item. "Well, we're going to demonstrate how the air in this bottle, which is rich in CO_2, heats up much more than this other bottle with just air in it. The CO_2 is trapping the heat."

All our team had their mouths gaping open, as this was basically showing the greenhouse effect which was going to feature in our film! I was pleased that they presented the science, yet so sad again to see how we're harming the planet. This was uncomfortable to watch, but when it came to the end, the clapping rang out.

Our film was going to follow the science project perfectly.

While our eyes were darting nervously from person to person, before we knew it, Kamlesh had introduced us on stage. We stood together in a line, with Femi near the back of the hall ready to click the 'play' button.

Kayleigh and I stepped forward to make the introduction. I was meant to begin, but the sight of such a huge audience was daunting. I took a step back as my focus shifted anxiously to the growing rumble of whispered comments and fidgeting in the audience. So many faces, all looking at us, at me, expecting.

In a split second, I felt a surge of confidence that propelled me forward to take three steps almost to the edge of the stage. I had this immediate sensation of standing on a shore, on my own, gazing far out to sea. I glimpsed the line of people in the back row and I knew that my message had to reach them.

"My name is Leah, and this project means the world to us.

"We've fought about it, shouted about it, got hurt, stormed out, come back in, got inspired together, angry together, laughed and cried a lot.

"And we found something that we didn't even realise we were searching for. We found respect."

The audience went quiet. I kept my gaze firmly on them.

"We then began listening to each other and appreciating each other's talents more. Yet, we only realised in our session this morning that becoming a team was the greatest success in this project."

A scattered round of spontaneous applause broke out, which surprised me. I could feel Kayleigh ready to burst, so I stepped back.

"Yeah, it's true," she said. "Hi, I'm Kayleigh. Up until now, I've only ever been able to trust one person. But as we got to make this film together, I realised in the end that other people in the team shared my passion, only in a different way to me. And although at the start I thought some of their ideas were rubbish, I began to see that each person had a powerful voice that needed to be heard. I started to trust."

The volume of applause went up a notch. I could understand it. Kayleigh was so herself.

"You know, I'm so passionate about sorting the climate crisis you wouldn't believe it. A foster mother told me about it when I was only ten years old and I was devastated. I couldn't handle it.

I didn't think that my generation had any hope at all. But this week, everything changed."

Kayleigh paused and passed the baton back to me as if we'd been practising.

"Yes. We changed the climate in ourselves and between us all. And suspicion changed into a climate of trust. Then we understood that changing the climate begins at home, here, in us, if we are ever going to heal our planet and rescue the future."

The audience applauded again, only much louder, a few even standing up.

"So, we called our film 'Home'," I announced with immense pride. I didn't explain further, because I hoped people would work it out for themselves after having seen the film.

There was now a growing sense of anticipation in the hall. The only sound I could hear was my own heartbeat thrumming into my ears. The lights went off. This was our moment.

▷

HOME TRUTHS

Home Truths

A starry night fills the screen as the mandolin and flute music of 'Innisfallen' plays softly.

The image of thousands of galaxies appears, while the soothing tone of Darweshi's voiceover comes in: "You can relax. You are here. At home in the universe."

Our blue planet gradually emerges from space, followed by an overlay of its protective magnetic fields, as arcs of silver.

Alongside, a picture of a human, surrounded by its energy field, in subtle lights. "This is the greatest technology on earth," I say.

Both pictures fade to grey. The screen goes black, the music stops. Suddenly, in quick succession, images of space junk surrounding our fragile earth appear.

"Oh my God," says Kayleigh. "We've made our oceans, land and skies into a rubbish tip. It's incredibly sad. Why do we ignore things just because they seem far away? They're not. They're close to home."

Focusing towards Planet Earth, the shimmering greens, pinks

and violets of the Northern Lights become visible, sweeping across the night sky like magical curtains.

In a nanosecond, we see a close-up of the red glove of a scientist holding a glass tube filled with snow. Kayleigh continues. "You're looking at snow from the Arctic. It contains thousands of microplastics. How did they get there? Is this the future for our generation?"

Scenes change, in shocking contrasts: from nature's wonders to the pollution of those wonders. Extraordinary beauty and ugliness side by side.

"We have a choice," says Helena.

Then, from a drone's great height, scanning vast areas of deforestation in the Congo Basin, Sumatra, Borneo, the Amazon... countless trees falling like dominoes, scarred land, huge mines, toxic streams and rivers. "The price of overconsumption," says Joe.

Faces of indigenous people appear. One of the elders speaks out. "They come like a disease, to scorch the land, even in the light of day. They do not understand respect, only death. The world watches as they steal our future; they do not understand that they steal their own future too."

"It's hard to take in the massive scale of destruction, both to humanity and the planet," says Kayleigh, her voice loaded with hurt.

The 'greenhouse effect' picture fades in, with graphs showing dramatic rises in global warming and sea levels linked to industrialisation.

"Ecosystems are not designed to absorb all our pollution. Roughly half of our carbon emissions go straight up into the atmosphere, trap the sun's heat and warm the planet. What are we doing to her lungs, and our own?"

The scene changes. A forest, insects busily crawling up and

around trees, the hedgehog happily foraging, the white barn owl soaring, majestic, into the night sky.

"The forest is their home," says Rhys. "We wouldn't let anyone destroy our home, would we? So why do we destroy theirs? Their home is part of our home. Planet Earth. Without it, we have nowhere to live."

Quiet acoustic guitar music follows as Kayleigh's face emerges in the foreground. "What's happening to our planet is because of the way we live our daily lives."

She pauses. "We've seen the sea turtles choking on plastic bits and fish netting. It breaks my heart. We also can't ignore air pollution just because we might not see it. My best friend, Callum, was…" She wipes her first tears away as she recalls how and why he died.

As she draws to a close, a photo of Callum, celebrating scoring a goal, comes on screen. Then the newspaper quote: 'High levels of air pollution – along a main road in his hometown of Lewisham – were most likely responsible for his asthma, resulting in his death'.

"I don't understand the apathy," says Kayleigh, fiercely.

My face appears onscreen as I follow on, "Everything that we do to ourselves and each other, we do to the planet. How much we harm ourselves and each other is how much we harm our own planet.

"We carry on like it's all normal. It never has been. The solution can't start out there. It's got to start in here. In us. What kind of people do we want to be? What kind of planet are we going to leave for the next generations… for my generation? Don't we all share this home?"

Then the sound and sight of Sarah surfing a wave as it rolls down onto the shore. Antonio narrates. "Some people feel at home surfing, or out in the wilds, or when they're among friends.

And some people feel at home in themselves, comfortable with who they are."

I continue, "There are also people who are in awe of the planet and the infinite universe, which for them is home. So, what is home for you? Is it wherever you feel safe and cared for? Is it wherever you feel like you belong?"

A few seconds of silence follow. Then Kayleigh adds, "No living thing can stay in a home where the climate makes it impossible for them to live there."

A black-and-white photograph of Tanguy's fishing village in the 1960s comes up, followed by photos of Lake Chad, shrunk by overuse and climate change effects.

"All over the world, sources of freshwater are drying up or are too polluted to drink. If water is life, how can we go on living like this?" I add. "The solutions are always closer to home than we imagine. So, I ask myself, what am I a home for? If respect, trust and co-operation lived in me, could that help bring change?"

A soundtrack of wind chimes and waves plays as our vast and beautiful Milky Way galaxy lights up the screen. Zooming slowly out, other neighbouring galaxies appear.

Then the scene of Natsuki, barefoot in the forest, eyes closed, doing the meditation. She breathes in rhythm with the movements, arms reaching up, then arcing down, as a folk song plays – a musical dialogue between a person and the planet, with a duet, harmonising the words, 'An Opportunity'.

"This is our opportunity now. And this is the music of our message," says Darweshi. "So, welcome home."

As our film faded from the screen, there was a moment of complete stillness in the hall.

What followed next was extraordinary. On waves of emotion, the whole audience rose to their feet in applause. This was no longer just a Presentation Day. It felt like, well, a demonstration, or a huge celebration of… I don't know… a celebration of hope? The clapping went on and on. I remember we were happily embarrassed to be standing there for around two minutes, as the congratulations continued to roll in.

When everyone was seated again, there was one woman still standing up near the front row, clapping and straining to stop herself from crying. For some reason, she was looking straight at Kayleigh. Astonished, Kayleigh jumped off the stage and ran straight over to the woman, squeezing carefully between knees and the backs of people and chairs. They hugged in front of everyone. It was like every ounce of hope in the hall came together in that moment.

We found out later that this was Sheila, the foster mother for both Kayleigh and Callum. She was so thrilled to see Kayleigh again, but overwhelmed when she saw the story of Callum's death in our film. Sheila was also the one who'd first told Kayleigh about the climate crisis.

"She was the only foster parent who I think really loved me," Kayleigh told us. "But I somehow blamed her for Callum's death, and after a blazing row I ended up back in care. I've never forgotten her, though." And clearly, Sheila had never forgotten Kayleigh.

☆ ☆ ☆ ☆ ☆

We came off stage flying high, inspired out of our skins and totally exhausted.

Emilia and Kamlesh then announced that the youth leaders and staff at camp would go backstage and vote for their favourite presentation.

It seemed to take them ages to decide, but when they came back into the main hall, I could hardly breathe…

"Every presentation today was of such high quality," Emilia declared. "And watching the teamwork among the dancers, the band, the scientists... everyone, has been so uplifting. It was almost impossible to decide a winner.

"You are all winners. I mean that," she said, turning to the teams.

"We believe, however, that one presentation stood out because it had a passion and a message that will resonate far beyond this summer camp.

"So, this year, we are giving the Bridgewell Camp Award and prize to... the filmmaking team."

Instantly, we bounced around like a bunch of happy kangaroos. Everyone in the hall was clapping and cheering, and it was an amazing sensation to watch all the other teams standing up and celebrating our win. That was special.

I was lit up head to toe like those coloured lights on Christmas trees. It was like the rays of a thousand stars were shining through everyone. Stardust.

Taka darted over and hugged me and Natsuki together. I saw Mum and Dad at the back of the hall bobbing up and down and waving, as was Aiden, whose team were near ours.

Somehow, though, it didn't feel right that the other brilliant group presentations hadn't received any award or prize. I mean, Emilia said that we were all winners.

"Hey, team," I yelled above the noise. "What do you think about sharing our prize with the other project teams? You know... how can you compare pottery or science to dance, music or our film? It's not fair. Each one is special in different ways."

"Sounds cool," Helena and Kayleigh chimed in. Everyone agreed, and because our prize was a whole wad of book tokens, we were able to share at least one with each team. Everyone in our team got two, though! First thing back in London, I'd be heading for my favourite bookshop in Barnet, to find a science book on energy and a new journal with dragonflies on the cover.

☆ ☆ ☆ ☆ ☆

With Presentation Day now over, the main hall was heaving with parents and the entire camp, in a clamour to meet and say hellos and goodbyes. Although dinner was scheduled in less than an hour, several families had to leave early to get on the road or catch flights.

Aiden and I had missed Mum and Dad, but I felt a bit distant. I wasn't sure how much of my experience I could share. Some of it felt very private.

I'd told my parents a lot about Natsuki whenever we'd been in touch, and when I introduced her, my mum kissed her on both cheeks and squeezed her shoulders. "It's great to finally meet you, Natsuki – I've heard many good things. And I'm delighted that you and Leah have become close friends. Please stay with us when you come to England again."

"Thank you, Mrs Greene. You have a home in Kyoto too," she replied, looking radiant.

We had a very animated talk, summarising three weeks of dramatic adventures into a few minutes. My parents were especially keen to hear about how we'd got on in our project teams. We each had something a bit crazy to share, and Aiden told us a hilarious story about an experiment that turned his white T-shirt red and brown. His description of each person in the science team, and what he thought of them, was even funnier.

I told Mum and Dad that our team was going to have a little farewell party in the gym before dinner, and Natsuki and I shot off. As we were exiting the hall, I turned around and saw that my parents had already found Taka and her mum.

Back in the gym, there was a lot of noisy chatter and laughing. Sarah, who'd come with Tanguy, told us how passionately she believed in what our film was trying to say. "It's truly impressive. And now I understand why you wanted that video clip of me surfing! I'd be very happy to help you promote the film after camp."

Tanguy said he'd help too, and then asked for everyone's attention.

"I'm so grateful to have met each one of you. Working with your team, and mentoring you through the challenges, has been one of the most humbling and inspiring moments of my life.

"We've all been on a great adventure, a real mission. You've become a true team – stronger, wiser and more respectful. And who knows what else you might achieve together in the future… for the future."

Kayleigh walked towards Tanguy and shook his hand. She had this soft and serious look in her eyes as she turned to face the team.

"This week has changed me.

"You know, most of camp has been so rough for me. I hated it from day one. But then this film project came along, and I met you lot. Making this film has been like someone flinging open the gates of a cage I was in… I couldn't see beyond it. But maybe the cage was always open, and I was just too scared to move on.

"And, well… I've really had enough of care homes, gangs and not having anyone to trust. That old life is not me now. Cheap thrills and fighting everyone wear you out in the end. I'm not that girl anymore.

"So, now… well, now I know who I am."

We all clapped. It touched my heart to see how she'd transformed. You can choose who you want to be, I remembered.

"You're a total inspiration to us all, Kayleigh. Thank you," said Tanguy, his voice wavering with emotion. "And now, before Sarah and I have to dash, I've brought a little something to show you my appreciation."

He presented us with this big chocolate and almond cake that he'd baked with Sarah's help. The two of them had obviously become much more than friends – everyone could see that. I mean, holding hands and staring lovingly into each other's eyes... come on!

In a flash, they were gone to help organise dinner in the hall, and we scoffed that cake down like we hadn't eaten all day.

Then came a flurry of goodbyes. It was a bit like a programme I saw on speed dating – just enough time to say a paragraph or two about how much we'd enjoyed being together and to swap contact details. We swore we'd stay in touch, agreeing to meet online later in the year.

Natsuki had to leave before dinner to get a taxi to the airport, and saying goodbye to her was tough. We didn't say much and didn't need to – we knew that our friendship would last.

Saying goodbye to Kayleigh was even tougher somehow. It felt like we were still in two different worlds, but those worlds were connected now in a way that neither of us understood. Our differences had probably made us both stronger. I was going to miss her for sure.

"Okay, dinner's beginning now," Femi reminded us, and within a minute, the gym was empty.

Back in the hall, everyone was scrambling around to find some empty chairs to sit with their families. My dad had reserved me a seat next to him and was interested to hear all about the youth leaders. He was captivated when I told him a bit about Tanguy's story and what a brilliant mediator he'd been. Suddenly, I had a lot to tell him.

I looked around a few times to see if I could spot Sean somewhere, and even snaked through the crowd once to search. But with parents and the whole camp, the hall was packed out and swarming now with over 200 people. He was either in a corner somewhere or he was already on his way back to Ireland. This pang of regret quivered coldly through me. I probably should have asked him if... no. I was imagining things. It was so sad.

☆ ☆ ☆ ☆ ☆

Dinner passed by too quickly, and I didn't have time to find the other people who I wanted to say goodbye to, especially Kamlesh and Emilia.

As I was leaving to go back to my cabin and pick up my stuff, I spotted Tanguy chatting with some of the youth leaders near the stage. I boldly ran across and wrapped my arms around him. He held me briefly, his strength pouring into me again. "We will meet in the future, Leah. You are a very special soul." I glowed.

By the time I left the hall, I was in floods of tears and struggling to hide them with my head down as I jostled past crowds of people.

Approaching my cabin, I decided not to go straight in. I needed to breathe in some of the fresh countryside air one last time and clear my head.

I looked up and scanned the darkening, red-tinged evening sky. There was such a deep longing in me to be there again, among the stars. In a flash, the last three weeks and camp disappeared. It was just me, the stars and... a question. The question. Maybe the answer was waiting for me in the forest clearing in Trent Park. After this week, however, my stardust question had grown.

I'd discovered so many new things about 'home' and I knew that this was my biggest clue.

I needed to meet Maia. We had to talk.

☆ ☆ ☆ ☆ ☆

There was no one and not much left in the cabin, apart from a few backpacks still waiting to be collected. I was hoping that I might bump into the twins again, but we did wave at each other across the hall before dinner.

As I went across to gather my stuff, I noticed a neatly folded little note on the table. And it had my name on it! I didn't recognise the handwriting, which was in blue ink, probably from a fountain pen. I use a fountain pen sometimes, but I'd never seen anyone else my age using one.

I felt lightheaded and my heartbeat quickened. It couldn't be. No way! I hastily slipped the note into my inside backpack pocket and zipped it up tightly. I didn't dare read it now.

I walked to the car park where my parents and Aiden were waiting for me. My heart was still pounding away, so I made an excuse that I'd left some hairbands in my cabin and headed back. I just needed a couple of minutes to calm down, and that's all it took. We were on the road.

☆ ☆ ☆ ☆ ☆

Although we were all chattering away non-stop on the drive back through Surrey, by the time we got on the motorway, Aiden and I were yawning and dozing off. It had been a very long day.

Gazing out of the car window, a few hilarious moments and familiar faces from the last three weeks flashed into my mind… including Sean, of course. Memories of some of the conflicts also came up, but they weren't half as scary as they'd felt at the time. "They are an essential part of growing up," my mum told me several times over dinner, as I rolled my eyes.

We finally passed the familiar shops along the parade in Oakwood, and as we turned into our road, that uneasy mixture of sadness and optimism stirred inside me again. I wondered if my life would always be this way. But one thing I knew. This experience had changed me forever.

I would never be the same Leah as three weeks ago.

The Note

The day after we arrived back in London, my mum got the tragic news that Chloe, her best friend from Ireland, had died from a stroke. She was only 41. My mum was devastated. She loved Chloe like a sister.

They'd grown up together in the same village in Killarney where they used to romp around on wild adventures, camping near the lakes and hiking over the hills. They made up poems and songs about fantasy worlds, which they used to sing in folk clubs when they were only sixteen. Chloe and my mum missed each other so much when we moved to London, but they'd kept in touch regularly and met up almost every summer.

For three days, Mum could hardly eat, and Dad took care of everything. It was weeks before she began to come back to herself. Mum had several good friends in London, including Maia, but no one who was a friend like Chloe.

So, we hardly spoke together about camp. In the meantime, faces of different people and special times played through my mind every day: Natsuki, Sean, Taka, Tanguy, Sarah, Kayleigh, Helena, the twins… in the gym, the main hall, the cabins, in the forest, out on the river. The memories were so alive.

During the week before school term was due to start, I had a chat in the kitchen with Mum and asked her about Chloe dying. She spoke with such warmth and value for her, and then paused in contemplation. Staring at a framed watercolour picture on the wall which Chloe had painted when she was about my age, Mum said a curious thing which has stayed with me.

"Chloe will live on. Bright spirits never stop shining."

It made me reflect again on what happens after death. Was Chloe still alive somewhere? Would Mum meet her again? What is the spirit? Is it different from the soul? Are they both made of stardust? What part of me had soared up into the sky that evening in the park?

I wanted to go back there… to stand in that clearing in the middle of the wood where I'd had my stardust experience. I wanted to meet my friends in the skies again. I wanted to tell them I'd grown up a lot in three weeks and become more self-aware.

I went up to my bedroom and stared at my cluttered desk with mementoes from camp – each one a little gem, like the pretty card from Natsuki and a new fire-making kit. I considered reading the mystery note that was now slipped into the back of my journal, still unopened. It was so tempting and I still didn't understand why my brain kept repeating, 'Not yet, not yet'. Maybe I didn't want to be disappointed or hurt.

But as I began doodling in my journal, a new question sprung up:

'If I can change the climate inside me, and I am made of stardust, will that change the universe in some way?'

I read out my question, hardly believing what I'd just written. Could I change the universe?! It seemed crazy. But if we are a part of the universe, then why not?

I closed my journal, a bit scared to read the question again. But it left me thinking that if a big question is really important, then it might lead to an even bigger question.

The park was calling to me now, though. I'd planned to go soon with Taka, but I wanted to be there on my own first – I had to reconnect with something...

☆ ☆ ☆ ☆ ☆

Early afternoon the next day, as I stepped through the main entrance, the park felt empty. I felt empty too. I missed the intensity of camp, being in a team, having a purpose... it was all fading. Was my experience with the stars fading too?

A few words then lit up in my mind. Actually, they weren't my words. They were an echo from those last minutes in the gym, when Kayleigh had told us, "I know who I am." I didn't get a chance to ask her what she meant.

As I gazed up into the treetops, those five words lingered and echoed louder now – they seemed to slip through the twisted branches above me like mist.

Cold, gusty winds rushed through the wood. A voice flew in, like a ghost murmuring into my ear, "So who are you, Leah? Who are you?"

I looked down at the scattered leaves, then up into the sky. It was daylight and the stars were hidden. As I watched a group of greyish clouds gliding past, I felt myself taking off in slow motion. I was rising up into the skies again... or some essence deep inside me was – travelling through the blue, the clouds, the winds, reaching towards the stars.

I was back in my other home, I thought to myself. Back where I came from. Back where I came from?

An image of Mr Eaton appeared. Having quoted from Hamlet,

he was calling out to me again, like from one end of a long tunnel. "Find out where you've come from… where your real home is."

Was this my real home? Maybe humans are made of stardust so that they can travel the universe… and find home?

I was now completely weightless, flying high, my feet no longer on the ground. As I looked down, the trees had shrunk into little green dots and the houses into tiny boxes.

But then I spotted the top of my head, which freaked me out. Instantly, I felt myself fall through the skies like a meteorite, dropping heavily back into my body. It happened so fast. My legs went weak, my hands were shaking.

Travelling so high had felt smooth, natural, light. Coming back into my body felt clunky and pressured.

Why was this happening to me? I had to know. This was the second time now.

I'd read about time travellers and superheroes with mysterious powers. Maia once told me that I had superpowers. "It's your ability to see through things, and deep below the surface of people's feelings," she explained. "You see meanings behind words and messages behind faces."

Our art teacher, Mr Kowalski, once spoke to us about the 'crystal children'. I remember him saying, "They have rare supernatural arts. They can read minds, build bridges between the old and the new, and sometimes travel to other worlds." So, was I one of them? I didn't think so. Isn't everyone born with some kind of magical power?

A hazy image then flashed into my mind. In it, I was hovering above the ruins on the island of Innisfallen and looking down on this little girl running and then trying to climb a tree. I looked closer. It was me.

I wondered how I could be in two places at once… and was my mind somehow able to travel back in time, yet stay in the present?

That didn't feel like a superpower… just something I could do. Maybe next time I could try doing it deliberately, by picturing a place or moment in time and going there. And could I travel forward in time too? I'd seen that in a movie and was excited to explore it in real life. What else would I discover?

I drifted over towards a bench near the exit. I felt lost in myself and had to sit down for a minute. My hands were tingling with tiny electric sparks – they felt charged. The presence was here again, moving somewhere nearby. I recognised that peaceful, warm sensation. It was beautiful. I wasn't dreaming.

My phone beeped, and I snapped out of it. It was a text from Kayleigh sent to the whole filmmaking team. 'Let's get together ASAP… make 'Home' into a full-length documentary?'

I leapt with joy when I read that, because that was exactly the same idea that I'd had the night before. Was that clairvoyance again? Things were getting so curious…

I texted back, 'Yes! Brill idea. How about we call it something like… 'Coming Home'?'

☆ ☆ ☆ ☆ ☆

I met up with Taka in the Water Garden on Friday that week. It hadn't been long since we'd got back, but I'd been really missing her.

We sat on a bench, creasing up as we shared outrageous stories about camp. I'd no idea that she'd already had a crush on Jaali from the first week. I'd never really noticed him around until I saw her dancing with him.

"Yeah. We sort of bumped into each other near my cabin. He was on his way to the lake to join the open water swimming group, and I was getting ready for our white-water rafting trip. We had a funny conversation about wet suits and zips!

"Didn't you spot him in the dance crew when he did that incredible solo breakdance, remember? He was a blur of twisting arms and legs… you know, his long black, wavy hair was sweeping the stage!"

"Er… I was watching someone else…"

Taka didn't twig that I was talking about Sean. It was all Jaali. On she gushed…

"We met up a few times in project week… went on long walks, danced and swapped phone numbers on the last day. We almost kissed, but… I'm not sure though. He lives up in Manchester, he's six months younger than me, and he never said anything nice about my drumming. We'll see. He's coming with his family to London for New Year's Eve celebrations."

I was so pleased for Taka, but as I was gearing up to tell her more about Sean, she raced on to give me a day-by-day account of the crazy stuff which had gone on in the band – almost as dramatic as in our group.

"I guess blazing rows always happen in bands, but nothing compares to that awesome feeling of playing together, in rhythm, in harmony, one tight band. You enter a different world… like you're in a floating bubble of sound, or a spaceship heading deep into space."

"Wow. I so know that feeling. I'm a frequent flyer in space!" I teased, launching myself from the bench as if taking off. Taka laughed as I dropped onto the grass.

"You know, we had that same feeling in our team, eventually, right after Femi showed us the first rough cut of our film," I continued. "It also happened the night before you arrived, when a group of us were in the forest, making a campfire together and singing our hearts out. Each time, there was that sparkly glow… a warm feeling of being part of something much greater than myself."

265

"Yeah, that's it, Leah. You feel the strength of everyone. You feel like you belong."

This was now the moment. I moved in a bit closer and told her in much more detail about all the things Sean had said and all the emotions I'd been going through. Taka kept wanting to know more, but there wasn't much more, yet. Then I told her about the note that someone had left in the cabin.

"Well, what did it say?"

"I don't know, I still haven't opened it."

"What? You're totally mad! It's from him. I'm telling you. He's crazy in love and wants to run away with you next summer to some secret place in Ireland. You idiot! Why haven't you opened that note?!" It was impossible to keep a straight face.

"I know it's weird, Taka, but as I was about to open it last night, I began worrying that it might be a nasty or creepy note from someone else, you know... remember those hate notes that girl used to send me last year?"

"Well, even if it is a hate note, who cares. Rip it up or burn it."

"Yes, but… okay, I'll open it tonight and text you."

"You better, Leah. Straight away. If it's a nasty note, I'm coming for them! But I'm telling you, it's from him. I know these things."

We left the park and walked back to our usual meet-up place near a roundabout. Before we parted, we hugged each other as she gently tugged my braided ponytail and I messed up her curly hair. It was our secret, playful way of saying that we'd always be there for each other.

☆ ☆ ☆ ☆ ☆

Later that night, when I was ready for bed, I sat by my desk and flicked through my journal. The note was still there, of course, almost begging to be opened. I followed the wavy lines and style of the handwriting very carefully, and wondered why they didn't write 'To Leah', rather than just 'Leah'. That wasn't a good sign. But the handwriting was really neat.

There was an elegant curl on the corner of the 'L'. Would a boy write in that style? If the note was from a girl, then probably… yes, it was from someone in the dance team who was jealous that I'd seen Sean four times. It must be. Maybe she hated me and wanted to tell me to back off. 'I can handle that', I thought, feeling my jaws tighten.

I hurriedly opened the note and stood up sharply. Oh My God. No. Yes. I stared at each one of the nineteen words, one question mark and a P.S., and analysed them like a police detective. There was also a phone number, but that could wait. The note said:

Do you want to be in contact?
  I love your voice
    Sean

P.S. Sorry, I should've asked for your number.

I read it about a dozen times and then put it down. I didn't know how to react. The writing was as neat as on the cover: it was well spaced, good punctuation and… totally amazing!

But I didn't like his 'I love your voice' bit. Was that it? Did he just want to get together to sing?

His handwriting, however, told a different story. The letters were thick, rounded, and flowed with a nice slant to the right. Plus, each of the eleven 'o's' was an almost perfect circle. It felt warm and showed a lot of care. And he'd apologised for not asking for my phone number. Totally right! Singing or no singing, he wanted to see me again.

I hardly slept all night, with questions rattling around in my head. What's he going to say when he finds out I don't have a smartphone? And when I tell him about my experience with the stars and my big question, he's going to think I'm half mad. And what am I going to write back? 'Oh, I'm really happy you love my voice. I love yours too. Goodbye'…?

Early next morning, I called Taka and woke her up. She screamed with delight when I told her about the note. I read it to her slowly three times, after which she cried out, "I told you, I told you! We need to talk boyfriends, Leah, ASAP."

"He's not my boyfriend!"

"You're insane. Did you read that note? Really? He's given you his phone number, yeah? Wake up, Leah! We need to meet up like now… er… but not now! Me and my mum are going away for the weekend before school starts. But first day back, I need to go through options with you."

"Options? What options?"

"Your options. I've already thought of three different ways of replying to that note."

"So, should I wait until we speak before contacting him?"

"Er… I'm not sure. Let's think about it and be in touch. I've got to get dressed and rush out now. Sorry, Leah."

When I came off the phone, I'd already decided to wait. No point in chasing, was there? You're not meant to do that anyway, are you?

☆ ☆ ☆ ☆ ☆

There were only two days left before school was starting, and I had a lot to prepare. But first, I wanted to reply to Natsuki, who'd already sent me a wonderful letter. It contained three paragraphs written in Japanese, with English translation underneath. I was so caught by the intricate characters, each one like a symbol or picture with a different story behind it.

'My experience at camp has made me more confident and daring,' she wrote, 'and my English is the best in class! Leah, you are my good friend and I miss you.'

Her friendship meant so much to me. I wished she was living next door.

Her letter was neatly folded around three photographs of the most awesome gardens I'd ever seen – with vibrant colours and exotic-shaped small trees and shrubs. She'd taken the photos at a Zen temple, Ginkaku-ji, near where her family lives in Kyoto. The picture which really lit me up was of a garden with meticulously raked and sculpted sand. I imagined myself doing Tanguy's meditation there… it looked so peaceful.

In my letter back to her, I started writing in detail about my stardust experience and my big question. But it sounded a bit like science fiction and I was worried that, like Taka, she'd think that it had been a dream. Maybe in my next letter. Anyway, I scrapped that and decided to tell her all about Sean's note, including the fact that I now had his phone number – she was going to love that!

I also wrote that I'd asked my parents if we could fly out to Japan to see her next year. Whether it was going to be in London or Kyoto, we were definitely going to meet again somewhere next summer… maybe back at camp?

In the meantime, the thought of going back to school the next day was like entering a dark tunnel with no light at the end.

WHO AM I?

Who Am I?

Monday morning, grey and drizzly, back at school. The long haul of studying for my GCSEs was beginning. The pressure was a shock.

In the first few days, I felt invisible and wasn't sure if I had anything in common with either the teachers or students anymore. All the talk in my class was of the mock exams at the end of the year and who fancied who. I didn't mind that, but who could I share all my adventures and burning questions with?

I did have Taka, and we were even closer now. And then there was Natsuki and my contact with the team at camp via texts. But I was starting to feel like I was slipping back into that old, depressing mood of being on my own. School was draining, and one of the teachers was already pressuring us into choosing what career path we wanted to take. To me, it was way too early to decide the rest of my life.

I was relieved when a lovely surprise arrived mid-week. It was a postcard from Maia, who was with her husband on safari in

Tanzania, studying giraffes… as you do! She mentioned that they'd be arriving in London on Saturday for a few days before leaving again to visit their son in Spain.

Maia texted me a short 'hello' as soon as they landed, saying that she hoped we'd be able to see each other soon. For me, this was urgent. We swapped texts, and she suggested driving over to meet me at the café in the park the very next day. She loved it there because they served her favourite tea – organic jasmine green. I couldn't wait to see her again.

As I walked towards the café that late Sunday afternoon, Maia ran towards me and tried to lift me up like she used to when I was younger. I was a lot taller now, so we ended up doing a little dance instead.

She was wearing a long, floaty dress with big, brightly coloured pictures of jungle animals and trees – that was so Maia!

"Here's your birthday present. Sorry it's late. It's from Mum, Dad, Aiden and me." The wrapping paper, which almost matched her dress, had big lions on it – well, she is a Leo.

"It's beautiful. I love the fine design. How original," Maia exclaimed, after carefully unwrapping a small box to reveal a silver-plated bracelet with little gold hawthorn buds.

"It was handmade by Mum's friend Alice, who's a jeweller. All her designs are inspired by flowers and shapes from nature, and the silver and gold are ethically sourced."

"What a gift! I will treasure it."

Once we'd sat down in the café with our favourite drinks, Maia mentioned that she only had an hour and a half. So I talked non-stop about the amazing events at camp and the people from many different countries who I'd met – everyone except Sean. That was for when we had more time… and after I'd discovered what his note was all about.

Maia just kept saying, "Tell me more," and I kept falling over my words because I was talking too fast. I could feel my brain booting up like a computer and busily scrolling down all the information on the spot.

Then I got to Presentation Day. As I connected to scenes from our film, I found myself welling up with tears and excitedly gasping for air. This was something I really believed in.

"The thing is, Maia, we made a whole new discovery about climate... you know, people talk a lot about climate change. They always refer to the climate on the planet, assuming that's everything. But in our film, we say that it's directly connected to the climate in people."

An explosive thought then dropped in.

"It's like sometimes people get angry, stressed and heated up inside, which is sort of, I don't know... 'human warming'? It affects how they make decisions. So, does that add to global warming too? I mean, leaders talking a lot of hot air isn't cool, is it?!"

We both chuckled away. "Your sense of humour has rocketed, Leah! Plus, you're really onto something big here. Press on!"

"Well, imagine if I asked you, 'What's the weather like in you today?' Is it stormy or calm, or is it... oh, I don't know... high pressure or low pressure?" This was all spilling out of me with images in my mind of the theatrical, arm-waving weather presenter on TV.

"I suppose that as you grow up, with all these changes in weather going on inside you, year after year, you get to know your own climate and how it changes. I mean, maybe you're basically a cool, chilled person. Or maybe people think that you're a very warm person, or even hot...

"The thing is, we found out that the climate *in* you changes the climate *around* you."

Maia looked riveted. "What you're describing carries such an intelligent and hopeful message. I can't wait to see how you managed to get this across on film."

I then began telling her about my new experience in the park, but after another few speedy minutes, I came to a complete stop and took a deep breath. Maia was watching me closely.

"So, what else? There's something you're not telling me."

Her instinct was right. I hesitated. Words escaped me for a few moments, until I found my voice.

"I believe that I have more than one home, Maia. I believe that I also have a home in the stars and out in the universe... because when I travel there... I mean, when my mind or my spirit or some part of me travels there, I feel really at home. And now I know that what the stars are made of is in me. So, I guess I'm beginning to feel at home in me too.

"And I... does this make any sense to you, Maia?"

She didn't answer. Maybe she thought I was out of my mind... although that was probably a good place to be! She raised her eyebrows slightly and shifted her chair forward.

"You know, I've never thought of home in this way, Leah. I've never imagined that I could feel at home in the universe, knowing that I'm made of stardust. That is so amazing. I love it.

"Most of my life, I've felt at home in myself and on this planet. Well, now I'm thinking that if we have many homes, perhaps that says that humans really are meant to be universal travellers."

Maia's eyes shone. I was startled. Was I actually teaching her something that she didn't know? Wow. I couldn't stop there.

"This still leaves me wondering... I mean... well, Kayleigh said 'Now I know who I am', which sounded so cool. The thing is though, I often feel like a loner, an outsider, even in a crowd and especially at school... so... I don't really know who I am."

Maia simply nodded. She went over to pay the bill and returned to where we were sitting by the café window. Placing her hand gently on my shoulder, we strolled off in silence towards the clearing in the middle of the wood.

When we arrived, we both looked up at the same time. The sun was low in the west, and to the east, I saw the faint white of the moon, surrounded by an infinite, blue sky. We stood there for a few minutes, the wind swirling briskly around us.

"I believe you already know a lot about who you are," Maia said softly. "Look inside."

"How do I look inside?"

"Close your eyes. Ask yourself your question."

I felt like I was entering a dark cathedral inside myself. But as soon as my question 'who am I?' appeared, shafts of blue, purple and green lights were showering down on me, like they were streaming through a rose window. I danced in those lights and some words bubbled up to the surface.

"I'm a dreamer, with big questions. I love the stars, trees, unusual words and plaiting my hair. I love learning new things and being out in the wild.

"I think I have good instincts and always try to be kind. If I believe in something, I'll give it everything. And I don't give up easily."

I opened my eyes. Light began flooding into me.

"That's quite a lot you know about yourself, Leah, although you forgot to mention how mischievous you are!"

"But I want to know more about myself."

"So do I!" Maia cried out, laughing and throwing her arms wide open. "You know, when I ask myself 'who am I?', I think of all the qualities, skills and values which I've grown inside me. They make up who I've chosen to be. They make up who I am, as a woman, as Maia."

"I love that," I smiled.

Maia paused, still looking up into the distant sky.

"There's a different question I ask myself first though… the question '*What* am I?'

"I always start with the fact that I am human, with a free spirit and a free mind, living inside this fine-tuned, intricately designed body. I am alive on this planet, sailing through space and time. I am connected to everything in the universe. So are you, Leah. It makes us not only human beings, but universal beings."

"Universal beings? Mmm. That sounds so cool."

"It is. Imagine how big this universe is. You can't. It's beyond measure. And we are part of it. It's staggering." Maia trailed off. She had to go.

Saying goodbye to Maia again left an empty space in my heart. She'd taught me so much without teaching me. But as I watched her leave, I realised I wasn't the same Leah she'd met before camp. This time, it felt so different with her. I felt more myself.

☆ ☆ ☆ ☆ ☆

Another week flew past, and I'd been so looking forward to the planned online meet up with the filmmaking team. But it got cancelled only two hours beforehand, when Kayleigh told us that she was being moved into a different youth care home. She didn't explain why. But we all still kept in touch and eventually agreed to connect during half-term, near the end of October. We already had some brilliant ideas for making 'Home' into a documentary, and Femi said she'd use the video-conference whiteboard to write them all up live. The enthusiasm in the team felt even more bubbly than at camp.

☆ ☆ ☆ ☆ ☆

I was building up the courage to respond to Sean's note. But how? Taka was my guru in this, and she'd now talked me through my options very carefully. But it seemed way too complicated and as he didn't have any of my contact details, there were actually only two options – send a text or phone him. Now I knew what I had to do.

The following Sunday, I sat at the desk in my bedroom with Sisu sleeping on my lap, staring at my phone for nearly half an hour before I finally felt brave enough to call him.

"Hello?"

"It's, er… it's L-Leah here," I stuttered, sounding strained and high-pitched.

"Hi, Leah! It's so great to hear your voice."

He paused. I smiled. Was this going to be all about my voice again?

"Thank you for your note," I said, to fill the gap.

"Well, it's so cool that you called. I'm not sure I'd have had the guts to call you."

We both laughed. It was a great way to begin a conversation, because his honesty quickly settled his nerves and mine. It made me think that probably everyone has a fear of being rejected.

We had a really good chat about camp, survival, folk songs, funny episodes in our teams and not wanting to go back to school. He was a year older than me and already had clear ideas about what he wanted to do after finishing his studies.

I found out that he loves fresh mint tea and dark chocolate too… how amazing is that?! It seemed like we were on the phone for an hour, but it was only 18 minutes and 25 seconds. We were speaking at the speed of light, though!

We arranged to talk again soon and possibly even meet up when school term was over. After we hung up, he sent me a lovely text with five very funny emojis, plus one green heart! I seriously wondered whether I was beginning to fall in love with Sean, or just with the status of nearly having my first real boyfriend. It could have been both!

I tried to keep a lid on my excitement, but that blew right off when I called Taka minutes after the call. She cut in halfway through.

"I told you, didn't I? This absolutely proves I've been right all along. You're going to move in with him after uni, get married in your twenties, and then go and live in an old farmhouse in Donegal!"

"Yup. That's so going to happen, isn't it?!" I joked.

Taka then got more serious and asked me all sorts of questions about him and his family. The more she asked, the more I realised I hardly knew anything about him.

☆ ☆ ☆ ☆ ☆

Apart from those moments with the few people who mattered to me most, I was still feeling quite lost, and pressures at school were building. Except for when I was with Taka, I still felt lonely.

My parents were a great support, but Mum was still grieving and Dad was working a lot of overtime. I wanted to be there for them both and did lots of extra jobs around the house. But it was hard to find any quiet time to talk to them about the enormous changes going on inside me... changes that were making me disconnect from most people.

Some of the images and new ideas which flowed through my head surprised and shocked me. There was such a wide gap now between my life at school and my world outside it. I needed time and space to think things through more clearly.

My old journal started filling up with notes of what was becoming a really unusual story of my life. My life in the universe.

I had dreams of it being made into a film, and Femi would help me produce it. But Taka told me that was 'insanely ambitious'. She was the first person, however, to encourage me to write my story as a book… that is, as long as she appeared in it sounding supercool! That was easy, because she is.

Over a few evenings, I read all my journal notes out loud in my bedroom. It was like I was reading the story of someone else's life. If my notes were accurate, then I was actually living a far more daring and confident life than I could ever have imagined!

But in the end, I realised that there was a crucial, obvious missing piece to my whole story.

Where was the answer to my big question?

WINDOW TWENTY

⚠

THE BIGGEST SHOCK
OF MY LIFE

The Biggest Shock Of My Life

It was a warm autumn Sunday during the half-term holidays, and Sean and I were texting. He'd now used that green heart emoji three times in nearly twenty minutes, which was now a total of five times since our first conversation following his note. I didn't know if he was being flirty, but I knew that if I asked Taka, she'd just roar something like, 'OMG. Are you really telling me you can't work that one out?!'

Sean had been booked to come to London with his parents this weekend. His mum had lots of old school friends in Hackney where she grew up. But Sean's grandmother had flown in unexpectedly from Scotland, so they had to cancel last minute. I was gutted and tried to hide my disappointment. I'd been hoping to see him on my birthday, October 22nd, in two days' time.

Now I was getting anxious – Sean's next text was overdue by at least two minutes. Ping. A message came through from Femi and I instantly perked up. She confirmed that all nine of us in the filmmaking team would be on our first video call next

Sunday. That meant connecting with seven different countries and various time zones, from New York eastwards around the globe to Kyoto. I worked out that's a distance of around 15,000 kilometres!

Our call would start in the early morning for Joe, late evening for Natsuki, and at various times in the afternoon for the rest of us. I couldn't wait to see everyone from across the planet, all on one screen.

More fantastic suggestions were flying back and forth for the documentary on 'Home'. The message that absolutely leapt off my phone, however, was a personal text from Kayleigh. She told me that she might be qualifying for a move to a shared apartment next year. 'Best news ever!' she wrote. But in the meantime, she was inviting me to come over and join her for next Sunday's call at her new care home! It was hard to believe how much things had moved on. I was counting the days.

Sean's next text finally arrived: 'Must go now – promised Dad I'd help him dig beds in the garden.' I loved the way he was always willing to help. And his text didn't sound like an excuse, especially as he ended it with a smiling emoji face with sunglasses. No more green hearts, however! I had to admit, I was missing him.

As I began catching up with new messages from the team, Aiden's voice boomed outside my bedroom, snapping me out of the frenzy of texts.

"Do you want to play Scrabble?" he shouted.

"Okay. I'll be down in five," I sighed, happy at the opportunity to take a break from being glued to a screen.

We were almost an hour into playing and I was feeling very smug, having just spelt 'euphoria' and scored mega points. But I couldn't stand being indoors anymore.

"I have to go out and get some fresh air now," I said.

"But we're almost finished!"

"Oh… you're going to win anyway," I grinned. He loved that.

I put on my old checkerboard-sleeved hoodie – which always made me feel tougher – and walked dreamily towards the pretty Japanese Water Garden. It was sunny, but the ponds still had a few patches of thin ice remaining from the unusually frosty night before. By a little bridge there, the arching cherry trees and tall bamboos still had some dewdrops on their leaves, which glistened with tiny rainbows in the sunlight.

There was a major change going on inside me since camp, and I needed some space to reflect. My mind was swarming over the big choices facing me now, especially as I'd be moving to a new school next year.

Going back to my local school had been like entering a machine. It was soulless. No one really talked about the bigger issues or opportunities. The experience of working in teams like at camp rarely happened. It was super-competitive, and all that mattered was who got top marks, who was a winner in sports, and who was into whom.

Still, it was a nice surprise to hear a rumour going around that I'd had a big crush at summer camp. I didn't deny anything and just let the gossip add a point or two to my previous non-existent street cred.

At least the culture of bullying wasn't causing the same anxiety in me as before, and I was proud of that. I kept myself to myself now and didn't react if one of the bullies tried to wind me up. Dad's Code of Five was finally working.

I was still being called 'the school weirdo', however, even by some of my classmates. Was it because I was an outlier to the culture at school, or because I still wasn't part of the ongoing perfect body image competition? Whatever. After my talk with Maia about beauty, I wasn't going to play that game. It seemed so childish now.

Anyway, I was always on edge there, and challenging the teachers with difficult questions, like I do, wasn't encouraged – other students thought I was just trying to be clever. Plus, the new English teacher, who'd taken over from Mr Eaton, was more focused on the classics than edgy young adult books or creative writing.

So I couldn't wait to move on, and even though changing school in the middle of an academic year was meant to be traumatic, anything was better than where I was. My parents believed that the new school, which promoted independent thinking and team projects, would motivate me and let me express myself more freely.

But it was life outside of school that was really calling to me. A life outside the tiny box of 'GCSE student Leah Greene'. A life where I could chase the burning questions and big issues.

At camp, I'd been shocked to not only discover more facts about the climate crisis, but also understand more about the refugee situation, poverty and other world issues. In our multi-cultural filmmaking team, there was this firm belief that we could really do things together to make a difference.

So, I was hungry for that sense of purpose and adventure I'd experienced in the team. I'd only felt that before on the climate marches I'd been on in central London… and after my stardust experience, of course.

Booshh! My train of thoughts stopped sharply. Before I knew it, my mind had completely switched track and was conjuring up scenes for our documentary…

Clips of each person in our team telling their story… the story of our generation and our passion for change; videos of people and wildlife from around the planet, showing the unique homes they build; an animated scene where I'd be travelling through space, talking to the stars, and then coming back to earth to tell everyone what it was like, because no one remembered.

After the documentary, people would leave, looking up at the sky, afresh, as if for the first time in their lives. Change would come.

New scenes and questions flooded my mind. The team call couldn't come soon enough.

But then I tensed up, anxious that I might lose Taka as my best friend when I changed schools. I couldn't bear that. And what if I didn't fit in at the new school? Plus, I was still worried about my mum, as the stress of losing Chloe had triggered an old back problem – worries, on and on, rattling around in my head.

I was getting a bad headache now, and that rarely happened to me. I wandered out of the Water Garden and zigzagged across the park, feeling disorientated. I shuffled out of the main entrance in a daze.

The next thing I knew, I was waking up in agony, in a hospital bed.

☆ ☆ ☆ ☆ ☆

It was the biggest shock of my life. My family were beyond distraught, and so were Taka and Maia when they found out. Sean, Natsuki and the team didn't hear anything about it for days.

Before I passed out, the paramedic told me that I'd been hit in my side by the front of a 4x4, which was braking and swerving to avoid me. It seems that I'd arrived at the hospital unconscious, with a long, deep gash across my left hip, three broken fingers on my left hand, a fractured ankle and cuts and bruises on my head, back and left arm. A bit of my hair had actually been scraped off because after being hit, I'd been dragged a metre along the road.

Later, a nurse described the scene of me being rushed into A&E covered in bloodied bandages. After checking my vital signs, they'd wheeled me straight into the ICU and put me on a ventilator. A young doctor had speedily removed bits of gravel from my head, hip and arm before they'd taken MRI and CT scans of all my injuries. I couldn't remember any of it.

"Very good to see you awake, Leah. You've been in a coma for four days," said the toweringly tall surgeon, Dr Pallana, in a friendly tone. I was in pain, drowsy, and struggling to process the news. On the other side of the bed, I could make out the blurry shapes and faces of my parents.

Leaning in close to me, I could see the hint of a smile on the doctor's lips when she added, "You got lucky, Leah. If you'd taken one more step, or the driver had been doing a few miles per hour more…" She didn't finish her sentence – she didn't need to.

Turning to face my parents, she spoke in a very professional tone. "It looks worse than it is. As you know, she had a traumatic brain injury, and the MRI showed a small brain oedema when she arrived. The swelling has responded well to the medication and, as she was stable, it was possible to take her off the ventilator yesterday."

'Who is she talking about?' was all I could think. But I was getting shooting pains each time I tried to move my legs and my throbbing headache was real. Dr Pallana was talking about me.

"We have done a CT scan this morning, and it shows that the oedema has reabsorbed and the brain is back to normal.

"The soft-tissue lesions are not severe, although the deep laceration in the hip needed a minor surgical operation – I'm quite confident there won't be any long-term effects. She'll need to start her first phase of physical rehabilitation soon as she's been several days without moving. She's what I'd call 'repairable in three months', and back playing football in perhaps six – hopefully. Although after being discharged, we'll still have to monitor her for a while as the physiotherapy progresses."

As Dr Pallana continued speaking with my parents, my mind drifted. I had a sudden flashback to what must have been the very last moment before I came out of the coma. There was this quiet, protective feeling of the presence beside my bed. It was sparkling with white sequins inside an electric violet haze. Had it been with me all the time? Had it saved me from...?

A searing pain across my hip brought me back to the moment. Dr Pallana had already gone and Mum was squeezing my right hand, which wasn't in plaster.

"You wouldn't know this, Leah, because of the coma, but it was your birthday two days ago... feels strange to say happy birthday... but happy birthday, my love," she said, shakily. "We've been worrying day and night, not knowing if we'd ever be able to say that to you again." With tears streaming down to her lips, she reached an arm across the bed and held me gently.

I'd completely forgotten about my birthday. And missing a birthday party seemed a bit meaningless now as it suddenly hit me that I could have died and they'd been agonising about it for days. Then an eerie voice from somewhere inside my brain said, 'But you did die'. I shut that voice right down as I shuddered at the thought and froze.

My vision sharpened now as I watched my parents just staring at me, their faces pale and weary, eyes baggy and dark.

"I... I'm okay now," I reassured them with my croaky voice, feeling so grateful that it hadn't been worse.

"You'll soon be able to get out of that bed, love. And we'll have an epic party once you're back home," enthused Dad, kissing my forehead.

"Yes," Aiden added, struggling to find his voice. "You know, Taka was here every day during your coma, sitting in the waiting room for hours…"

"My best friend… like a sister."

"… and she's already been in contact with your friends from camp."

"And Sean?" I cried out, not thinking.

"Who's Sean?" Mum asked.

"Oh… ermm… just a friend… from camp."

Mum knew that wasn't the whole truth, but she smiled sweetly, and Aiden knew better than to answer my question. This was getting too emotionally sticky for me, and my eyelids were getting heavy with sleep. Mum didn't need a hint.

"We'll see you in the morning, love, with Uncle Jake. Sisu misses you too. Keep resting please." Before leaving, she gave me a card from my grandad in Norway and some birthday gifts. "I always wrap presents too tightly, as you know, but I'm sure the nurse will help you open them later if you want. And here's your journal and your phone, fully charged. Please call us right away if you need anything."

When my family left, I tried to claw open one of the presents with my right hand. But I was in too much pain. The ward nurse, Katerina, prepared my medication as she watched me pulling feebly to get the tape off. She offered to open my presents, which she did while chattering away happily about her fascinating life as a nurse. I was too knocked out to really follow her story, and all I remembered afterwards was her explaining that coma means 'deep sleep' in Greek… and that's exactly what it had felt like.

Using only my index finger, I managed to text Sean and the team about my accident. I imagined each of their caring expressions on reading it, which relaxed me into falling fast asleep.

By the weekend, I wasn't feeling so tired or sick. I was able to sit up and stretch both my legs out from the edge of the bed. That's when I knew I had to continue writing my story as soon as possible, from the hospital, looking out of the window of my ward. I was scribbling away in spite of my bandages, plaster and pain.

☆ ☆ ☆ ☆ ☆

Monday morning. The best surprise! A postcard arrived from Sean with a photo of the beautiful landscape by the coast in Donegal. His note was not original, but very sweet.

'Send yourself!' I immediately thought, and had to stop myself from texting him those two words.

Sean's message inspired me to walk further than before, and when my family and Taka arrived in the afternoon, Katerina helped me hobble to the end of the corridor. My ankle plaster cast was heavy to drag around, even on crutches, and I couldn't grip properly as the fingers on my left hand were also in a cast. My strength was coming back though, and so were my questions about 'stardust' and 'home'.

☆ ☆ ☆ ☆ ☆

A week later, when Maia was back in London, she visited me briefly with some gifts from her trip to Tanzania. One was a beautiful silver necklace with a little hanging silver baobab tree and three tiny aquamarine stones in its branches. She helped me put it on straight away and I never took it off for weeks.

She asked me again about camp, and this time I told her about Sean. She was just like Taka and worse than my mum, asking for every detail, especially about his handwriting and the way he danced. I think she wanted to interview him ASAP!

I also told her more about my special friendship with Natsuki, and the recent letter she'd sent right after hearing about my accident. She'd asked her grandparents, who used to be top herbalists, to send me a list of natural herbal treatments for my recovery. They also sent me a bottle of disgustingly smelly black liquid, but it was helping to build up my stamina.

As Maia was leaving, she asked me if I would like her to do some mental healing on me. I instinctively nodded, but then frowned, not knowing what that was. Seeing my expression, Maia's lips widened upwards into a little grin. "Remember the tuning forks, Leah."

Two and a half weeks after the accident, I was able to stand up and plod down the stairs to the hospital garden without having to grip the handrail like I was holding on to the edge of a cliff. I could move around now with less pain, except when putting too much weight on my ankle. Inside, I felt stronger than ever.

☆ ☆ ☆ ☆ ☆

Over four months have passed now, and the physical therapy has helped so much – I'll soon be playing football, just like Dr Pallana said I would. I'm doing well at my new school so far, and although I don't see Taka as often, we're still best friends. I hope we will be for life.

What I haven't written up yet is something out of this world, literally, that happened when I was in the coma… very difficult to explain. It's taking me ages to remember any details as everything's still so hazy, although the feelings aren't.

How do you describe feeling like you died? Maybe I did, just like that eerie voice had told me. I was still alive somewhere, though, moving far into another dimension. But where was that… where did I go? Did I travel through that portal in the Summer Triangle of stars, or a black hole, entering another universe? And how did I come back?

Uncle Jake's now sure that I'd been through a 'near-death experience'. So, maybe I spent four days in the place where you go after you die. Uncle couldn't explain any more, so I'm just waiting to ask Maia as soon as she gets back from her latest trip. But if she's never had a near-death experience, how will she know?

In the last two days, a strange memory and pictures from my time in the coma have flashed into my head. So, I've begun doing some sketches and making a few notes. I don't want to forget whatever extraordinary journey I've been on.

I'm also going to ask our family friend in New Zealand, who's a famous illustrator, if he could paint or draw clearer images using my rough sketches and descriptions. Because I've no idea if what happened to me has ever happened to anyone else.

I'm planning to write about this during the Easter break,

and also about what's been happening with our documentary film on 'Home'. I managed to join the last two online meet-ups and we've already agreed who's going to be contributing what. And so far, we've only had one argument... and I wasn't part of it!

As for Sean, well, that's getting really exciting. I heard through Taka yesterday, who heard it through Jaali, that he does like more than my voice. That piece of evidence was confirmed this morning! He texted, inviting me to Donegal – with or without my brother. I'm staying calm, so far, and looking forward to seeing Taka tomorrow to go through every detail of his text. I don't even know if he's discussed this with his parents, but his invitation did end with another green heart.

☆ ☆ ☆ ☆ ☆

My big questions have been going crazily around and around in my head for almost a year now. They began that night in the park, followed me all the way through summer camp and have only become more urgent since my accident. They're always with me. The deeper they go, the more revealing they become.

But last night, something major happened, and it's changed everything... literally, everything.

It began when I was in the school library studying images from *The Atlas of the Universe* for a science essay, which I called 'What do stars see?'. At the end of it, I wrote about stardust and the words danced into life in front of my eyes, just like once before.

My essay got the second highest mark in class, which totally surprised me. I thought it was very scientific, but not like the science they teach in school. My teacher actually read out the last two paragraphs to the whole class yesterday.

*'I know we are made of stardust. Look at all the gases, chemicals,
energy and elements out there in stars which are here, inside
our bodies (see list below). It's a scientific fact.*

*But humans can also shine their creativity, genius and love.
And if humans don't shine, then how will the stars, or anyone
or anything out there in the universe, know we are here? How
will they know that we care? How will they even see us if we
don't light up?'*

This was a vital clue to my questions about stardust and home.
I was so close to the answer now. It was like breathing in a fresh,
salty breeze, knowing that the whole seaside is waiting for you
around the corner.

Just before I went to sleep last night, I was watching an astronomy
video in my bedroom about how stars are formed. The images were
spectacular... bursts of colour, energy, light and power. The photos
of new stars forming in the vast Orion Nebula were so beautiful...
and all these 'star babies' are being born out there right now.

Well, after watching it, I could hardly keep my eyes open. My
mind began conjuring up pictures of all the most significant
things that had ever happened to me over fourteen and a half
years of living on this planet.

Yet, when I woke up today, I couldn't remember anything more
about it. But as I turned on my side to get up, somehow, my big
notebook was lying open right next to my pillow. And there it
was. Incredible.

I swear I have absolutely no memory of ever having written a
poem. I'm not exactly sure, but I guess it looks like my
handwriting... except that it's much neater and more stylish than
how I usually write. Plus, I've never spoken or written down some
of these words before.

A memory comes sharply to mind from last night. It's of the presence. I was standing up inside it this time. I was a part of it and it was a part of me. We were breathing the same air and speaking with the same voice.

As I read the poem back to myself now, the words sound like a message from somewhere else.

Now I realise.

The poem must be the key that will unlock my questions… and a signpost to where I must travel next.

I am made of stardust
promise, longing

I make diamonds in myself
to do what darkness cannot do
to shine light

Brave people inspire me
to stand by my principles
I will be brave

I don't want to be like anyone else
I will paint my own colours
to become what I was made for

My home is a quiet place
I find inside myself
or with a true friend
or close to Mother Earth
or travelling with starlight

I want to love, give, be curious,
grow trees, wildflowers, breathe pure air
radiate wonder, kindness
light up the runway
fly the open skies
on sapphire breezes
with ruby heart

Stardust must fulfil
the purpose of its arising
so I will go to the stream
to watch the wings of dragonflies
as they unfurl from their homes
hoping the chameleon
will then show me its secret

And when the green emerald
is dimmed by the shadows
of old stealing new
I will be its light

No one can prevent me

except myself

Let me be

please

I am forever

a free spirit

My name is Leah

Appreciation...

... this word is in my top three favourites from the whole dictionary. Its two meanings do a sort of passionate tango. Because when you truly recognise the value of someone, you also add to their value in your eyes and theirs.

So I deeply appreciate the belief and guidance of everyone who's generously contributed to 'Home'. They've been like the village which raised a child, or in this case, helped in Leah's coming of age.

Without Grant MacDonald, the illustrator, this book would only be available in two dimensions! You've not only brought the special moments and characters to life, but you have believed in Home since day one and worked tirelessly on every detail of your art. Your wise advice and calmness have been a refuge.

Thank you so much to the teenage editors from around the world. You have used your sharp pencils and red pens on the text with unrestrained enthusiasm! I hope that Leah's story is for those who, like you, are becoming the change that the world so needs. Great appreciation therefore to: Olivia Ravé, Ruby MacDonald, Clio Siegel, Sage Patterson, Ella MacDonald, Beth Marsh and Grace Marsh. You've inspired me more than I can express.

Then there's the adult team of editors – a wonderful mix of seasoned professionals, authors and people who understand and love working with youth. Thank you: Mark Siegel, Sophie Deen, Macarena Mata, Eleanor Hawken, Becky Stradwick, Rosamond Rolleston, Julie Glover, Alexis Siegel, Natasha Rozenberg, Kathy Patterson, Maiko Takemoto and Julie Hoyle. Your skilled wordsmithing and belief have transformed Leah's story.

I've also loved working with the Eminent Productions team and freelancers who have produced, formatted and been midwives to the birth and inspired promotion of Home. My thanks go out to: Macarena Mata, Viv Mullett, Nick Ross, Saira Aspinall, Claire Morrison, Julie Glover, Enrique Spacca, Jessie Meenan and Julie Pond. Your belief has motivated me to go all the way.

☆ ☆ ☆ ☆ ☆

To those students, teachers and librarians who I met with at schools – Chancellor's, Queenswood and Dame Alice Owen's – you enabled me to see Leah's story through your eyes. That was precious.

A special mention also to all the young people and staff at Six Hills Children's Home for a truly memorable meeting. You helped me to understand Kayleigh and how she overcame her greatest fears and challenges. Thanks also to the team at Refugee Action, who enabled me to interview Musa for Tanguy's character, giving me the opportunity to hear the uplifting story from someone whose journey in life has been so profoundly testing and liberating. Your words Musa, and the tears I cried afterwards, opened a greater compassion in me, I believe, to better understand the meaning of being brave.

☆ ☆ ☆ ☆ ☆

I have so valued working as a team with everyone I have mentioned and more who added their support – my family included of course! I hold a vision of teamwork – minds and sentiments in natural harmony – and believe in its transformative power in the world. Teams working together for a cause greater than themselves are an essential part of the legacy and future of this human race.

☆ ☆ ☆ ☆ ☆

In life, it is rare to meet people who, unknown to you at the time, unexpectedly become your lifelong mentors. Not because they're trying to teach you something, but because they are a living example of what it is to lead a free and purposeful life. My profound gratitude to Leo & Ruth Armin and Ethra McKay. You've shown me a rare freedom to grow and be myself, and to truly appreciate the gift that life is.

☆ ☆ ☆ ☆ ☆

So now, how to find words when the feelings extend so far beyond them. For this goes out to my life partner, closest friend and greatest inspiration. You are, and forever will be, the strongest, brightest and most enduring light of my life. Your beauty, within and without, lights up everyone who knows you.

And how inspiring to have the ultimate editor of my words and behaviours so close! Thank you for your great forbearance and care. Tu eres mi amor para siempre.

Look out for the next phase in Leah's incredible journey...

For breaking news, stay tuned to
#LeahsUniverse & leahsuniverse.com

#LeahsUniverse